FINAL TABLE

PATI NAGLE

Other Books by Pati Nagle

Pet Noir
Kokopelli and the Virgin

Blood of the Kindred series
The Betrayal
Heart of the Exiled
Swords Over Fireshore

Immortal series
Immortal
Eternal

Short Story Collections
Many Paths: Stories of the Ælven
Coyote Ugly and Other Tales

Wisteria Tearoom Mysteries
(written as Patrice Greenwood)

A Fatal Twist of Lemon
A Sprig of Blossomed Thorn
An Aria of Omens
A Bodkin for the Bride

FINAL TABLE
PATI NAGLE

Evennight Books
Cedar Crest, New Mexico

(a partner of Book View Café)

Final Table
copyright © 2008, 2016 by Pati Nagle
*(Originally published as **Dead Man's Hand**)*

ISBN: 978-1-61138-605-9

Cover illustrator: Aaron Hover, mountainofstrength.net

Published by Evennight Books, Cedar Crest, New Mexico, USA, an affiliate of Book View Café Publishing Cooperative

Book View Café Publishing Cooperative
P.O. Box 1624, Cedar Crest, NM 87008-1624
bookviewcafe.com

for all my poker buddies

Acknowledgments

Many thanks to the following people for their invaluable assistance with this novel: to Laura Anne Gilman and Nancy Jane Moore for editorial advice; Deborah J. Ross for proofreading; Sally Gwylan, Pari Noskin, D. Lynn Smith, and Jerry Weinberg for their valuable input; and to Chris Krohn for his indispensible support and for nagging me about the poker details.

Thanks also to Aaron Hover for the beautiful cover art, and to Book View Café for being the best writer's support system since sliced bread.

~ James ~

Deadwood, South Dakota

James awoke to the sensation of flesh creeping onto his bones. It had been a long time since he'd worn any such thing and the feeling was disconcerting.

So was finding himself seated with his back against something cold and hard, dressed in his favorite buckskin jacket and trousers, hat and boots, gun belt with his .36 Colt Navy pistols— all the traps he'd been buried in. That jacket and all the rest had rotted away a long time ago, along with any expectation of ever feeling alive again.

But he felt alive now.

It was a moonlit night and he was sitting inside a little fenced rectangle. When he craned his head around he saw that the thing he was leaning against was a big old gigantic pillar of bronze. He stood up and turned around to get a better look at it. It was taller than him by a good few feet, and at the top was a giant bust of a man's head. His.

"Oh, Lordy!"

He became a bit self-conscious standing there, so he stepped over the fence and looked the whole thing over from the outside, as a visitor might do. It was impressive, certainly. He stared at the words on it:

WILD BILL
J. B. HICKOK
DIED AUG. 2, 1876 BY PISTOL SHOT
AGED 39 years
CUSTER WAS LONELY WITHOUT HIM

He reached out a tentative hand, new-grown flesh all pale in the moonlight, and touched the metal surface bearing his name. It was cold.

He knew where he was. He had some vague memories of being moved once or twice, a bright light and someone staring down at him saying "Look at that!" He'd been here for a long time, up on the hill, only now somehow he'd gotten outside of the grave and acquired a new set of duds—or a resurrected set— along the way.

There was a dead bouquet of flowers at the foot of the pillar, crushed. He'd been sitting on it. Lot of dry leaves blowing around; the smell of them woke memories. He glanced up at the moon and saw a cloud scudding over it, blown by a chill wind. Autumn, and a cold night to boot.

Another cairn stood a little behind his, with a plaque. Agnes?

Heart thumping, he hurried over to it, but the name on it was not his wife's. It was Calamity Jane's.

He shook his head and sighed. That gal was crazier than a hoot-owl. Why they'd put her next to him he could not imagine, unless it was because the stories she told about herself were even more exaggerated than his own reputation.

All he'd ever wanted was a simple life. A chance to make a living, maybe set him and Agnes up comfortable. That was why he'd come to Deadwood, hoping to stake a claim and strike it rich. Hadn't worked out that way, though.

Memories came crawling back to him, buzzing around inside his head like a mess of fireflies. A game of cards, a hand he thought sure to win: aces and eights. Gunfire, pain, darkness. He knew he shouldn't have taken the chair with its back to the door. He knew it; why had he gone and done it?

He stepped over to Jane's marker and squinted to read the dates. She'd died a good twenty-seven years after him, and the carved numbers looked alarmingly worn.

Underneath her name it said "Martha Jane Burke" in smaller letters. He'd never heard her called Burke. Maybe she'd married and settled down, though that didn't seem too likely from what he knew of her. He stepped back and looked all around to make sure Jane hadn't shown up, too.

Nobody else in the graveyard. He was alone.

"What the hell is this, anyway?" he muttered aloud.

The question seemed to agitate those fireflies in his head. His brain must've grown back too, he guessed, and something inside it was itching.

He frowned, looking east. Something was calling him. He didn't know who or what, but now that he was paying attention he felt the most insistent urge to follow it.

Agnes. What had happened to her, after he'd died? Was she dead, too, by now? He swallowed senseless hope that she wasn't.

Maybe that was why he felt the need to go east. Back to Cincinnati, maybe, to find her—to find her grave.

He looked up at the sky again, where the wind pushed the ripped-up clouds across the cold moon and carried the smell of snow. Better get moving 'fore he froze, standing here.

He made his way out of the graveyard, which was large and looked to be housing more dead bodies than the whole mining camp of Deadwood had housed live ones. It was a great deal grander than the boot hill in which he had first been laid to rest —if you could call it that; he hadn't found it especially restful.

Being dead was a fair bit confusing, and not all it was cracked up to be. He'd seen nothing of pearly gates or such glories. He'd spent a lot of time remembering all the stupid things he'd done in his life. Over and over, with the feeling there was something he ought to understand about it all, but he never had done. Above that, the constant murmur of living people coming around—people he couldn't understand and didn't want to understand, but who tickled the edges of his awareness with their presence—had kept him from any sense of peace.

Death for him had been a vague sort of existence, and compared to the brilliance of all the physical sensations he was suddenly feeling again, it was like being in an uncomfortable dream world. He couldn't say as he'd care to go back to it.

He followed a path down to a roadway—flat black and

curiously smooth—that led downhill toward Deadwood. It entered a vast field of the same paving, and there stood a stagecoach, all black, with a team of black horses hitched to it.

James's heart sank at the sight and he hastily withdrew in among the pines alongside the road. That coach was here for him, he knew, and seeing as how he hadn't requested a coach, he was disinclined to get into it.

He made his way through the trees, following the road downhill, through a smaller field of black, and down into the valley. A glow of light came from the valley bottom and he heard some vague rushing sounds and what might be a distant scrap of music.

A slow smile came onto his lips, and his left hand came up to smooth his mustache. Deadwood was still hopping, it appeared.

The road was painted with a yellow dotted line down the middle and white stripes on the sides. He'd seen avenues planted with fancy bushes and rows of tall trees alongside, but he'd never seen a decorated road before. It occurred to him as he walked along the dotted line, trying to fit his pace to it so it took exactly two steps for the length of each stripe, to wonder how long it had been since he'd died.

He heard a sound and paused to listen. It was like the rushing sounds from below but much louder and closer, kind of a roaring growl. Reminded him a little of a locomotive, only lighter, and angrier somehow.

A pair of blinding white lights came up the hill and the roaring grew more intense as they rushed upon him. He threw up an arm to block the light and heard a banshee shriek as the lights wavered side to side, then stopped a little way past him.

He turned, heart pounding with the fear of almost being hit by whatever that was. Some kind of vehicle—looked vaguely like a boxcar only smaller. Built out of metal and all shiny, with the light glaring off down the road. It sat there, still rumbling but quieter now, like a giant cat purring.

He heard a heavy "chunk," then a man's voice started yelling. "What are you, crazy?! You could have been killed! Jesus,

I almost hit you!"

James's right hand hovered near his pistol. He cleared his throat and warily addressed the man, whom he could barely see in the dark after being blinded by the vehicle's lights.

"I thank you kindly for not doing so."

A bright light hit him in the face and he blinked, startled. The stranger let out a groan of disgust.

"Not another one of you nut-cases. Look, the cemetery's closed. Come back and pay your respects in the morning. Meanwhile, let's not get killed walking down the middle of the road, all right?"

"Beg pardon," said James. "I didn't know it wasn't allowed."

"You drunk, mister?"

"No, sir, I haven't had a drop."

He said it a bit wistfully. He was getting to think a glass of whiskey would be a comfort.

The bright light was lowered, and James blinked, trying to see the man in front of him. The clothes he was wearing were strange. The pants and boots looked all right, but he had on some kind of jacket that was all puffy like a featherbed, only it was blue. He wore a black hat over short-cut dark hair and frowned as he stared at James, as if doubtful of his condition.

Having nothing to hide, James looked frankly back at him. Finally the stranger sighed.

"All right, where's your car?"

"Car?" James laughed at the suggestion he owned a railroad car.

"No car? How'd you get up here?"

"I-I was brought here."

"Lemme see your I.D."

This was getting awkward, and James was beginning to be annoyed. He kept his voice polite, though. "I'm sorry, sir, I'm afraid I don't know what that is."

"Don't be a smartass. What's your name?"

James swallowed and gave a deferential cough. "Hickok."

"Yeah, I get it. I mean your *real* name."

"It is Hickok, sir. James Hickok."

The stranger frowned at him. "OK, fine." The light came up again and played across the gunbelt at his hips. "Those loaded?"

"I don't know," James said truthfully.

"Right. Take off the belt and put it on the ground, nice and slow."

He swallowed. "I must decline to do that, sir. You would not expect a man to disarm himself, would you?"

"I expect you to do what I say if you don't want to wind up in jail! You're halfway there already, buddy!"

"Might you be the sheriff, sir?"

"That's right, I'm the sheriff. See?" The light swung aside and glinted off a metal badge the man held up, then hit James in the eyes again. "Now take off the guns and put 'em down."

Swallowing his growing resentment, James did as he was told. He didn't suppose a night in jail would do him any harm. There were worse places, certainly more dangerous places, to be.

"OK, now step over here and put your hands on the car."

The light swept toward the coach and back, so James gathered the man meant that vehicle when he said "the car." James placed his palms on the slick surface above the window and frowned. He'd been a sheriff himself, and while he'd certainly had to dispense forcible justice from time to time, he had always been civil to those who were civil to him. Times had changed, it seemed.

Startled by the sheriff's hands touching his hips, he turned. "Now, see here—"

"Hold still! Face the car and don't move, buddy. I'm losing my patience."

James turned around again, silently tolerating the swift brush of the sheriff's hands over his limbs. Searching for hidden weapons, he supposed. He swallowed his ire. He would have to get used to the way people acted, if he wasn't going to end up dead in a fight. Again.

"Got anything in your pockets?"

Saying he didn't know was probably a bad idea. "See for

yourself," he said instead.

The sheriff stuck his hands into James's coat pockets, then his trouser pockets. Apparently he found nothing.

"Where's your wallet?"

James would like to know that himself. Before he could answer, the sheriff gave a disgusted grunt and stepped back.

"Don't suppose you have a permit for the guns, either. OK, turn around."

James did so, and stood still for a long moment with the sheriff's hand-held light in his eyes. The man leaned close, and James had to fight the instinct to push him away. Finally the sheriff stepped back and lowered the light.

"You don't look drunk or stoned. I assume this whole act is an attempt to get into the show down at the Number Ten."

James drew a sharp breath. The No. 10 Saloon was still around? And hosting some kind of show, apparently.

He had only ever been in two shows: Bill Cody's play, and his own disastrous "Buffalo Chase." He hadn't done so well in either case. He wasn't really cut out for a showman, but it might be a way to make some money, just temporarily. He'd need money to pay his way east, and for necessities. He could use a drink, for example, though he wasn't especially anxious to get it at the No. 10.

"Here's the deal," said the sheriff. "I'm taking you to the station where you'll take a breathalyzer test. If you're clean, you're free to go. If not, you can sober up in the drunk tank. If I have any more trouble with you it's three days in the slammer for vagrancy. Got it?"

"I—yes."

He hadn't understood half of what the sheriff said, but he had the strong impression that cooperation was his best bet for staying out of jail. The part about vagrancy he had understood. He'd been locked up on that charge many a time.

"OK, get in the car."

The sheriff pulled open the second door of the coach and gestured toward the seat. James stepped toward it, wishing his heart would quit thumping so. He was a little wary of riding in this great roaring thing. A strange, green light was glowing inside it. That was nearly enough to change his mind, but he did want to get down to Deadwood and it would be a long, cold walk, and anyway it didn't seem as though he had much choice.

"My guns?" he said.

"I'll get 'em. Go on, get in."

James climbed onto a long seat like a couch, as plush as any he'd ever had the pleasure to sit upon. There was a large wheel mounted to the front wall of the car and the green light came from in front of the wheel, where a scatter of lights decorated the wall. A couple of dials looked like clocks but didn't have the right numbers. Some of the other lights looked like words, but they were tiny. James leaned forward and squinted, trying to read them. His eyes hadn't been so good for a while.

The sheriff opened the front door and climbed into the seat in front of James. A metal screen divided them. The sheriff put James's gun belt on the empty shotgun seat, then took hold of the wheel and pushed a lever.

The car growled in response, then leapt forward with a force that pressed James into his seat. "Awp!" he said, then clung for dear life to the metal screen.

Through the wide window at the front of the car he could see the painted stripes on the side of the road, writhing before them like ribbons in the wind, while the dotted line in the middle flashed by like the flicker of a magic lantern. James stared over the sheriff's shoulder at them, breathing hard, stiff with fear.

"You're not from around here, are you?" the sheriff said.

"No."

Better maybe to say he wasn't from around now, but that would only cause confusion. He wondered, in an idle kind of way, what year it was. Should have checked some of the newer headstones in the graveyard. He had a feeling it had been a lot more than twenty-seven years.

"You sure have the lingo down right. What were you doing up in the cemetery, just communing with old Wild Bill?"

"Ah—you could say that."

"Well, do it during business hours from now on."

"Yes, sir."

He'd have to find out what they were. There was a lot he didn't know about this time.

His reputation had survived him, though, it seemed. That was mighty flattering, but he was beginning to see difficulties ahead. Convincing people of who he was, just for starters.

Maybe he'd better let that lie. It was more important to get east. The buzzing in his brain about that wouldn't quit. In fact, it seemed to just get stronger every minute.

The car took a swerve to the left and he closed his eyes, feeling slightly sick. He'd done some fancy driving in his day, but this sheriff was intent on killing them both, or so it seemed.

"Done many wild west shows?" the sheriff asked.

"One or two," James answered cautiously.

"You sure got the look right, I'll give you that."

"Thank you kindly, sir."

"Yeah. Give it a rest, OK? I can't get you the job."

James fell silent. The car was running on the straight again, so he opened his eyes. They were descending pretty fast down a steep hill. Off to the right, unearthly bright lights flickered between the pine trees. He'd never ridden so fast, not even on the railroad.

Finally the vehicle slowed as they reached the bottom of the valley, and rolled to a halt next to a large red sign labeled "STOP" in white letters. Stage stop, James wondered? There didn't seem to be a station or even a shed. The stage hadn't even come to Deadwood in his day, but it looked like the place had grown a considerable lot since then.

A light started blinking on the front wall and the car started moving again, turning right onto a larger road, more of an avenue. There were buildings here, houses and such with big, fine lawns out in front. Deadwood had proved its promise, it seemed. Lot of folks must have made a fortune in gold to afford such nice houses as these. Some of them looked to belong in a big city, like Chicago or New York.

Chicago. That would be a good place to head for, he decided. If he could make enough to buy a horse he could ride there, then sell the horse and get a railroad ticket to Cincinnati, to look for Agnes. He frowned, wondering if maybe the stage would be cheaper, only he didn't know if the stage came to Deadwood. There had been that stop, but it didn't look like it was in use.

The sheriff made a couple more turns, and though James continued to cling to the wire screen, their pace was not so fast any more. They passed more houses—street after street of them. He was amazed, and a little frightened, at what Deadwood had become. It looked to be a city now, a full-blown, fancy city!

There were lights shining everywhere, brightening up the place like daylight, brighter than the gas lamps he'd seen in the cities. Some of them were brilliant colors and others flashed on and off. At a crossroads a bright red light was hung out over the street on a wire. The sheriff stopped the car there, giving James a chance to admire all the lights around and the buildings.

Another "car" came hurtling toward them and James flinched, but the sheriff drove on without even acknowledging the other vehicle or slowing down at all. It passed in a blur of bright lights and a glimpse of red, with a whoosh that reminded James of the sounds he'd heard from up on the hill. He swallowed, trying to get his heart to go back down into his chest where it belonged.

At last the sheriff turned the car into a small field painted with stripes. He rolled the vehicle to a stop between two of the stripes, then pushed his lever forward and did some other things with the controls. The purring of the car stopped, and with it the vibration that James had scarcely noticed but had become accustomed to. It was suddenly dead quiet.

The sheriff got out, bringing James's guns with him, opened the door beside James, and gestured for him to get down. The drive had shaken James up some and he had to steady himself against the car. The sheriff gave him a suspicious frown.

"Come on," he said, gesturing toward a building nearby.

"Gunslingers first."

Bright lights illuminated the building and shone out through its windows. James would have liked to look it over but the sheriff behind him was impatient, so he went up to the front doors, figured out which part of them were the handles and pulled one open.

Inside, the place was warm and lit up bright as day, with some kind of hanging lamps that put out more light than anything he'd ever seen. He gave up trying to figure them out, or where the heat was coming from since he didn't see a fireplace anywhere. It was magic, pure and simple.

"In there," the sheriff said, gesturing to a hallway as he shed his featherbed coat. Beneath it he wore a tan shirt and trousers, the shirt decorated with a couple of badges.

Another fellow in a similar tan shirt looked up from a desk as they passed. The sheriff exchanged a couple of words with him, and he shot a grin at James, then went back to writing on some papers on the desk.

The sheriff took James into a room with whitewashed walls bare of any paper or even pictures, and made him blow some air into a piece of arcane apparatus that he couldn't begin to fathom. He consigned that to magic as well. It was a handy way to think of the things he didn't understand.

"You're clean," the sheriff said, frowning at the contraption. "OK, you can go, but stay out of trouble."

"Thank you kindly, Sheriff," James said, then stepped toward the counter where the man had set down his gun belt.

"Whoa, hold on there, I didn't say you could take that."

James looked him in the face, biting down on his own impatience. "It is my property, sir, and I need it."

The sheriff gave him a measuring stare. "Yeah, I suppose you do, for the show."

The sheriff pulled one of the pistols from its holster and opened the cylinder. He took out a round and looked at it, then whistled through his teeth.

"Man, these are antiques! Where'd you get these?"

"Had 'em a while."

The sheriff gave him a skeptical glance, then took the rest of the cartridges out of both guns. James clenched his teeth on his growing anger as the sheriff swept the cartridges into a pile.

"I'll have to keep these. You can take the guns. Don't get into any trouble with them, all right?"

"No, sir," James said quietly, accepting the gun belt. He buckled it on and felt better with the Colts back on his hips, even unloaded. He'd have to get some more cartridges once he earned some money.

The sheriff opened the door and gestured for him to go out. James walked in silence back through the building to the front doors, with the sheriff following him. He pulled the door open and winced at the sudden cold.

"Stay out of trouble, now," said the sheriff.

James gave him a measured look, then a single nod. Bracing himself, he stepped out into the chilly night.

He walked over to the field where the sheriff's car sat silent and dark. He hoped to hell he wouldn't ever have to drive one of those things. It might be that he'd have to go east in one, but he'd much prefer traveling by rail.

If they still had railways. He shivered, glanced back at the jailhouse, then stepped out into the street.

He had no idea where he was. This didn't look anything like the Deadwood he remembered. Deciding to head for where the most light and sound was, he walked across the street and headed toward some tall buildings.

The street had boardwalks of a kind on both sides, though they weren't covered. They weren't made of boards, either, but of some hard, gray mortar, all sculpted to a perfectly even surface. James followed one to a crossroads where there was another set of the hanging red and green lights. A fellow in a ten-gallon hat was standing at the corner with a young woman whose short skirt—higher than her knees—proclaimed her to be a soiled dove. Both of them wore puffy featherbed coats, and both grinned at James as he joined them.

"Yee-haw, pardner!" said the man.

James touched the brim of his hat. "Evening," he said.

"Great getup!" said the soiled dove, and gave him a saucy smile.

James smiled back. For all the differences, it looked like Deadwood was still his kind of town.

"C'mon, change!" said the man, looking at the lights across the way.

There were more of these than James had been able to notice from the sheriff's car. Now that he had the time, he saw that all four corners of the crossroads had lampposts with glowing light pictures on them. People here and now sure liked to decorate the right-of-ways.

As he was admiring an orange picture of a hand—fortune teller's shop sign, perhaps?—it went out and a different picture came on, a stick-figure of a man leaning forward in glowing blue-white light. The fellow and the soiled dove started across the street. James followed them.

The man turned his head to address James. "Going to Saloon Number Ten?"

James tried to ignore the sinking feeling in his stomach. "Might look in there."

"You in the show?"

"Not tonight."

The fellow looked disappointed. The soiled dove whispered something in his ear, then giggled and shot James a coy look.

James thought about whether he might try to take her away from the other fellow, but he had the severe disadvantage of empty pockets. She looked like a choice piece, so she wouldn't be cheap. Maybe at the saloon he'd find a woman who was a little older, a little more inclined to be sympathetic with a fellow who was down on his luck.

Maybe he could get into a game and make some money that way. He'd have to find someone who'd give him a stake.

The thought of a card game sent a queer sort of shiver down his spine. He loved to play, loved nothing more in this world than a good game of bluff poker, but the last time he'd sat down at a card table in the No. 10 Saloon he hadn't been so lucky.

He'd just keep his back to the wall, that's all. He'd never make that mistake again. To hell with courtesy, and to hell with the game if the other players wouldn't give him the seat he wanted.

A car whooshed by in the street beside them, startling James so fierce he jumped. He stared after it, fascinated by the long, low shape of it and the red lights hanging on the back, like the lanterns on a caboose. The fellow with his gal kept on walking, and they went around a corner just as James glanced up at them. He hurried after them, noting a street sign that announced he had arrived at Main Street.

Turning the corner, he was astonished. There was light and color everywhere, even more than on the other streets. Music blared out of doorways that stood open despite the cold — strange, loud music with a fast, thumping beat. There were cars, big and small and painted every color of the rainbow, lining the sides of the street. More cars were driving back and forth, and crowds of people walked along the boardwalks.

The women amazed him more than anything. Not a one of them was properly dressed. Those in skirts wore them indecently short, and the rest wore trousers, like crazy old Calamity Jane. Most had painted their faces with licentious abandon. He saw several women wearing black leather jackets decorated with strange silver studs, usually over denim trousers. Quite a few of the men wore these as well.

The fellow and his soiled dove had vanished into the crowd. James stood on the corner staring down Main Street, trying to fit what he was looking at into his memory of Deadwood. The way the street lay looked about right, but everything else was changed. All the buildings were taller, all lit up so bright. Some ghost of the rowdy mining town he'd known might still be here, but it was only a ghost.

He looked up toward the hillside, but the bright lights in town kept him from seeing the shape of it. If he guessed right he was facing northeast, which meant the No. 10 Saloon would be on the right up ahead. He started walking, looking all around in the hope of seeing something familiar.

There were gaming establishments and restaurants, hotels, shops, and signs advertising tours. He reached another street and started across it when a blaring airhorn and a familiar screeching sound made him jump back onto the boardwalk.

A large red car had stopped in front of him. The driver yelled obscenities out of his open window, then drove on. James started after the car, his heart pounding.

"Better wait for the light to cross, dude," said someone near him in a laconic voice. "Traffic is crazy in this town."

James turned and saw a sleepy-eyed young man in a black duster and denim trousers that were much too large for him. The fellow was regarding him with a lazy stare that brought his instincts alert.

James kept a wary eye on him, his hands twitching near his guns despite their useless condition. He wished the sheriff had left him even one round.

He watched the people around him, and when a group of them started across the street together he followed. Cars had stopped to let them cross. He didn't bother puzzling why. He just wanted to get to the saloon.

On the corner was a tall building with a lighted green sign. He walked past it and stopped in front of the next building.

The sign called it Saloon No. 10, and it was in about the right situation, but it didn't look at all as he remembered. The No. 10 had been a ramshackle wooden shack. This place was brick, with a lot of signs loudly proclaiming it to be the place where he'd been killed, which he thought a might tactless.

WILD BILL HICKOK
MURDERED BY JACK MCCALL
1, 3, 5, 7, 9

It was pleasing to be remembered, but a little disconcerting to find that one's most memorable act had been dying. He frowned as he gazed at the sign. Those numbers made a pretty useless poker hand, if that was what they were supposed to be. No pair, only an ace. He'd won on less, but not often.

He went in, glad to get out of the cold. Like the jailhouse, the saloon was lit up brighter than day. Chandeliers hanging from the ceiling and lights with glass chimneys on the walls all burned with a steady, unnatural whiteness.

The saloon was crowded, rowdy with laughter and the music of a piano hidden somewhere he couldn't see, sounded like it was right overhead. James made his way deeper in and paused beside a glass case holding an old chair. A neatly lettered sign identified it as the chair he had been sitting in when he'd died. He stared at it, trying to remember. Hadn't really noticed the chair, except that it was in the wrong place.

Another case on the wall displayed the nine of diamonds, with a sign labeled "Dead Man's Hand" in large letters, claiming the nine was the kicker card in the hand he'd been holding when he was shot. That he *did* remember—he'd had aces and eights, and the kicker was the queen of hearts. He chuckled, pleased to find that showmen were still the same blustering liars they had ever been.

He really ought to find out what year it was. He looked at the walls, where there were a lot of other things on display including every photograph ever taken of him, or so it seemed. There were no calendars, however.

He turned his attention to the bar instead, wondering if the barkeep, a weaselly looking fellow in a vest and string tie, would be sympathetic. The bar was new and different, a long, massive thing of highly polished wood, and there was a poker game going on at a table nearby.

A chill went through James as he looked at the table. The men sitting there were dressed more normally, in buckskins or frock coats. And wearing guns, he noticed. In noticing that, he realized that none of the other patrons wore guns. The sheriff had worn one, a strange little black snub-nosed item, but no one else in the town seemed to carry a weapon.

One of the players glanced up at him and got a queer look on his face, then went back to the game. A few other people were standing about dressed in familiar styles, including a couple of soiled doves who by comparison with the rest of the women looked positively prim. These all seemed to be watching the game.

In fact, pretty much everyone in the place was watching the game. There must be some high stakes on the table.

James drew a little closer to get a better look. Across the table from him another fellow drew closer, too. Maybe it was that the other fellow happened to be coming from the direction of the door, or maybe it was the look in his eye, but James suddenly felt a dread warning in his bones. He opened his mouth to call out even as the man was reaching for his gun, then the pistol fired and all hell broke loose.

James's gun was in his hand. People had screamed at the shot, and now, strangely, some were laughing.

A man at the table collapsed forward. The fellow who'd fired ran out of the saloon, and the other players got up and chased him. No one bothered with the man who'd been shot. James holstered his gun and hurried to his side.

The man was wearing buckskins, a big hat, and a string tie to his starched white shirt. James knelt by him and put a hand on his shoulder.

"Where're you hit?"

The man opened his eyes and gave him a startled glance, then moaned loudly and collapsed again. Someone grabbed at James, shoving him aside.

It was the barkeep, who shot James a dirty glance, then turned to the man sprawled on the floor. After a cursory examination, he stood up and pronounced, "He's dead! Wild Bill is dead!"

The soiled doves let out a chorus of "Oh, no!" and commenced to making weepy noises. James stepped back, cold realization pouring through his limbs.

The "dead" man had spilled his cards artfully across the

floor. Aces and eights, nine of diamonds.

Everyone else in the place started applauding. James felt queasy. He swept the room with his gaze, saw smiling faces, nodding at him. They thought he was part of this macabre farce.

He needed a drink. Shoved his way to the bar, then remembered he didn't have any money.

Behind the bar a young woman stood grinning at him. She was dressed like the soiled doves. Her face was painted like a harlot's, but she didn't inspire any lust in him, not at the moment.

"That was an interesting little ad-lib," she said. "You had Marty scared for a minute."

She nodded toward the card table. James glanced that way and saw the barkeep and the two soiled doves carrying the "dead" man away. The crowd had gone to chattering and laughing, and a lot of them were leaving the saloon. The show was over.

"Like your outfit," the gal added. "What can I get you?"

"I don't have any money, ma'am, but I sure could use a glass of whiskey."

She cocked an eyebrow at him. "All right."

James watched her reach behind her to a row of bottles and pour a small glass of golden liquor. She put a little square of tissue paper in front of him and set the glass on it.

"On me. You deserve something for spicing up the show."

"I thank you kindly, ma'am."

James lifted the glass and admired the whiskey's clear golden color. None of the rot-gut that Nutter and Hall had poured in shameless libel of the name of whiskey. This looked to be first-rate stuff. He smelled it, took a sip, and then drained the glass, setting it down on the bar with a sigh as it burned down his throat and lit a fire in his belly.

"Ambrosia," he said, nodding to the gal pouring drinks. "Thank you."

"You're welcome. Just don't expect a free drink every night."

"Every night?"

James glanced at the card table, which another gal was

clearing, taking away the cards, empty glasses, even the coins the players had been betting. He looked at the woman behind the bar again. She was filling glasses of beer from a tap mounted right there on the bar.

"They do this—show—every night?"

"Five times a day. One, three, five, seven, and nine. This is the last week of that, though. Drops back to three shows in the winter."

She set a filled glass on a tray with some others and one of the other gals picked it up and carried it away. James looked after her, wishing he had the money for a glass of beer or better yet, another whiskey.

"You know, you're a dead ringer for Wild Bill," the gal at the bar said.

Dead ringer. James couldn't help a weak smile. Dead, anyway, or had been.

Come to think of it, he was none too sure about his present status. He gave a cough of unwilling laughter.

"You interested in doing the show?" she asked. "I know Marty's been talking about taking some time off."

That was what the sheriff had suggested, that he come do this show. That was why he'd come here, wasn't it? To try for some gainful employment, only he hadn't realized it would involve reenacting his own murder.

He didn't know if he could do it, even once, let alone five times a day. The very idea made his stomach twist up in a knot around that fine whiskey. He blinked, swallowed, and managed to speak.

"Who would I see about that?"

~ Ned ~

Las Vegas, Nevada

Ned rolled over and tried to go back to sleep, which was when he discovered he was lying on the floor. He was fully dressed in his best silk suit, and he was sweating. Wherever he was, the air conditioning wasn't working, and these clothes were much too hot for Vegas, even at night.

A glint of light from something metal made him look up, and suddenly he recognized the place—narrow space like a hallway to nowhere, marble wall rising on one side, with big metal name plaques. His family's names.

"Fucking Christ!"

Either he had taken too many drugs or not enough. Probably not enough.

He was in the fucking mausoleum, Eden Vale, where his family was stashed. There they were, looking down at him—Daddy and Mama and the whole Runyon crew.

He scrambled to his feet and out of the space in front of the vaults, into the little chapel area with its token rectangles of colored glass. The air was stuffy and no lights were on. A vague noise of traffic reached him from outside.

He went to the glass doors and saw outside the familiar palm trees: three to the right, three more to the left, confirming where he was. He tried the door, but it was bolted.

Definitely not enough drugs.

This was some asshole's idea of a great joke. Randy, probably. Fucking bitch! It was just her kind of trick. Man, would she be sorry when he ran her down!

He stood fuming, trying to remember when he'd last seen her. There was something about her...he couldn't remember. He'd been having nightmares, maybe that was it. He needed a hit. He always thought clearer when he was high.

He searched his pockets. Absolutely empty. Fucking Randy had even taken his wallet, goddamn bitch. She was probably out spending the cash right now, or blowing it on the tables.

His money. His money. She had said something about his money. She and fucking Dick Tabbet, they'd come to his house. Flaunting their affair in his face. Tabbet had been his friend, goddamn back-stabber. His friend and his mistress, lovers.

Anger and pain came stabbing at him. Ned rubbed his eyes, trying to will the misery away. He needed some horse. He had to get home, get some cash, get some drugs. Then he'd fix fucking Randy and Dick.

Yeah, he had to get out of here. He had the strangest desire to go to Atlantic City. That made no sense, but what the hell did make sense in this screwy world?

He searched the mausoleum for a back door. Found one, but it was bolted shut, too. Didn't they have fire regulations about that?

He jogged back to the front doors. Just that little effort got him sweating. He needed to lose weight, get back in shape. Doctors were always nagging him. Probably they were right, but he just didn't care enough. He had money, so he could get what he wanted without being young and beautiful. Good thing, 'cause he was neither any more.

Once he had been. Once the girls had hung on him just for his looks, forget the money. Of course, it didn't hurt to be the son of Ronny Runyon, founder of the Rabbit's Foot Casino. Old Ronny had been one of the friendliest gamesters in town and one of the meanest SOBs if you crossed him. Living in his shadow was a hell of a drag, but the perks made it tolerable.

Daddy Ronny was long dead, though. He was up there in the marble wall. Ned had succeeded him as owner of the Rabbit's Foot, but he'd lost the casino, along with his gaming license, in a power struggle with his siblings. He now had nothing left to do in life except indulge his appetites.

The drugs, the women, the gambling. They would kill him someday, but he was resigned to that. He enjoyed the hell out of them, and had no reason to go looking for another kind of life.

His gaze fell on a fire extinguisher mounted to the wall by the hallway. He grabbed it and swung it at one of the glass doors. It took two tries to break through, and a few more swings to clear enough glass so he could get through the opening. Alarm bells clanged the whole time, but he ignored them. He tossed the fire extinguisher aside and stepped through the door.

A big, black limo sat at the curb. Lincoln town car, had mob written all over it.

Ned's heart started pumping and he turned around, heading behind the mausoleum. He hustled his steps and was out of breath by the time he'd got the building between him and the car.

He sneezed and rubbed at his eyes some more. A hot breeze was blowing, and there was always some obnoxious, high-allergen weed blooming in the desert.

Maybe he *should* go to Atlantic City. Might change his luck. Get away from Randy, find a less sadistic bitch to warm his bed. Randy was a fucking psychopath. Not that she was warming his bed much anymore. She only came around when she wanted something from him.

He frowned, trying to remember whatever it was that niggled at him. Randy wanted money.

She always wanted money. No, that wasn't it. He'd figure it out later. First he had to get home.

He dashed to the wall that surrounded the grounds, keeping an eye peeled toward the limo. No sign of movement there. He climbed on top of a dumpster and hopped over the wall, then hustled up the street, keeping off the sidewalk as much as he could.

When he got to the corner he looked cautiously around. No limo, but no taxis either. Not much traffic; this time of night all the action was downtown and on the Strip.

He really didn't want to walk anywhere, but it looked like he'd have to find a phone, 'cause there weren't any taxis around here at night. Cussing under his breath, he crossed the street to a convenience store, keeping a wary eye out for the black limo.

He could see the lights of Fremont Street and the tower of the Rabbit's Foot. He felt a pang for the old casino, even though these days he preferred the Palms. He squinted at the tower. For a minute it looked like the big rabbit's foot was gone, replaced with a giant "R."

Hallucinating. He shook his head and rubbed at his eyes, but it didn't go away. Annoyed, he went into the convenience store.

His feet were killing him. The shoes he had on, Armanis, were new and expensive and uncomfortable as hell, not meant for hiking around in. He was getting a blister on one heel, he was pretty sure.

The scrawny kid behind the counter gave him a look like a startled deer. Ned was in too foul a mood to make nice.

"Lemme use your phone," he said.

"Pay phone's out front," the kid said.

"That's fucking great, except I don't have any money. I've been robbed, OK? And I need to call a cab."

The kid's eyes went even wider. "Should I call the cops?"

Ned hated cops. "No, just call me a fucking cab, all right? Jesus!"

He paced away while the kid made the call. He maybe could have called a friend instead, except it was late.

He looked at his wrist, but he wasn't wearing his watch. Fucking Randy probably took it and pawned it.

Glancing at the clock behind the counter, he saw it was after two. Party time. Some of his friends would be out and around, but he figured it was better just to get a cab. He didn't much want to explain how he'd come to be in need of a ride.

For that matter, he *couldn't* explain it; he didn't fucking remember how he got to the mausoleum. A cabbie wouldn't care, and Ned could pay him when he got home.

"Cab's on the way," the kid said. "Say, you look a lot like that guy who got killed a few years ago."

Ned turned away without a word and walked out the front

door. He was in no mood for a sick joke like that. He'd had one sick joke too many already tonight. He was even having trouble remembering what day it was. Not that that was unusual.

It was hot outside and he almost turned to go back in and wait in the store, but he saw a cab pulling into the parking lot and hurried toward it instead. Pulled open the back door and got in, sighing gratefully for the cold blast of the air conditioner.

"Where to?" said the cabbie, a chubby middle-aged woman with red hair out of a bottle. She snapped her gum and looked at him expectantly.

He gave his address and leaned back, closing his eyes. His head was aching. What a fuck of a night.

"Say, you related to that Runyon guy? You look like him."

Ned opened his eyes a crack. "Runyon?"

"Yeah, Fred Runyon. Used to run the Rabbit's Foot. Got killed by his girlfriend and her boyfriend. Or his ex-girlfriend, I guess. Didn't you see it on TV?"

Ned felt a chill on the back of his neck. Must be the air conditioner. "I don't watch the news."

"Oh, it was all over the place a few years ago. His ex and her boyfriend, they killed him and took all his money, only the court overturned it on appeal and they got away scot free. Ask me, they're guilty as hell."

Ned sighed and closed his eyes again. He didn't know what the fuck she was talking about, and he didn't want to know. He just wanted to get home and get high.

Fortunately, the drive didn't take long. The cabbie shut up after a while and just drove. Ned didn't open his eyes again until the car stopped at the curb in front of his house.

"That'll be fifteen-fifty," she said. Snap.

"I don't have it on me. Wait and I'll bring it out."

"What the fuck? You trying to rip me off, buddy? Gonna screw me for a lousy fifteen bucks?"

No, you'd have to pay me a lot more than that, Ned thought.

"I'm not gonna rip you off, but someone took my wallet. I have to get cash from inside."

"Well, you can leave your jacket here, then," she said crankily. Snap, snap.

God, what a bitch. But it was hot anyway. Ned got out of the car, shrugged out of his jacket, and tossed it on the back seat.

"Be right back."

He turned to the house. Didn't have his keys, so he'd have to punch in the code on the gate. He walked up to it and jabbed at the security panel. The gate didn't open.

"What the fuck?"

Had Randy changed the code? That was going too far! He tried the code again with no luck, then peered through the gate. Two cars sat in the driveway, a green truck and something yellow that looked like it should have clowns coming out of it.

The truck could be Dick's, but who the fuck's was the clown car? Randy wouldn't be caught dead driving that thing.

He was about to start yelling when he noticed something else on the driveway. A red and yellow plastic trike.

Holy fuck. Someone else was living in his house.

He looked up at the windows, all dark. A sudden dread descended on him, along with that urge to drop it all and go to Jersey. Fuck, fuck, fuck! He must have had a bad crash. Must have been out for days. Weeks, even, long enough for them to fucking sell his fucking house!

He turned back to the cab. The driver sat snapping her fucking gum, looking bored. His suit jacket was neatly folded beside her on the front seat. He climbed into the back again.

"I changed my mind. Take me to the Desert Inn."

"The Desert Inn?" The driver turned around and gave him a weird look.

"Yeah, the Desert Inn. What, are you deaf?"

"What are *you*, stoned?"

"I wish. Just drive." Ned leaned back and sighed. His head was starting to ache.

The cabbie kept staring at him, snapping the gum. "You got money at the Desert Inn, eh?"

"I got friends there. Don't worry, I'll pay you. Fifty bucks. If not, you can keep my jacket."

The cabbie shook her head. "OK, pal. Whatever you say."

She turned around and took off, muttering something into her dispatch radio. Ned glanced back at his house as the cab pulled away from the curb. He'd get whatever fucker had pulled this. If it was Randy and Dick, they were both dead.

He tried to remember what had happened, but could only conjure vague dreams. Wandering around lost in the Rabbit's Foot's casino, watching the World Series of Poker and cussing the winners. Spacing out on the floor of his house. He'd been chasing the dragon, and he couldn't tell the nightmares from reality.

Too much horse. Not enough.

He swallowed the saliva that rose to his tongue. God, he needed a fix.

Don't think about it. He had to talk to Donny. Donny'd lend him some cash and help him sort out this mess.

The cabbie turned down the Strip and Ned looked out at the lights. They seemed even brighter and more crazy than usual. He stared out the window as they passed the sci-fi shape of the Stratosphere, the carnival pinkness of Circus Circus. All the glitz that hid the dark stuff underneath this tawdry town. God, he loved this place.

The cab pulled across the street into a long drive that led up to a hotel he didn't recognize. It was Bellagio-shaped but slick and modern, with a lake out front and landscaping out the wazoo and a honkin' sign that said "Wynn."

"That fucker Wynn," Ned muttered. "Buying up the whole fucking Strip."

The cab pulled to a stop at the lobby entrance. The cabbie turned around and looked at him.

"What the fuck is this?" Ned demanded.

"Desert Inn's gone, buddy. They tore it down ten years ago. Where've you been?"

Ned looked behind them at the other side of the Strip. He could see the corner of the Fashion Mall, but the Frontier was fucking gone. Desert Inn, too, was gone.

He looked back at the giant Wynn hotel. It was sleek and modern, whispering of huge amounts of money.

His stomach churned. This was getting fucking scary. His house they could sell in a few weeks, but tear down the Desert Inn and build this? It would take years. What the hell had happened?

"So," said the cabbie, grinning, "about that fifty bucks—"

"Wait here."

Ned got out of the cab and walked into the hotel. Cool air washed over him. The lobby was huge and expensive, the ceilings painted with weird flowers. It was quiet, unlike the older hotels where the sound of the slots was an ever-present jangle in the background of the lobby. This place oozed class. Ned went over to the concierge desk, occupied despite the late hour.

"I want to speak to Donny Salgado."

The concierge, a smart-mouthed looking spic kid in tailored charcoal silk, raised an eyebrow. Ned bit back an insult and tried again.

"Mr. Donny Salgado. He was a resident of the Desert Inn."

"Ah. Well, sir, I suggest you might try Planet Hollywood. Starwood owns that property."

What the hell was Planet fucking Hollywood? Never mind. Starwood was the big conglomerate that had owned the Desert Inn. Donny had an interest. He had his fingers in a lot of pies in Vegas.

"You got a phone I can use to call over there?"

The guy's polite smile wilted a little, but he picked up a phone and dialed, then handed the receiver to Ned. After a couple of rings, a woman's voice answered.

"Planet Hollywood."

"Yeah, is Donny Salgado staying there?"

She hesitated. "I'm not able to give you that information, sir, I'm sorry."

"OK, if he's there, I want you to connect me to his room."

"It's after two in the morning—"

"I know that!" Fucking bitch. "Just connect me."

"Please hold," she said in a voice gone frosty.

He held. The concierge was shuffling brochures on his desk, obviously wishing Ned would leave. Ned turned his back and leaned against the desk.

Finally the phone started ringing. He counted seven rings before the sound of someone fumbling to pick up on the other end.

"What?" said a cranky voice.

"Donny, it's Ned. I need your help."

"What the fuck? Who is this?"

"It's Ned."

Silence. Then a click. He'd hung up.

Ned turned to the concierge. "We got disconnected. Could you redial it?"

The smile was gone by now, replaced by the beginnings of a frown. Ned smiled instead, the ho-ho-I'm-just-a-big-overgrown-kid smile that usually made points with the chicks. The concierge barely stifled a sigh and punched the phone. Ned gave him a big grin and a nod, then turned around again.

This time Donny picked up after three rings. Ned shouted over Donny's cussing.

"Donny don't hang up. It's me, Ned. I need your help, buddy."

"Whoever the fuck you are, this is one sick, tasteless joke!"

"Don, it's me, Neddy! C'mon, pal, I need you! Look I'm coming over, all right? What's your room number."

"Fuck you, that's my number."

"Wait, wait, wait! OK, I'll meet you in the lobby, then. Please, Don old buddy. I really need a friend right now. And could you lend me a hundred? I gotta pay the cab."

A pause. "You sure do sound like Ned."

Ned laughed. "Yeah, well, what do I gotta do to convince you?" He dropped his voice, cupping a hand over the phone. "Look, I'm not dead, OK? I'm alive and I need your help."

"Fffuuuck."

Ned waited, shifting from foot to foot. He could feel the

concierge's eyes boring into the back of his head.

"OK," Donny said slowly. "In the lobby, then. Fucking Christ."

Donny hung up and Ned handed back the phone with another big smile. "Thanks."

The concierge hung up the phone, glanced at Ned's hands, and saw no tip forthcoming. His face turned sour and he said nothing. Ned hurried away, out the big glass doors that slid aside with a whisper, out into the sweltering night. He was half afraid the cabbie would have left, but she was still there, snapping her gum and watching the meter tally up the bucks.

Beyond the cab sat the black Lincoln. The back of Ned's neck prickled as he froze in his tracks.

The back door of the limo swung open and a woman leaned toward him, her cleavage drawing his gaze. Something sparkled there, a pendant of diamonds or rhinestones. She was dark, Mexican maybe, and small. She smiled and beckoned to him.

His body said "yes," but his brain screamed "no." He'd been hijacked once already.

He jumped in the back seat of the cab and told the driver to go to Planet Hollywood. She looked over her shoulder at him and rolled her eyes.

"My friend moved over there, OK? I talked to him, he's bringing some money. You'll get paid, all right? Now move it!"

Move it she did. Ned had to grab the Jesus bar to keep from sliding off the seat. He looked back at the hotel as the cab sailed down the very long, sloping drive. Definitely a New Vegas style place. He preferred Old Vegas.

The limo followed.

Ned wished there was more traffic. The Strip wasn't so crowded this late, though there were still plenty of people shuffling from casino to casino with their cups full of tokens. Most of the tourists had gone to bed, and the hard-core partiers owned the town from now until dawn. Ordinarily he loved this time of night, but the Lincoln prowling behind him killed his pleasure.

Trying to distract himself, Ned gazed at the lights of the casinos, looking for differences now. If he'd been gone long enough for the Desert Inn to go down and that slick bastard to go up in its place, he'd lost a few years.

Jesus. Years. Holy crap.

He didn't want to think about that. Instead he looked at the hotels, seeking familiar places. Bellagio and Paris were both open —they had been under construction last he knew. The heap next door to Paris was vaguely familiar, then he saw the sign that said Planet Hollywood and almost pissed his pants. It was huge, a three-armed thing that looked like the old Aladdin on steroids, swollen to three times its normal size.

That's right. They'd torn the old Aladdin down. He'd watched the demolition with some friends. Donny had been there, come to think of it. Ned had been feeling down because he'd lost his gaming license. They'd mourned about that and about the loss of another Old Vegas hotel, about how the new Aladdin was going to be a mega-resort like Wynn's new Bellagio, with a mall built in so the gals could shop while the men played the tables.

Had they scrapped that plan? Built this slick, white Planet Hollywood thing instead? Ned wouldn't have thought Donny'd be caught dead living in a place like that.

The cabbie pulled up to the entrance and gave him a bored glance. He told her to wait and hurried into the lobby. Soft, thick carpet hushed his footsteps. He looked anxiously around for Donny and spotted him next to a big potted palm.

Donny looked as wiry as ever. There was a lot more gray in his curly black hair than Ned remembered. He was dressed in a rumpled red jogging suit, and looked less than happy. Ned put on a smile.

"Donny. Thanks, pal, I knew you'd come through for me. You got the hundred?"

"Fuck, it *is* you!"

"Of course it's me! Listen, somebody's done a number on me. Give me that cash so I can pay the cab and then we'll talk about it."

Donny slowly put his hand in his pocket, eyes fixed on Ned in a puzzled frown. He pulled out a small wad of twenties and handed it over.

"Thanks, pal. You're the man. Be right back."

Ned hurried out to the cab and ransomed his jacket with three of the twenties. He looked for the limo but didn't see it—which didn't make him feel any better. He shoved the other bills in his pocket, slung the jacket over his shoulder, and went back to the lobby.

Donny led him to a bar where they retired to a booth in the back and ordered double whiskeys. Low music thumped in the background, and the place was cool and dark. Ned took a large swallow of his drink and sighed, then loosened his tie and unbuttoned his cuffs, turning them back a couple of times.

"I can't believe it," Donny said, shaking his head. "You were dead."

"So I heard. I don't know how they did it, but somebody put me on ice and gave it out I was dead."

"You *were* dead, man! I came to the viewing. You were wearing that same tie."

Ned glanced down at the tie, a striped number, pale blue and white with a kind of silvery sheen. He didn't remember it, but then he had about a billion ties.

"Must've been some poor schmoe they dressed up to look like me. Whoever did this is a sick fuck, you know? Obviously it was a threat."

"A threat? Put you on ice fourteen years as a threat? Man, who'd go to the trouble?"

"I don't know. I thought at first Randy'd done it, but I don't think she could pull this off. Maybe I pissed off the mob. They been after me anyway, ever since they did Fat Herbie."

Donny glared at him over his whiskey glass. "Piss off the mob, they ice you permanent. No, it'd take some weirdo with a lot of cash and too much imagination to dream up something like this and pull it off."

"Yeah, but Hughes is dead."

"He wasn't the only rich weirdo in Vegas."

They both took slugs of their drinks. Ned rolled his glass between his palms and looked for a waitress to order another round.

"Somebody's living in my house."

"Yeah, well. You were dead."

"So my assets are all gone."

"Yeah."

"I've got some silver stashed."

"No, you don't. Dick Tabbet dug it up."

Ned stared at Donny. Donny took another pull at his drink.

"That's why he and Randy were taken to trial," Donny added. "They also tracked some of your coins and stuff back to Tabbet. I assume you heard about the trial?"

Ned frowned. "Some."

"They were accused of burking you for your cash."

"Son of a bitch."

Ned finished his drink in one large swallow. A red haze was beginning to form around the edges of his vision. Unusual on only one drink, but then god only knew what the kidnappers had doped him with. He didn't feel too bad physically. He was getting angrier by the minute, though.

Donny caught the eye of a passing waitress and called for another round. "So, what did happen?"

"Fuck if I remember."

"Oh. You don't remember anything for the past fourteen years?"

Ned shook his head. "I remember sending Connie off to college. I remember telling my lawyer to take Randy out of the will. Had the feeling she was going to try something. Did he do that?"

Donny shrugged. "She was convicted, so she didn't inherit anything. Only they overturned the conviction, so I don't know what happened."

"Sonofabitch! She got off?"

"Both of 'em got off. Some of the evidence was thrown out, something about button-marks on your chest. You got any of those?"

Ned glanced at his chest. He didn't know, and he wasn't going to strip in the bar to find out.

"I'll fucking kill 'em!"

"Ch, ch, ch," Donny said as the waitress came up. She set down their glasses, shot a questioning glance at Donny, then left.

Ned gulped down half the new drink. "You gotta help me, Donny. You gotta help me get my life back."

"Afraid that's beyond my scope, buddy. Talk to your lawyer."

"Yeah. I'll call him in the morning." Ned took another swig, frowning at the table top. "You ever been to Atlantic City?"

"No. Why?"

"Just wondering. Been thinking about it."

"If the mob's after you, I'd stay out of Jersey."

"They're not after me. I'm dead, right?"

"Christ, Neddy."

"Think about it. It'd be like starting with a clean slate."

"OK, I'm too tired for this. It's three in the fucking morning, Ned." Donny finished his drink, then stood up, pulled a couple of crumpled bills out of his pocket, and dropped them on the table. "You want a place to crash? I got a spare bed."

Ned looked up at him and managed a smile. "Thanks, Donny. You're the best."

"Come on."

Ned followed his friend to the elevators and they rode up in silence. The mirrored elevator wall gave Ned his first good look at himself since he'd woken up at the mausoleum. Rumpled suit, tie loose and askew, face round and flushed and the silver hair fading back from his temples. He looked like a fucking chipmunk. When had that happened?

He was fifty-five. In the prime of life, right? But he looked like shit and he felt strangely adrift. His house, money, mistress, all gone. Frankly, he didn't care if he never saw fucking Randy again.

"What happened to the silver?" he asked.

"I think it went to Connie after they caught Tabbet digging it up."

"Good, good."

If Connie had the money, that was all right. He'd wanted it to go to her anyway. He could call her—no, that wouldn't be good. He could go out to her school, explain what had happened, and she'd give him some money back. She was a good kid, and she loved her dad.

Only she must have finished school by now. Donny was right, he should talk to Tom White in the morning, find out what the hell had happened.

He sighed. More than ever he wanted a fix. Smoky white dragon rising from the heated foil. He could practically taste it.

The elevator doors opened on a hall with plush carpets and gentle lighting from lamps on the walls. Donny led Ned to his suite and dropped the key card on a table by the phone. Ned strolled past him into the living room. The picture windows looked out on a prime view of Bellagio with a glimpse of Paris to the side.

He ambled over to the coffee table, which held a couple of big picture books of the kind useful for impressing chicks. "You got anything about the murder trial?"

Donny stifled a yawn. "Nah. It was all over the papers. Been a couple of books written, too. You're fucking famous, now that you're dead."

"Not dead. I'm getting better." Ned glanced up at Donny, but the joke had missed. "Maybe I'll go pick up one of those books. Give me more of an idea what the hell happened."

"None of them mentioned alien abductions as far as I know."

"Ha, ha. Can you lend me a thousand?"

"I just gave you a hundred."

"Yeah, but I had to pay the cab—"

Donny came toward him suddenly like a bull at a red flag. Ned instinctively took a step back.

"I will give you another hundred," Donny said in a fierce,

low voice, "but you will not bring any drugs back here or I will kick your ass down the elevator shaft."

Ned laughed, a kind of sorry, apologetic laugh. "Sure, Don."

"And if you get busted for doing smack in some doorway, I will not bail you out. You get into that shit, you are on your own, bro. Got it?"

Donny's eyes were on fire. Ned nodded.

"Yeah. Got it."

Donny stomped out of the room, into his bedroom. Ned watched him out of sight, then his gaze drifted back to the window.

Glitter Gulch. Beautiful town.

He looked up when he heard Donny coming back. Pocketed the bills Donny pushed into his hand.

"Thanks, Don. I won't get in trouble. Can I borrow your key?"

"Just knock on the door when you're back. I don't mind."

Implication being he minded giving Ned his key more than he minded being awakened. It felt like a slap in the face, but Ned swallowed it and let the subject drop. He put on a grin.

"OK. Thanks Donny. You're a great guy."

Donny didn't smile. "Yeah. Take my advice, buy a couple of books and come straight back."

"Right."

Ned gave a thumbs up sign and headed for the door. When it closed behind him he paused for a moment as the hush of the hotel hallway descended on him.

In the distance he imagined he could hear the siren call of the slots, beckoning him to the casinos. Game of Hold'em to settle his nerves. Maybe stop by a strip joint, find a cutie, score some horse. He sucked in a deep breath and let it out with a happy sigh, then headed for the elevator.

~ Clive ~

Bloomfield, New Jersey

He woke from one nightmare to find himself in the middle of another. He'd been dreaming of Orson Jones, the captain of the *Silver Slipper*, who had taken exception to his success at cards in the *Slipper's* saloon and pursued him into Bloomfield.

Clive remembered quite clearly running from the captain, who had been rendered unreceptive by drink and who, most unreasonably, demanded the return of the monies Clive had won. Memory clouded after that. The dream had been terrible, and seemed to have repeated itself over and over. There was always a knife, a wicked blade in the captain's right hand. The other details were unclear, but the blade shone sharp and bright, though it had felt much the same as a punch, going in.

Clive moaned and rolled over. The ground he was on was very hard. He put a hand beneath his face to shield it and tried to recapture sleep, but it was hopeless. He would only dream again, and he had been caught in that dream far too long.

Over and over, the knife, the blow, falling and more blows, Jones's hands rifling his pockets, the chink of gold as the captain took his winnings. Then the dragging, the endless dragging.

He put a hand to the back of his head, expecting to find it sore. It was not. The night was silent except for the occasional swish of water from the paddlewheel of a passing steamboat. He listened for the creak of wagon wheels on the towpath. It never came.

Strange. Clive opened his eyes. There was an odd, smoky smell in the air. He had an intuition things weren't right.

He lifted his head, and in doing so became aware that he was not in Bloomfield, at least not in any part of it he remembered.

The road beneath him was peculiar, like pressed gravel coated with tar. He sat up and found that it was not a road at all.

He'd been lying between two monstrous machines, somewhat like locomotives though smaller, and not sitting on any rails. They were painted identically with shields labeled "New Jersey State Police" on their sides. Clive sat still for a long while, listening and pondering.

It occurred to him to check the wounds Jones's knife had given him. He wasn't able to find them, which rather annoyed him after all that endless dreaming. He felt perfectly all right.

Had it been a trick knife, then? The sort used on stage, with a disappearing blade; it must have been. Jones had used it to catch him off guard and had robbed him. And he'd fallen for it!

His pockets were empty of everything, valuable or not. A glance around where he'd been lying informed him that Jones had apparently taken his valise as well. And his beaver hat.

That was the last straw. He'd find that miserable bastard and have his hat back. It was a good hat, it fit him well, and he wanted it.

Let Orson Jones beware! Clive's dignity had suffered a worse blow than his person, and he brooked no insults to his dignity. He wanted his own back on that rascal.

He stood up and looked around, trying to get his bearings. He saw a building, large and blockish, lit very brightly by what had to be electric lights. He'd seen those in Manhattan, but not in Bloomfield.

Doubt shook him, stopping him in his tracks. This building was no part of Bloomfield, either. Though to inquire within seemed the simplest way to get help, his intuition warned him away from it.

Go south, a silent urging told him. South, to the coast, to the sea. To the Atlantic.

A seaside resort, yes. Pleasant weather, pleasant company, civilized folk who might enjoy a friendly game. A smile tugged at the corner of Clive's mouth.

The thought of such company was certainly more alluring

than the idea of confronting Jones, knife or no knife. He'd get his own back, make no mistake, but at present he was disadvantaged. If he could build up a stake, he could hire a lawyer to harass Captain Jones, and perhaps extract additional damages from him.

Clive's eyes narrowed even as his smile widened. Yes, that would be the way to handle that brute. The gentleman's way.

Parentage aside, Clive considered himself a gentleman in every respect, saving the minor detail that he was not above turning a card to win a pot. A fellow had to make a living, after all.

The night sky was starless, heavy with cloud. With a last glance at the strangely lit building, Clive turned away and walked out into the darkness, toward the swishing sounds that must be coming from the canal. There he'd find passage with the next willing boat captain.

Jones and his *Slipper* were probably long gone. He knew Jones had been heading down to Jersey City, so he might as well head that way himself. If the *Slipper* was not in evidence, he'd proceed down the coast, restore his finances, and then come back and find Jones.

Happy to have this plan settled, he dared to whistle a tune as he strolled down a street toward the canal. Houses on both sides —strange, boxy structures—unfamiliar, but never mind. The rushing sounds were growing louder. They came and went, stopping and starting, which Clive found rather disturbing. No steamboat he'd ever been on had operated in that way. He found himself revisiting his nightmare, realizing this sound had been in it, sometimes. Not every time.

The more he listened, the less it seemed like any sound he'd heard associated with a riverboat. Some other kind of machinery, then? Locks, or something? He knew the Morris Canal was fully contraptionized to an extent that bored him silly. Engineering had never interested him. He was a man of opportunity.

There were more lights ahead, electric lights on top of preposterously tall posts that he could see even above the buildings and trees. A drizzling rain began to fall and he turned up the collar of his jacket, wishing for his greatcoat that, alas, had been in his valise. He uttered a curse at Orson Jones's expense.

The rushing sounds grew louder as he crossed a final street. On the far side he found not the canal, but a wall, a good ten feet high or better, and made of concrete. The noise came from beyond it, a river of sound, and a line of the lights on tall posts stood beyond it as well. A road of the same tarred gravel upon which he'd awakened ran alongside the wall.

Hearing a mechanical growl to his left, he turned and saw two bright white lights barreling toward him at phenomenal speed, raindrops sparking in their beams. He caught his breath and stepped back, blinded. An air horn sounded, making him jump even more, then the thing swept past him, spattering him with water. It resembled the locomotives he'd woken among.

Perhaps he was still dreaming. He knew of nothing like that contraption, even in Manhattan.

Suddenly his knees felt weak. Not wanting to faint, he squatted at the side of the road. He rested his face in his hands and took deep breaths, trying to calm himself. After a moment he had a sense of not being alone, and looked up.

To his right, a riverboat was gliding toward him where a moment before there had been nothing. The boat was black as soot all over, with lanterns flickering orange on its upper deck like evil, winking eyes.

Clive shuddered. Another dream? He almost hoped he was asleep, but reason told him he was not. Reason could not explain the steamboat, though, floating along without any water beneath it.

The boat was coming for him. It was Charon, come to take him across the river Styx, to the underworld. Come to claim his life. A sense of doom washed over him, and endless sadness.

He heard the rushing of another locomotive from the left. He had time to do no more than glance up before it was upon him. This one slowed, rolling to a gentle stop beside him. A woman's voice called out from it.

"You OK?"

Clive slowly stood up, blinking rain from his eyes. The lights were pointing off into the night, raindrops glinted in their twin beams until they fell upon the riverboat which swallowed them into its blackness. The boat was closer now, and he could see a young man dressed in black standing on its deck, the orange lights from the torches glinting in his eyes. The youth waved to him.

"I-I was looking for the Morris Canal," Clive said, turning away from the boat.

"You're right next to it. It's the JFK Parkway up here, mostly."

Her face, dimly seen in the darkness, seemed kind but her words made no sense to him. She turned her head away and he heard her talking in a low voice. A man's voice answered, then she looked at Clive again and smiled.

"Lousy night for a history walk. Want a lift to someplace dry?"

Clive's heart rose at the suggestion. He glanced at the riverboat bearing down on them and hesitated no longer. "Thank you. Much obliged."

"Climb in."

He stepped toward the vehicle and hesitated. It was smaller and lower to the ground than the locomotive things. He had no idea how to get into it.

"You sure you're OK?" the woman asked.

"I-I'm sorry, I—I was robbed."

"Oh, you poor thing! Let me help you."

"Sheila—" called the man's voice.

A hatch on the side of the contraption swung open and the woman stepped out, wearing a greatcoat over trousers and boots. She pulled open a second hatch behind the first, then took Clive's elbow and guided him toward the vehicle.

"Watch your head," the woman said, putting a hand on the vehicle's roof above him.

Clive obeyed, ducking his head as he sat on a cushioned bench. The woman bent closer to him.

"Let me find the seat belt for you. It likes to slip down behind the seat."

He sat completely still, afraid to move while she leaned across him. In the front of the vehicle, a large, heavyset man sat looking back at him. Clive couldn't see his face in the darkness, but knew the fellow was keeping an eye on him. Beyond him, through the rain-dappled glass window at the front of the vehicle, the orange eyes of the riverboat loomed. Clive drew a sharp breath.

The woman stepped back, and Clive found that she'd lashed him into the seat with a couple of broad straps. He was about to protest when she shut the hatch, startling him. The vehicle sagged as she climbed into the seat in front of him. Instead of facing his as it should have in a carriage, it faced forward, like a rail car's.

Ahead was the riverboat, still coming nearer. Would it crush them? Didn't these people see it?

The young man on the boat's deck put his hands to his mouth, calling out, "Mr. Sebastian!"

The vehicle rumbled, then started forward, rolling smoothly over the road. The riverboat vanished, the vehicle passing swiftly through the space where it had been. Clive stifled a gasp.

"Do you want to go to the police station?" the woman asked. "There's one close by."

Clive shook his head, weak with relief. "No, no. I just want to get to the coast."

"Where are you headed?" the man asked.

"Atlantic City," said Clive, naming the first seaside resort that came to mind.

The man harrumphed in his throat. The woman spoke to him in a low voice again. Clive let the sound wash over him as they conferred. It was marvelously warm in the vehicle, so warm it made him realize how chilled he'd become.

"We can drop you at the bus station in Newark," the woman said. "That OK?"

"Oh, yes, thank you."

"I think there's an evening bus to Atlantic City," the woman continued.

"It may have left already," said the man.

What was a bus, Clive wondered? He'd find out, he supposed. If it was a means of conveyance and would take him to Atlantic City, he'd be satisfied. He had an intuition that his troubles would be solved if he could hie himself to that resort.

A spell by the sea would soothe his soul. A game or two of bluff would restore his pocket, and he might find some pleasant feminine company. All would be well.

"We're Bob and Sheila Dickerson," the woman said, turning her head to speak to him. He could hear the smile in her voice.

"Clive Sebastian."

"Nice to meet you, Clive. I'm sorry it's under such unhappy circumstances."

"Thank you kindly, ma'am. And thank you for your assistance. I'm most humbly grateful."

The vehicle was accelerating at a frightening pace. Clive was suddenly glad of the lashings holding him to the seat. He bit down on a scream of terror as they hurtled forward into the night.

"You really ought to report being robbed," said the man sternly.

"If he doesn't want to, that's his choice," said the woman.

Clive couldn't answer, as he was still occupied with fighting not to scream. Lights of other vehicles sped toward them, then just when he was sure they would collide they swept past, so close he could hear the rush of wind. The car leaned from side to side as the man, who was driving, followed the road that disappeared before them into the dark.

It was a nightmare after all, Clive decided, which might be a blessing. Eventually he'd have to wake up.

"Sometimes the police aren't any help, I'm sorry to say," the woman added.

Clive had an intuition these were God-fearing people, in spite of how the woman had been dressed, how familiarly she addressed him and how intimately she'd touched him while lashing him to the seat. He knew how to speak to such folk.

With an effort he swallowed, then unclenched his teeth long enough to say, "The Lord giveth and the Lord taketh away."

"Amen," said the woman.

Aha. He'd been right. He revised the little plan he'd been making of suggesting a game of cards to the gentleman when they stopped. He'd been hoping to begin repairing his pocket. Not with these folks, though, and just as well. Their generosity should not be repaid with despoiling their financial resources. Clive made a silent vow, in case Mr. Dickerson did want to play cards, not to cheat.

"Where are you from, Clive?" asked Mrs. Dickerson.

He cleared his throat. "Tennessee, ma'am. Clarksville."

"And what do you do?"

That question posed him a difficulty. To admit that he made his living by gambling would not win him any favor from these good folk. He decided on an answer that was truthful while avoiding the mark.

"I am a traveler, ma'am."

"A traveler?" said Mr. Dickerson, sounding displeased. "You mean a migrant?"

"Bob, please," said Mrs. Dickerson.

Clive sensed he was on dangerous ground. "I have been a stevedore, a fireman, and a roustabout," he said. "I make my living where I can, sir. It may not be glamorous, but it's honest work."

"Of course it is," said the lady, her tone reproachful toward her husband. "And how terrible that you've been robbed! Oh, my goodness—are you hurt? I didn't even think to ask!"

"No, I'm all right," Clive said, even as a memory of Jones's knife flashed in his mind.

"We could take you to a hospital—"

"No, no. Thank you, ma'am, but I am unhurt."

Reminded of how unexpected that was, Clive fell into silent pondering. Where had Jones got hold of a trick knife? If indeed that was what he'd used. Maybe Clive should get one. He had a general dislike of weapons, but an item like that might prove to be handy.

The vehicle leaned to the left, following a curve in the roadway. Clive's stomach protested. He closed his eyes, hoping the queasiness would subside.

"What's a stevedore?" said Mr. Dickerson after a moment.

Clive took a deep breath and swallowed. "One who loads and unloads freight from a boat, sir."

"Oh, a dock worker. Longshoreman?"

"I've worked on the rivers, mostly."

"You a union man?"

"Absolutely, sir, of course. Though I was too young to fight in the war." He didn't bother to add that his father and elder brother, who had fought in the war, had been Confederates.

A long, uncomfortable silence stretched out. Clive had the feeling he and the gentleman had not quite understood one another properly, but never mind. They would not be in company together for very long. An hour at most; Newark was a matter of six miles from Bloomfield, and this vehicle was traveling inordinately fast.

Even on the thought, the vehicle slowed and he cautiously opened his eyes again. There were more lights now, everywhere on both sides of the road. Lighted signs flashed by, too quickly to read. Trying made his head ache, so he kept his gaze forward.

"You said you'd been a fireman," said Mrs. Dickerson in a kindly voice. "That's a hero's job."

He hadn't quite thought of it that way, but then womenfolk tended to have romantic ideas. Maybe the thought of a man shoveling coal into the belly of a steamboat's boiler appealed to her.

"Why did you quit, if you don't mind my asking?" she said. "Was it nine eleven?"

"Ah—no, ma'am," he said, wondering what the time of day had to do with anything. The thought made him reach for his watch chain, which he was unsurprised to find missing. He'd give Jones what for when next they met.

"I suppose I just got tired of all the soot," he added.

"Oh, I see."

"I'd do it again, if I needed work and the opportunity arose," he added for the benefit of the husband.

"I'm sure you could find a job," said Mrs. Dickerson. "They always need more firemen. It's such dangerous work."

"Yes, ma'am."

That was one of the reasons it wasn't his favorite way to earn a few dollars. He'd been on one steamboat whose boiler had exploded. On that occasion, he'd been traveling as a passenger, fortunately, and had escaped the misadventure intact, but a couple of the firemen had been scalded to death.

The vehicle slowed suddenly, and Clive instinctively grabbed at anything his hands could reach. The lashings held him to his seat as the vehicle swung hard around a corner. His stomach protested again. Had there been anything in it, he would surely have disgraced himself.

"Well, here we are," said Mr. Dickerson.

The vehicle rolled to a stop. Clive peered out the window beside him and saw a long, low building with several peculiar-looking rail cars sitting in a row beyond it and one standing in front of it.

The rail car was uncoupled, sitting by itself on its strange, rounded black wheels. It was made of shiny silver metal, curved on all its edges, and had two bright lights on the front of it like the Dickersons' vehicle and all the others that he'd seen on the road.

Was this a railroad station? That was all right—he could get a train down to Camden, and from there take the spur out to Atlantic City. Except that he saw no tracks.

His benefactors were conferring in whispers again. Clive gazed around, trying to make sense of the lights and all the rest. Through the rain trickling on the window beside him, everything looked dreamlike, divorced from reality.

Mr. Dickerson shifted in his seat, then reached an arm over

the back of it toward Clive. "Here's fifty dollars, that should be enough to get you a bus ticket and some breakfast and what not," he said gruffly. "Don't gamble it away."

"N-no, sir! Thank you, sir!" stammered Clive, amazed at both Mr. Dickerson's prescience and his generosity.

Fifty dollars! More than most poor fellows made in a month! Clive had had the good fortune to win as much or more at the gaming tables, but for charity it was an enormous sum.

"This is most generous of you, sir," Clive said as he took the bills. They crinkled crisply in his fingers. "I am deeply in your debt. Might I have your direction? I'd like to repay you when I can."

The gentleman harrumphed again and reached into his coat pocket. "Here's my card," he said in a milder tone. "Good luck."

"God bless," added the lady.

"Thank you, and may God's blessings shower down upon you both," Clive said, meaning it from his heart.

It was a satisfactory farewell all around. Unfortunately, Clive didn't know how to get out of the lashings, or the vehicle for that matter. He fumbled at his left side, where the lady had reached around him earlier.

"Push the orange button," she said helpfully.

He saw no buttons anywhere, save on his own clothing. The only thing orange he could see was a square on the middle of a stub into which the lashings were tied. He obediently pushed on it, and the connection gave with a mechanical pop that made him jump. He untangled his arms from the straps and they slid away behind him as if pulled by some helpful ghost.

Clive shivered, reminded of exactly how strange all of this was: the vehicles, the roadway, the lights, the phantom steamboat. Yet other things were familiar, like the comforting crackle of the new bills in his hand.

He fumbled at the hatch, looking for a way to open it. Again the lady helped him, directing him to pull upward on a metal lever. The hatch popped open and Clive stepped out. The rain had subsided to a drizzle, and the strange electric lights gave a blue-gray cast to the buildings and the street and the rail cars.

"Goodbye, Clive," said Mrs. Dickerson through her open window. "Good luck!"

The vehicle rolled backward away from him, then swerved to the side, its lights flashing in the puddles on the road. Clive could see Mrs. Dickerson smiling at him. He waved a hand in farewell, watched the vehicle execute an impossibly tight turn and drive away, then looked at his surroundings.

The low building had a strangely glowing sign that read "Bus Terminal." He supposed he would be more comfortable inside it than out here in the drizzle, and maybe he could learn about the train timetables.

He cast a doubtful glance at the rail car. Now that he was outside with it, he could hear it rumbling in a way rather like the Dickersons' vehicle had done. Could rail cars now move under their own propulsion? He had spent a lot of time on riverboats lately, but he didn't think he'd been so very out of touch.

Maybe this was another dream. That made sense of all the things that didn't make sense.

He walked toward the building. The doors on the front of it were glass and had no handles that he could see. As he came near they slid apart to either side. Look as he might, he couldn't see who'd done it.

He walked into a large room lit by glowing panels set into the ceiling. Some were pink, some bluish, and one was flickering like a guttering candle. Rows of curiously rounded, unupholstered chairs sat mostly unoccupied, though there was a tramp hunched in one of them, softly snoring.

Clive walked over to a counter where an old negro clerk was punching at what looked like an accordion's keyboard. It made no music, only clicked. Perhaps it was intended for practice. Clive cleared his throat, and the clerk ceased tapping the keyboard and looked up with tired, watery eyes.

"Can I help you?"

"Yes, I want to travel to Atlantic City."

The clerk gazed at him. "Going to the casinos?"

Clive blinked, unsure how to answer. The clerk went back to playing on the keyboard and looking at a box that emitted a glowing light. Clive was about to take him to task when he spoke.

"Your best bet is to go up to the Port Authority and catch the casino bus. The casino gives you a bonus."

Lost, Clive swallowed. "How much?"

"Five dollars to Port Authority. Then the casino bus will run you around thirty-five."

"Thirty-five!"

Clive had thought Mr. Dickerson had been overgenerous. Apparently he had not.

"The bonuses are good. Twenty, twenty-five on the slots or the tables, depending which casino." The clerk eyed him. "You want the ticket?"

Clive drew himself up haughtily. "Perhaps you could direct me to the nearest railway station."

"Train's gonna cost you more. 'Bout sixty dollars."

"Sixty!"

Clive bit back a curse. It was a dream, only a dream. A very bad one. His fifty dollars was dream money, so why not spend it extravagantly? He could always dream up some more.

He wished, most sincerely, that he might wake up now.

He coughed. "Five dollars, you said?"

The clerk nodded. Clive handed over one of the crisp bills Mr. Dickerson had given him, though it cost his heart a bitter pang. The clerk paused to play at his accordion a little more, then handed Clive a small ticket printed with blue ink.

"Thank you."

Clive stared at the ticket, trying to make sense of what it said. Newark, New York, and the times were understandable. A lot of other numbers weren't, and the date, "October 16, 2012," was preposterous.

"This isn't the correct date," Clive said.

The clerk took the ticket, peered at it, and handed it back. "Yes, it is."

He gestured toward a calendar hanging on the wall behind him. Clive was momentarily distracted by the apparel—undergarments, and obscenely scant for those—of the woman pictured at the top of the page, then his gaze descended to the calendar heading: "October, 2012."

"Oh," he said.

Suddenly his mouth was filled with liquid fear. He swallowed, feeling weak.

"Don't forget your change," the clerk said helpfully.

Clive numbly watched his hands move to pick up the bills, fold them, and slide them into his coat pocket. The feeling of the fabric on the back of his hand was very real. Nothing else seemed to be.

Hanging beside the calendar was a clock face that read 9:26. That was perfectly normal, nothing wrong with that except that the face seemed to run without the benefit of any workings of a clock. He watched the second hand tick its way around. It frightened him. Everything frightened him.

He put the little printed ticket into his other pocket and turned away from the counter. Walked slowly to the nearest row of chairs, touching one to make sure it was real. It felt solid enough, so he sat down in it, after which his limbs turned to water.

This was a very, very bad dream. If it was a dream at all.

That was what frightened him the most—the slowly dawning realization that all this strangeness was part of a waking truth he did not have the heart to face. That he might not be dreaming, but had somehow been transported over a hundred years into the future.

Could Orson Jones have done that to him? No. Jones was an unremarkable river pilot. This madness was more like the concoction of a storyteller. Like Mark Twain's Connecticut Yankee, only in the wrong direction.

Clive laughed under his breath. Thinking of that yarn made him feel unexpectedly better. The story was a complete fabrication, so much balderdash, yet it gave him a sense of context. As if the place—the *time*, he amended—where he found himself were not so completely outlandish.

Not Twain. Washington Irving. Rip Van Winkle.

Had he slept a hundred years and more, untouched by time? He doubted that. He remembered distinctly Orson Jones's attack —and maybe it had not been a disappearing blade after all—and he also remembered the sensation of being dragged. Dragged along the roadway, then into a field. Dragged for a long time, during which he had lost consciousness, for it was the last thing he remembered before awakening tonight.

Could Jones have killed him, after all? A shiver went through him and he closed his eyes. His mouth was dry, his breathing short.

Come now, Sebastian. Come, pull yourself together, man. If you were dead you wouldn't be here. Heaven perhaps, hell more likely.

This was neither. This was…strange.

A hundred years in the future everything should be perfect. There should be no filth, no tramps sleeping in hard chairs, no dinginess to this room beneath the flickering light, no faint smell of urine in the corners. If the future was so dismal, he wanted no part of it.

Atlantic City would be better, perhaps. He was going there, certain. He took out the ticket again and held it in his hands, staring at it as he tried to convince himself it was real and not part of a dreadful dream.

~ Arnold ~

Queens, New York

Arnold Rothstein awoke with the sound of an automobile engine in his ears. He opened his eyes and saw nothing—he was wrapped in a sheet.

Fighting panic, he struggled until he got the sheet loose enough to free his arms. He had to roll back and forth, and in doing so realized he was outdoors.

It was cold. Hard to breathe.

He got his hands free and untied the hood from around his neck, pulling it off along with the scrap of cloth that was covering his face. He sat up, annoyed, and disentangled the sheet from his legs. Underneath he was dressed in a plain white shirt—two shirts, actually—and pants with a strip of white cloth for a belt.

A moment's reflection changed his mood to bewilderment, because he'd been pretty sure he was dead. If that was so, he should be lying in the ground, not on it.

He remembered the shooting, remembered the hospital. He'd begged Carolyn not to leave him alone, that was the last thing he remembered clearly. The rest was sort of hazy, like a dream. He was pretty sure he'd tried to haunt George McManus.

He looked around, saw gravestones in tidy rows. A cemetery. His stomach did a slow flip-flop as he realized what that meant. He was dead all right, or should be. From the looks of things he'd been buried, but wasn't anymore.

Another car engine roared by, out in the distance. It was night, and cold clouds drifted across a pale moon. Arnold shivered and got to his feet, kicking away the sheet that had been wrapped around him. A purple striped prayer shawl fell out of it. With a grimace of disgust he kicked that aside, too. Who the hell had dressed him like this?

Carolyn, probably. She'd given him a Jew funeral, a gesture to his father.

Screw his father, Arnold thought savagely. Bastard had hated him, and the feeling was mutual. He turned around.

Yep. Grave marker with a lot of goddamned Jew gibberish on it. In English, "Departed November 6, 1928." That fit.

The weather fit, too; it was cold. He picked up the sheet and wrapped it around himself like a blanket.

Why the hell couldn't Carolyn have buried him in a suit and tie, like decent people? Here he was, Mr. Big, the Man Uptown, the Brain—dressed in a goddamn sheet.

Things didn't look quite right. Didn't sound right either—the car engines had a strange tone, quieter and faster than he remembered. There were weird colored lights out along the street.

He stood still, his back to the gravestone, coldly thinking what was best to do. What he wanted was to go down to Atlantic City, take in a nightclub act, enjoy the sea breezes. That was crazy, though. He must be disoriented on account of having been shot to death by that idiot McManus.

First order of business, get some decent clothes. Damn, he wished he'd been buried in a suit! He'd have had one of his stickpins to pawn for cash. Now he had nothing but this stupid sheet, not even his wedding ring.

He bent down and picked up the prayer shawl. It might bring him a dime or two. He needed everything he could get. He glanced at the hood and the cloth that had been over his face. Wouldn't get a cent for those—not like the Jews would use them again.

He started toward the street. A glint from the ground caught his attention. Photograph in a frame, sitting at the foot of a grave. He picked it up, frowning.

The photo was of a young woman wearing strange clothes, and even in the dim light from the distant street he could see that the picture was tinted with brilliant colors. He opened the frame, pulled out the photo and dropped it on the grave, then put the frame back together. He should be able to get a few cents for it.

Glancing at the headstone, he saw the woman's death date and drew in a hissing breath: 1996! Holy crap!

That meant things were more complicated than he'd thought. No wonder the cars sounded strange. He'd have to catch up on stuff.

It also meant Carolyn was almost certainly dead. She'd be buried in some Catholic cemetery, probably with her family.

Arnold flinched at the sharp pang of loneliness. He couldn't afford it. Survival came first. He'd miss Carolyn, but he had other problems to deal with.

Atlantic City called to him, sea breezes, good gin, and hot honeys. A place to forget about things. He would dearly love to forget about the miserable way his life—or former life, perhaps he should say—had ended.

He began combing the graveyard, adding to his collection of items for the pawn shop. A nice vase, a couple more picture frames. He found a small gold ring on one of the graves, a jackpot for him. Probably not left by a mourner, unless in a fit of anger. Didn't matter. It would be worth a few bucks. He wished to hell these damn clothes had some pockets. Wished to hell he had some shoes, too, or socks at least—his feet were freezing.

He stuck the ring on his pinkie and continued scrounging. When he had as much junk as he could carry he left the graveyard, glancing back to look at the name on the gate. Union Fields. That was in Queens. Damn, a long way from Manhattan.

A car sat by the curb, a long black Packard. The headlights came on as he looked at it. Arnold turned and walked the other way. The car followed.

Crap. Just what he needed.

He switched directions, staring a challenge at the car as he walked toward it, then hurrying past. Before the car could turn around, he crossed the street. There were houses here, a lot of them. He zig-zagged through the neighborhood until he was sure he'd lost the car, then started looking for a pawn shop where he could sell his loot and maybe pick up some real clothes.

He wasn't a vain man, but he liked to look respectable, and preferred to look elegant. He hated sticking out. He had never courted attention; in fact, he avoided it whenever he could. Making waves just made trouble.

After walking for what seemed like forever, he finally started coming into a business district. The houses gave way to auto shops and delis, all of them closed. Nothing looked familiar. The signs were all lit up, some looked like colored glass lit from inside, pretty snazzy.

He found a pawn shop but it was closed, the whole front of the shop covered with a metal grating. Other shops had similar barriers. Things must've gotten rough.

He kept walking, his feet now sore as well as frozen. A brightly lit building turned out to be a restaurant that was actually open. He passed it by, not wanting to make a scene in his outlandish clothing. He had no money for food anyway, though he was beginning to get hungry.

He found a park and put down his collection on a bench, sitting beside it. Tucked the bottom of his sheet around his feet and tried not to shiver. He must look like a damned vagrant, and that made him angry.

Never mind. He'd fix things. He'd always been able to fix things, always relied on his wits. A few bucks from the pawn shop he could turn into more, easily enough. Find a craps game or a card game, play the odds. He was good at numbers. He always had been.

Sitting on the bench, he mused about George McManus. Why the hell had that idiot lost his cool and shot him? Stupid thing to do. McManus was worried about collecting for his goddamn poker game, which had been a goddamned crooked game, and Arnold wished he'd known that to begin with. He'd never have played. Instead he'd refused to pay up, and that drunken idiot McManus had tried to threaten him, and then shot him. Probably pulled the goddamn trigger by accident.

He wondered if McManus had been tried. Sent to prison. Serve the stupid jerk right, he supposed.

He wondered if Carolyn had been all right. He'd stood to win a cool half million on bets on the election, but they'd be a loss since he'd died. His other interests would have been snapped up by the wolves—Luciano, Lansky, Siegel. He hoped to hell Carolyn hadn't died poor.

He shook his head. Best not to think about her. She was gone.

A movement off to the side caught his attention, brought him suddenly alert. Someone coming toward him through the dark. Arnold turned his head and fixed a cold stare on the skinny figure that emerged from between two trees. A kid, probably no more than twenty. Eyes big with fear, and a knife in his hand. Not good.

"Gimme your money," the kid said.

"Do I look like I have any fucking money? Get the fuck out of here."

Arnold stayed where he was, arm thrown across the back of the bench protectively over his pitiful little pile of junk. He shifted slightly to face the kid, at the same time curling the finger with the ring out of sight.

"I mean it, man! I'll cut you!"

The kid was shaking. Arnold stood up, letting the sheet fall to the ground. He wasn't a giant, but he was taller than this little punk. He squared his shoulders and bunched his fists. The kid should back down, unless he got stupid.

"I got no money. Try your luck elsewhere, bucko."

"Gimme your wallet, man!"

He was panicking. Arnold roared back in his face, all the while keeping an eye on the blade. "I don't have a fucking wallet! I don't have a fucking pocket to keep a fucking wallet in! Now scram!"

The kid made a move with the knife. Arnold knocked the hand aside and gut-punched him, sending him to the ground. He stomped on the kid's wrist until he dropped the knife, then bent and picked it up, stuck the point of the blade in the kid's nose.

"Get the fuck out of here and don't come back."

Terror filled the kid's eyes. He was trembling all over. Probably high as a kite. Arnold stepped back, keeping the knife. He watched the kid roll over and get up on his hands and knees. Just as he was getting to his feet, Arnold planted a foot on his butt and gave him a shove to get him going. The kid stumbled away, out of the park and down the street. Arnold watched until he disappeared around a corner.

Well, now he had a nice knife. Might come in handy, too.

He grimaced. He preferred to leave the violence to others, but at the moment he didn't have a choice in the matter. Without money, he had to do everything himself.

He decided a couple of changes were in order. First, for the sake of privacy and mobility, he took off the outermost of the two white shirts he was wearing and used that to tie up his junk in a bundle. He was colder, but could now move in a hurry. Moving was the second change—he didn't want that punk kid to find his courage and come back for him, maybe with a gun.

The knife was a problem. He didn't have anywhere to stash it except in the bundle. He'd rather have it to hand, but walking down the street with it in his hand was a bad idea. Cops didn't take kindly to that sort of thing, and the last thing he wanted to do was piss off some cop.

He put the knife in the bundle, placing it carefully between two picture frames so it wouldn't cut the cloth. Then he tied the gold ring into the knot in his belt so it didn't show, and wrapped the sheet around himself again. Hefting the bundle, he started off. Probably looked like fucking Santa Claus. He left the park in the opposite direction to where the kid had gone, regretting the loss of the place but not sorry to be moving. At least walking warmed him up some.

What he should do was find a mission or someplace. Sisters of Charity, maybe. Someplace that would give him a meal and a place to flop.

He laughed under his breath. Arnold Rothstein, the Big Bankroll, sleeping in a goddamn mission. His associates would have laughed, if they hadn't been dead.

Well, he'd started from nothing before, he could do it again. He'd have to make connections, but he was good at that. He was the best.

A bright light flickered along the sidewalk ahead of him. He stopped, frowning, and realized the light was coming from behind him. He looked around and was blinded by a spotlight. Behind it he heard the purr of a car engine.

"You are the cleanest damned vagrant I ever saw," said a man's voice.

Cop. Arnold shaded his eyes with his free hand, trying to see the cop's face. The car's headlights were huge and wide apart.

"What's in the bag, ice-cream man?"

"Just my things, officer."

"Yeah? Cold night for taking your stuff for a walk."

"Someone tried to rob me in the park."

"Figures."

With the bright light in his face, Arnold could barely make out the shape of the car, long, low and wide. He had an idea, and put on a humble expression.

"Officer, can you tell me where there's a mission or someplace? I'd like to get out of the cold."

"Yeah, I bet you would."

The car door opened and the cop got out, shining yet another light in Arnold's face. This guy was big and built like a gorilla, looming over Arnold on the sidewalk. The sort of man Arnold liked to have around for protection. He wondered fleetingly if Tammany Hall was still operating, then dropped the thought. Even if it was, all his contacts there would be dead or so old they'd be worthless.

"Goddamn, you're clean," said the cop. "Whatcha doing roaming the streets in the middle of the night?"

"Just trying to stay out of trouble, sir. I'm just a fellow down on his luck."

"Uh-huh. OK, you got a driver's license?"

"No, sir."

"ID card?"

Arnold shook his head, lowered his gaze and did his best to look miserable. He wanted the cop to think he was just a sad case, harmless.

"What are you, some kind of religious nut, or did you escape from a toga party?"

"Sir?"

"What's with the white getup?"

Deciding the crack about religion was as good a cue as any, Arnold followed up. "We walk before the Lord in humble simplicity," he said, and shifted his feet a little so the cop would notice he was barefoot.

"Yeah, right," muttered the cop. "OK, Jesus buddy, climb in the back. I'll give you a ride to the Salvation Army shelter."

"Thank you, sir. May God bless you."

The cop opened the back door of the car and Arnold got in, setting his bundle on the seat beside him carefully so it wouldn't clink. The door shut with a heavy thunk, and the cop got in the driver's seat.

The car glided off smoothly, sparking an instant desire in Arnold to own one of these new automobiles. Soon enough, he thought. Soon enough. He'd have a whole fleet of them, and men like this gorilla cop to drive them.

It occurred to him to wonder why he was alive. Second chance, on account of his dying from George McManus's stupidity? Why the delay, then? Why dump him here in nineteen-fucking-ninety-whatever, with nothing?

No answers occurred to him as he watched the streets whiz by. His mind wandered back to Atlantic City. Goddamn if he wouldn't get there. He needed some R and R.

In a very short time the cop had pulled up in front of a blocky brick building. Dingy lights lit up the Salvation Army shield—that hadn't changed, or not much anyway. Arnold hid a grin as he looked for a handle on the car door. The cop opened it from outside before he could find one, and Arnold got out, clutching his little sack of junk.

"Thank you, officer."

"Yeah, all right. Stay off the streets at night, huh? And stay clean."

The cop chuckled as he got back in the car and drove off. Arnold went up to the Salvation Army's door, but it was locked. A sign said to ring the bell after nine. He didn't see a bell, but there was a button next to the sign so he tried pushing it. A buzz sounded somewhere inside the building, and after a minute someone opened the door.

The young fellow who looked out was tall and lanky, wore a faded checked shirt and dingy pants, and peered at him with a calculating look. "Can I help you?"

"I need a place to sleep," Arnold said, trying to look humble.

"You eaten today?"

"No, sir."

"Dinner's over, but I can get you some bread and peanut butter. Come in."

Arnold followed him down a hall lit by long glowing tubes overhead. They passed an open doorway to a large, brightly lit room with tables and benches along one side and people lying on mattresses in the middle. The ones that weren't sleeping were sitting in small groups, talking in low voices. The muttering faded as Arnold followed the guy in the checked shirt down the hall to a kitchen.

It was huge, obviously designed for feeding a lot of people, with two stoves and lots of storage and counter space and several big pieces of fancy equipment whose function Arnold couldn't guess.

The man opened a cupboard and took out a half loaf of bread in a wrapper of something clear and flexible. From another cupboard he took down a jar, then got a butter knife from a drawer and smeared some of the jar's contents on a slice of bread. He handed it to Arnold.

"I'm Dave Stewart, I'm the night supervisor. What's your name?"

"Arnold. Roth—" Arnold stopped there and hastily took a

bite of the bread while he wondered if his name was still well known. Maybe not, but better not to take chances.

The peanut butter was salty and sweet and very sticky. He swallowed and it went down like a lump.

"Could I get something to drink?"

"Sure."

Stewart got out a glass and poured some milk into it. Arnold took a big swig, shivering a little as the cold hit his stomach.

"We'll get you signed in and get you a bed. You can stay for three nights temporary, then if you still need help you can apply for a long-term shelter."

"Thank you," Arnold mumbled through another mouthful of food.

Stewart's gaze traveled over him and an eyebrow rose. "Maybe you'd like a change of clothes."

Arnold nodded enthusiastically. "Please!"

"Where'd you get those? Were you in a hospital or something?"

Arnold grimaced and shook his head. "Long story. I'd love to have some decent clothes, though. And some shoes."

"We'll get you fixed up."

Arnold nodded his thanks as he chewed the last mouthful of bread. He finished the milk and handed back the glass. Stewart put it and the knife in one of two gigantic metal sinks that were molded into the metal counter.

"OK, let's get you settled in. There's a little bit of paperwork."

He led Arnold down the hall to an office and gave him a form to fill out, which Arnold cheerfully started covering with lies. No permanent address was about the only true thing he put on there. Some of the items he didn't understand. He left a lot of it blank and handed it back.

Stewart glanced over it. "We do need your social."

"My what?"

"Your social security number."

"I don't have one."

Stewart frowned. "You never got a card?"

Arnold shook his head, then glanced down as if ashamed. He wondered what this card was for. If it was good, maybe he should get one.

"All right. Come on, let's get you some clothes and a bed."

Within half an hour, Arnold was dressed and in the big room. Within an hour, he had pinpointed the power brokers in the room: the drug dealers, the hustlers, and one pimp who offered him half an hour with a scruffy little boy. Arnold hid his disgust and tried to look regretful as he declined.

There were no women in the room, he realized. Either they had another room to themselves somewhere or this place only accepted men.

The clothes he'd been given were a workman's clothes, worn but clean, with a pair of shoes that fit his feet closely and were amazingly supple. He had gladly abandoned the white junk except for the sheet, which he kept to make a better bundle for his things. Rather than expose his valuables to the greedy eyes in the big room, he'd just tied the sheet up around the whole bundle.

Stewart returned carrying a thin mattress and a couple of threadbare blankets. He handed the blankets to Arnold and flopped the mattress onto the floor at the end of a row. On the mattress next to it a grizzly old man twitched in fretful sleep. Arnold spread the two thin blankets over his mattress, then set his bundle on top.

"Breakfast is at six," Stewart said. "You have to clear out by eight, then you can come back at five for supper. Good luck."

"Thanks."

Arnold watched him go out, then sat down on his bed and listened, waiting for the room to settle. The murmur of voices gradually increased. Arnold glanced up at a clock mounted high on the wall, saw it was ten to ten. They'd probably turn the lights out then, unless they just stayed on all night.

Last call for pimps and hustlers. Arnold stood up, tucked his bundle under one arm, and strolled toward a half-dozen guys who'd been playing go fish with a battered deck of cards. The game had changed to blackjack, and small piles of coins were changing hands. Arnold watched from a respectful distance. One of the hustlers was dealing, keeping the bank, which said something right there. Arnold had no interest in this particular game—that deck was as good as marked, and the dealer was probably cheating—but the players might answer some questions he had.

After a couple of minutes the dealer glanced up at him. "Fifty cents to get in the game."

Arnold smiled. "I don't have it. I'm a poker man, anyway. Know where I could find a game?"

One of the players gave a huff of laughter. "Atlantic City."

A tingle went through Arnold. Could be a coincidence, but it seemed strange Atlantic City kept coming up, first in his thoughts, now in conversation.

He squatted down as if to watch the card game better, and also to make himself less intimidating. "Where in Atlantic City?"

"Anywhere. All the casinos have poker."

Casinos. Sounded like Ben Siegel's kind of setup. Seigel'd always been shooting off his mouth about how Monte Carlo was so great and they should bring casinos to the states. It would have required some political fixing, on account of gambling being illegal in Jersey. If it had happened—and it sounded like it had—then some big money had changed hands.

Arnold watched the game a little longer, then wandered away. He checked out a couple of other groups, turned down an offer of a bag of cocaine for ten bucks, noted the dope dealer's size and appearance in case it might come in handy later. He hoped it wouldn't. He didn't plan on spending any more time than he had to in this hole.

The lights were indeed shut off at ten. The blackjack game resumed after a decent interval, illuminated by a flashlight.

Arnold lay down fully dressed on his wretched bed, between the blankets as he couldn't bring himself to lie directly on the mattress. With his arms around his bundle he dozed lightly, alert to any sound of danger.

When morning came, he lined up with the others for a serving of pasty oatmeal and burned toast, accompanied by watery coffee. He ate it in silence, sharing a table with a dozen assorted lowlifes, then left the shelter at a brisk walk, heading for the pawn shop.

An amazing amount of traffic was cramming the street. The cars had gotten smaller and more colorful, quieter but throbbing with power, and a lot of them seemed to be playing music. As he gazed in wonder at the chaos, his attention was caught by one car that seemed out of place.

The Packard. Long and black and menacing. He saw it coming toward him, and ducked down a side street and into a shop, hoping he hadn't been seen.

He waited a good while, pretending to read a magazine while he watched out the shop window for the car. It passed, and after a few more minutes he put back the magazine and ventured out, peering up and down the street.

No sign of the car. He got his bearings and headed in the direction of the pawn shop. By the time he got there it was open, metal gate gone, windows filled with glittering junk.

Arnold walked in and set his bundle on the counter. An overweight, bulb-nosed clerk shuffled out of the back, shot him a skeptical glance, then looked at the bundle in distaste.

"A fence is expected to be a little subtle about presentation."

"This is stuff from my grandmother's attic," Arnold said, untying the sheet. "She wouldn't give me a box."

"Yeah, sure. OK, what do we got here?"

Arnold spread his haul out on the counter. The clerk poked through it, shaking his head. Arnold glanced around the shelves of goods for sale while he waited.

"This is crap." said the clerk. "I'll give you five dollars for all of it."

"It's worth at least ten," Arnold said, based on his past knowledge and understanding of the species of pawn brokers. He pointed to a table of nicknacks. "You're going to sell the picture frames for five apiece."

"What, you're not going to rush back and claim them? OK, seven-fifty, and that's it."

"What about the prayer shawl?"

"It's no good. See, the fringe has been cut."

The clerk held up an end of the shawl. Arnold ignored it and gazed steadily at the clerk instead.

"It's still decorative. You can sell it."

"OK, three bucks for the shawl. That makes ten."

"Ten fifty," Arnold said.

Ten-fifty seemed like a lot, but who knew what things cost these days? If a cruddy little used picture frame went for five smackers, then ten wasn't going to take him very far. The clerk counted out the dough and Arnold stuffed it in his right pocket, feeling a new gratitude for the existence of pockets. From the left he took out the little gold ring. The clerk's eyebrows went up as he reached for it.

"Nice," he said, nodding. "Gold plate."

"Solid gold," Arnold said.

The clerk gave him a sidelong glance. "Nice little piece. Give you ten for it."

"You think?" Arnold reached to take it back. "Maybe I ought to have a jeweler take a look at it."

The clerk pulled his hand away. "OK, I'll make it twenty."

"You'll make it fifty, or no deal."

"You're killing me. I got kids to feed."

"Then you better keep your money." Arnold reached for the ring again.

"All right, fifty it is."

Arnold suspected he was still being cheated, but fifty bucks was a start, anyway. The price of gold must've gone sky high. He accepted the cash, pocketed the pawn ticket out of courtesy, and left the shop.

He returned to the restaurant he'd seen the night before and paid probably too much for a decent breakfast of eggs and bacon, with coffee that was both strong and hot, to wash the taste of oatmeal out of his mouth. Then he found a newsstand where he picked up a paper.

"What's the cheapest way to get to Atlantic City?" he asked the proprietor.

"Bus, probably. Station's on Hillside Street."

Arnold got directions from him, then started off walking. The air was chilly but the sun was out, and he was a lot warmer than he'd been the night before despite having no coat. The new shoes he'd acquired at the Salvation Army were amazingly comfortable to walk in. His mood was picking up, too.

Soon he'd be in a game, double his cash. Build up a bankroll. As soon as he could afford it he'd buy a decent suit. Then he'd see about this casino business. Might be he could get in on it, streamline the business, improve management. These were his gifts, and he'd used them to build an empire. No reason he couldn't do it again.

Atlantic City had been a whoopee spot when he knew it, one of his favorite getaways. The gambling that had gone on there was illicit, though there was plenty of it. The jazz and the gin were equally as big, and had drawn the Hollywood crowd. Shows would open on the piers for test runs before going to Broadway. The Miss America Pageant had brought beautiful girls from all over the country—he wondered if that was still going.

The black car pulled out of a cross street just ahead of him. Arnold's stomach did a flip. He stepped backward into an alley, heart racing. Who the hell was following him?

He turned to head down the alley and flinched back. Standing in his way was a woman, tall and slender, black hair cropped in a bob, dressed in something long, black, and slinky that shimmered with beads, with a stole of black fur draped over her arms. A regular sheba, and for a second Arnold stood frozen in admiration.

"Mr. Rothstein," she said in a low voice. "I've been looking for you."

"Yeah? Why?"

She tilted her head, her jet black hair brushing her jawline. Her eyes glittered green and cat-like. He was relieved to see she wasn't holding a weapon, at least none that he could see.

"Do you want to go to Atlantic City?" she asked.

Arnold suppressed a shiver. "What if I do?"

"I'm your guide. I'm here to escort you."

"That's nice. Who sent you?"

"Simon Penstemon. You won't recognize his name."

"You're right, I don't, so why should I accept his hospitality?"

The sheba smiled. "Mr. Penstemon is hosting a poker game. You're invited to play."

"I don't have a stake."

"You don't need one. The game isn't for money."

"Then why the hell should I play? You know, the last poker game I was in didn't turn out so well."

"That's why you've been invited to this one. It's a chance to rectify that unfortunate incident."

"Rectify?"

"Mr. Penstemon will explain it all when we get to the casino. Shall we?" She gestured toward the street with a hand, and he heard the car's engine behind him.

Arnold stared at her narrowly, thinking hard. It sounded nuts, but then it was nuts that he was alive, so what the hell. He didn't have much to lose at this point, and he wanted to check out the casino action anyway.

"OK, sugar. I'll play."

Arnold squared his shoulders and offered his arm. She smiled and laid a hand on it, and he felt as if a chilly mist had touched him. Ignoring that, he walked her to the car. The back door swung open as they reached it. That right there almost made him bolt, but he restrained himself and handed the lady into the back seat. Her green eyes glinted up at him as he got in beside her. The door swung shut, and the car glided forward.

"Nice car," he said.

"I'm glad you like it."

"A little conspicuous, though, isn't it? Wouldn't a modern car be less noticeable?"

The sheba smiled. "Not at all. I guarantee you no one will

notice this car."

"I noticed it."

"That was the point."

She leaned forward and pressed a button on the back of the front seat. A panel opened toward them, revealing a small bar stocked with tumblers, wine glasses, decanters, and an ice bucket, all fine cut crystal.

"Would you like a drink?"

Arnold leaned back, deciding to enjoy himself. "Don't mind if I do."

"Champagne or bourbon?"

"It's early. How about the champagne?"

He watched her open a split and pour from it into a flute. "Aren't you joining me?"

"I don't care for champagne."

He eyed the crystal flute she'd handed him. "There wouldn't be anything else in here, would there?"

"Come, come, Mr. Rothstein. What would be the point of restoring you to life only to kill you again?"

His eyebrows went up. She was implying that this Penstemon guy was responsible for his being alive.

"I don't know. Sadistic gratification?"

She pursed her dainty lips, then took the flute from him and sipped, leaving a faint haze of lipstick on the edge. "Satisfied?"

"Sure, honey."

She sneezed. Hiding a smile, Arnold filled his mouth with champagne, enjoying the sizzle on his tongue. It was good stuff, as good as the best he'd tasted, and he'd drunk some pretty fine wines in his day. The memory brought a pang of loneliness for Carolyn. He frowned and took another swallow.

"Tell me about your boss."

She raised a finely arched brow. "My boss?"

"Mr. Penstemon. Isn't he your boss?"

She smiled slyly. "He might tell you I'm his boss."

"That so?"

She stretched luxuriously, then smoothed her hair with a

hand. "He takes care of me."

"Ah."

Nice of this Penstemon to send his play-toy to fetch Arnold. Too nice, so Arnold didn't trust it. Maybe she was supposed to get him all comfortable and tipsy, so he'd have his guard down. Arnold took a tiny sip of champagne. He'd get comfortable, sure, but not careless. He was never careless.

Almost never. He'd been careless with McManus.

He looked out the window, which was smoked glass and hard to see through. He had to concentrate to see out of it, and when he figured out where they were he nearly spilled his champagne.

"Hey! We're not driving on the road!"

"The side is less crowded," said the sheba.

The traffic to his right was a mess of shiny blurs. Arnold looked toward the driver to tell him to slow down, and his heart nearly lurched out of his chest. There was no one in the driver's seat!

"Shit!"

"Calm down, Mr. Rothstein."

"There's no fucking driver!"

"Yes, there is, you just can't see him. He's a will-o-wisp."

"The cops are gonna be all over us!"

"I assure you they won't."

There was a car on the shoulder up ahead. Modern car, with red and blue lights flashing on its roof. Arnold's stomach clenched as the car he was in slowed, then swerved into traffic. They passed the car with the lights and Arnold saw "Police" in big letters on its side. Another car was sitting in front of it. Arnold's ride swerved back to the shoulder again when they were past.

Maybe it wasn't such a good idea to look out the window. He leaned back and looked for a place to put the champagne glass. His stomach was complaining. The sheba took the flute from him and handed him a newspaper instead.

"You might want to see today's news."

Arnold closed his eyes until his stomach was settled, then looked at the paper. The date was an astounding 2012. That would make his age 130, if you counted from his birth date.

The news was confusing, some of it, and other than that pretty much like it had been in his day. Politicians were still bullshitting. Movie stars were still the subject of endless gossip, and they were doing something called television, some new kind of theater, it sounded like. The country was fighting a war in some godforsaken place he'd never heard of, near another conflict in a place called Israel, which seemed a sorry joke to Arnold.

Airplanes had become a big thing. There were new diseases, old cons, and all the usual flap. The world was still itself, which was comforting.

By the time he'd finished skimming the paper, the car had started to slow down. Risking another look out the window Arnold saw they were in a city. He didn't see anything he recognized, but it must be Atlantic City, because they crossed a street marked Pacific Avenue. It was crawling with scum. Down-and-outs, hookers, and hustlers, mostly negro. Not classy, not at all like the exclusive place he remembered. Town needed cleaning up.

The light changed, making Arnold look up. It was morning —or not much later than noon, anyway—but now the sky was twilit.

The Packard eased to a stop in front of a high-rise building. The door next to Arnold opened. He flinched, then got out. He could smell the ocean.

They were at a hotel, as elegant as the rest of the town was shabby, all glass and chrome and velvet ropes to retain a non-existent crowd. A black velvet awning stretched out over a blue carpet that extended into the hotel.

The building rose into the sky, a tower of black glass with glowing blue outlining its edges. On top was a gigantic playing card, the queen of spades, all made of light and brilliant against the indigo sky.

Arnold swallowed. Nighttime, not day. What the hell?

Just go with it, he told himself, ignoring the pounding of his heart.

The sheba was standing next to him. Arnold turned to give her a looking over.

She was sleek and glossy, a sylph all in black with pale ivory skin and those green eyes. She had a beaded belt at her hips that he hadn't noted before, fastened in the front with a large triangular clasp crusted with diamonds that flashed and sparkled in the sunlight with every move she made. Black beaded fringes dangled down from the clasp to tickle her knees. She was one classy-looking dame, and Arnold couldn't help but smile. He offered his arm again as the car glided away.

"What's your name, honey?" he asked, suppressing a shiver at the chill of her touch.

"Mishka."

"Pretty name. Russian, isn't it?"

"I believe you're right."

They strolled toward the hotel. Despite the weirdness, Arnold was enjoying himself. It was nice being driven in a classy car and drinking champagne, especially after the way he'd spent the night.

Forget about that, he decided. It had just been a bad dream. He'd pick up some cash in a game or two—after finding out exactly what Penstemon wanted to play for—and then start getting himself established. Maybe Mishka would like to help him out, help him find a place to stay and get it set up nice. She could decorate it if she wanted.

He was getting ahead of himself. Mishka was Penstemon's girl, and until he had built up some clout he had nothing to offer.

Uniforms opened the doors for them. Just uniforms. There were no heads beneath the caps that seemed to float in the air above the black coats with polished silver buttons. More whatchacallems, Arnold presumed. Like the driver.

Quiet, jazzy music played as Arnold followed Mishka into the lobby. An albino woman and a bald-headed guy with long, pointed ears stood talking to a young woman behind the counter. Both wore dark leather pants and jackets with a lot of silver zippers and studs.

The albino turned her head, fixing ice-blue eyes on Arnold as he passed, then whispered into one of her companion's astounding ears. He glanced at Arnold and grinned, revealing teeth as long and pointed as the ears. Arnold tensed, remembering stories his grandmother had told. Dubbyks and golems. Stuff to frighten unruly children.

"What the hell kind of place is this?" Arnold muttered as he followed Mishka to the right.

"It's a resort," she said. "A top-shelf hotel and casino that caters to alternative lifestyles."

"Alternative? Is that what you call it? Did you see the ears on that guy?"

Mishka smoothed her hair over her own ears and ignored the question. "This way," she said, leading him along a wide corridor that twined snake-like through the hotel.

He swallowed his misgivings. "They still have good jazz here?"

Mishka shook her head. "Not like you would remember. Most of the emphasis is on gambling these days."

"Too bad."

"Mr. Penstemon sponsors good concerts now and then, or so I've heard. I'm not a music lover."

"Just who is this Penstemon, anyway?"

She gazed back at him, eyes wide with innocence. "He's the owner of the Black Queen. You'll meet him soon."

They passed some weird abstract sculptures and a couple more fountains, then went through a lounge area where people were sitting on plush sofas and chairs, listening to a trio of piano, sax, and string bass on a glowing blue dais. The instruments appeared to be playing by themselves.

The music was good, though the people listening to it were all a little odd. Too tall, too short, too pale or too dark—or too green—to call normal. Some wore strange clothes. Arnold knew he wasn't up on the current fashions, but he was pretty sure the Thomas Jefferson getup wasn't a hot fad.

A red-haired woman in a silvery dress pointed at Arnold and said something to her friends. Heads turned as he and Mishka walked past. Arnold got the feeling these people knew who he was, a feeling that he was used to, but that had been distinctly absent since he woke up in the cemetery.

Leaving the lounge behind, they followed a curving hallway through an arcade of shops. Tobacconist, liquor store, even a book shop was unremarkable, but some of the other places gave Arnold the creeps.

One marked "Apothecary" looked more like a zoo. It was full of critters in cages and funny-looking plants. Another simply labeled "Boutique" had the weirdest assortment of clothes he'd ever seen. They seemed to be for women, sort of, but there was nothing frilly in there. Most of it was black, and Arnold didn't like the look of the tall, skinny guy who was holding a shiny black dress up to himself in front of a mirror.

Mishka led him into a shop beside a small, tasteful brass sign that said "Gentlemen's Attire." Racks of suits, from casual to tuxedo, lined the walls around a central display case filled with silk shirts, ties, handkerchiefs, and other fine accessories. Arnold let out a small sigh of satisfaction. The place reeked of money.

A small, wiry young man with sandy hair and a foxy look to his sharp eyes came forward to greet them. Mishka smiled at him.

"Alphonse, this is Mr. Rothstein. Please help him choose some more comfortable clothing." She glanced at Arnold and quelled his half-hearted protest. "Mr. Penstemon's compliments. He wants you to be comfortable for the game."

"Very nice of him. Tell him thanks."

She smiled. "I'll be back in half an hour."

Arnold watched her stroll out, then looked back at Alphonse, who was regarding him as a sculptor might look at a chunk of marble. "This is not my usual style," he said.

"Of course not," said Alphonse. "I could tell that

immediately. You belong in silk, of course. A classic cut, I think. Let's look over here."

Alphonse turned and with quick, busy steps led the way down a wall of suits. One small section was a bouquet of pastel colors that made Arnold want to gag. Another ranged from dull gold to rust to brown. Alphonse passed both by, to Arnold's great relief, and paused before a rack of suits in varying shades of gray and black, with one or two dark blue for variety. He reached in and took down a hanger.

"This one?"

Arnold gazed at a suit that could have come out of his own closet. "Sure."

Alphonse held the jacket out for Arnold to try on. He hesitated, doubting it would hang right over the heavy shirt he was wearing. Alphonse's brows went up.

"Oh! Stupid of me."

The tailor waved a hand and a cold wind whirled around Arnold. A second later it stopped, and Arnold was wearing a white silk dress shirt. Goose bumps rose on his arms, and not from the breeze.

"That's better. Here, now."

Numbly, Arnold slid his arms into the sleeves and stood still while Alphonse walked around him, twitching the jacket and tut-tutting.

"A little longer in the sleeve, I think," said Alphonse, taking hold of the left jacket cuff, which rode above Arnold's wrist. He gave it a sharp tug, then smoothed it. The sleeve now brushed the back of Arnold's hand.

"Better," said the tailor, and tugged the other sleeve to match, then passed a hand along Arnold's upper back. "And a little wider across the shoulders, I think. You do have fine shoulders, if I may say so."

Arnold didn't bother to thank him. He wasn't sure he could get his tongue unstuck from the roof of his mouth. He tried to decide if he was hallucinating, or in hell. Neither seemed to fit.

The jacket was fitting better, though. Alphonse muttered and ran his hands down the side seams, and Arnold could feel the cloth shifting to conform to his shape.

"Now the trousers."

More breeze, and more adjustments. Arnold tried not to shiver as he stood there. It was not just the wind that had made him cold and caused his balls to retreat. It was the whole situation. What the hell had he let himself in for?

"There you are," said Alphonse from the floor where he'd been kneeling to take up the trouser cuffs, a process that seemed to involve caressing the cloth. "Much better, if I may say so. Let's just get you some shoes and then you can have a look."

He put his hands on Arnold's supple walking shoes and a small flash like lightning made Arnold jump. His feet were now cased in fine leather. Alphonse smoothed his hands over the shoes and they hugged Arnold's feet while the hair on his legs stood up.

"C-could I keep those other shoes?" Arnold asked, noticing with pride that his voice didn't quaver.

Alphonse stood up and brushed his hands. "Of course. I'll have them sent up to your suite. Did you want the other clothes as well?"

"Uh, no."

"Good. I'll send up a selection of casual wear for you, and some additional shirts and so forth. Would you care to step over here and choose a cravat?"

Arnold obediently followed him to the display case and picked out a pearl-gray tie with matching pocket square. A sea-blue silk set caught his eye as well, and Alphonse set it aside for him. Arnold was half afraid he would conjure up another windstorm, but instead he turned a mirror on the counter toward Arnold and waited while Arnold tied the gray silk around his neck. That brought Alphonse up a notch or two in Arnold's esteem. A good tailor knew that a gentleman tied his own tie.

His hair was a mess. Arnold smoothed a hand over it, then accepted a silver hairbrush and comb from Alphonse and used them to groom his dark hair into submission.

"Very elegant, sir. Would you care to take in the whole ensemble?"

A sharp "pop" startled Arnold as a full-length mirror appeared beside him. "I wish you'd quit doing that," he said, then turned to the mirror to appraise himself.

"My apologies, sir," murmured Alphonse. "It's just quicker."

Arnold adjusted the necktie. "Yeah, like the way you tailor a suit is quicker."

"I hate fussing with pins. Oh, that reminds me."

Alphonse reached under the counter and brought out a small case lined in black velvet. In it rested half a dozen stickpins, each tipped with a sizable jewel. Arnold selected one with a diamond head and carefully placed it in the exact center of his tie.

"Perfect," said Alphonse. "You look much better, if I may say so, sir."

"Yeah, you may."

Arnold turned to the mirror. He felt better, too, though he wondered if the suit would turn into a pumpkin at midnight.

"Tell me about Penstemon."

Alphonse's eyebrows twitched upward. He blinked, then carefully put away the case of stickpins. "What do you wish to know?"

"Who is he? Where'd he come from?"

"He is originally from Florida, I believe. As to who—" The tailor paused to brush the shoulders of Arnold's suit with a silver-handled clothes brush. His golden eyes met Arnold's in the mirror.

"Being in his employ, I might be considered biased, but I think it is fair to say he's the most powerful warlock in the country."

~ William ~

Hertfordshire, England

William Weare sat up, much annoyed, and took the coins from his eyes. He had been in the middle of a perfectly good haunting when a peculiar sensation had gripped him, rather like to being drawn into a maelstrom, though the underwater feeling of it may have just been his imagination. He was dry now, in any case, though rather chilled. That, upon reflection, was unusual.

He looked around and saw that he was in the Elstree churchyard, right enough. There was the obnoxious Burton monument just near. He was sitting on his own grave, dressed in his Sunday best. He frowned, stood up, and noticed a stray leaf on his sleeve. He brushed at it and it fell off. That was when he realized he was in a living body.

Disturbing; he'd forgotten how heavy it felt. He took a deep breath and marveled at the smell of mouldering leaves and damp night air. He hefted the two coins in his hand. Guineas, antiques by now. Probably worth a pretty penny. He dropped them into his coat pocket.

Alive again. He supposed he should be pleased, but he still felt faintly annoyed. He'd got used to being dead. He could go where he liked without anyone bothering him, and if he got bored he could frighten a few good people out of their wits for a laugh. How was he to frighten anyone now?

And these clothes—the ones he'd been buried in—well, they were absolutely out of fashion now, he knew that much. Frock coat and breeches belonged at a fancy dress ball nowadays.

The young people he had been haunting were nowhere in sight. Scared off, perhaps, by the maelstrom or whatever it had been. They had gone home, or off to the pub to brag about daring the graveyard. He felt cheated.

The sound of horses' hooves clopping on pavement made him turn his head. Outside the churchyard fence he saw a black coach and pair coming down the street. The matched black horses raised their hooves high as they trotted, very showy. The coach pulled up to the gate and stopped.

William gazed at it with narrowed eyes. He'd never seen the coach before, but it didn't belong in the middle of 21st century Elstree any more than he did. That meant it must have something to do with the maelstrom and his sudden return to flesh. Well, he might as well have it out with the driver.

He strode through the churchyard to the gate and went out. Still frowning, he accosted the driver.

"You there! What's your business with me?"

No reply, and he noticed now that there was no face beneath the top hat. He grimaced. He wasn't fond of magical creatures, preferred to avoid them. They cramped his style.

The coach door opened and a young man stepped out. He was slender with dark hair and eyes of greenish gold, and wore a black driving coat with several shoulder capes. Very dashing for 1823, but a little out of place now. The fellow bowed to William.

"Good evening, sir."

"Well? What do you want? And what do you mean by coming here in that museum piece?"

The youth looked at the coach, then back at William. "It's meant to make you feel at home."

The accent was American, definitely. William knew it from watching the telly; he had also seen American tourists often enough, even haunted a few.

"Feel at home? It's a bloody antique! Where do you think I've been the last hundred and eighty-nine years?"

The youth looked disconcerted. "Well…you've been dead."

"Yes, but that doesn't mean I'm completely out of touch!"

William eyed the coach with displeasure, partly born of the remembrance of his departure from this mortal coil—or some other mortal coil, more likely. This one was in too good condition to be the same.

He'd been dragged out of a coach—a gig, actually, smaller than the monstrosity before him—by his boon companion, John Thurtell, who had proceeded to murder him. Thurtell had taken exception to losing at cards, accused William of cheating (true, but Thurtell had no proof of it), and bludgeoned him to death. With the help of friends, he had then dropped William in the pond at Gills Hill Cottage, but being nervous that he'd be discovered, they had moved him to another, more remote pond, and then to the river.

After all that sloshing about, William's remains had been in poor condition. He remembered. He had watched.

He'd watched the trial, too, and a rare sensation it had been. He had been a solicitor in life, and professional interest, not to mention having little else to do, had drawn him to take in all the many blustering hours. He'd been at the hanging as well, there to greet his old companion and hasten him to his own personal hell. Thurtell hadn't liked seeing him, William recalled with a smile.

The young man in the driving coat cleared his throat. William glanced up at him.

"Mr. Weare, I'm here to invite you to join a card game."

"A card game? Is that why I'm given a new body, so that I can play cards?"

"Well, yes."

"And to whom to I owe this honor? If it's Thurtell, you can get back in that rattletrap and begone."

"No, no. It's Mr. Simon Penstemon, an American. The game's in America."

"And why should I journey to America merely for a game of cards?"

"Don't you want to keep that new body?" said the youth.

A feminine giggle drew William's attention. Two young ladies, a plump redhead and a petite brunette, both wearing fuzzy jumpers over their blue jeans, were walking toward him along the street. They had their heads together and were obviously amused by William's attire. The brunette cast a coy glance at the young man in the driving coat.

"They can see you," William accused.

"They can't see the coach," the fellow replied in a whisper, then he nodded and smiled to the ladies.

"Hello, boys!" said the redhead. "Off to a masquerade? Can we come?"

"No masquerade," said the fellow in black. "We're just talking."

The redhead pouted. Her friend was staring at the young man in open admiration, but he appeared not to notice. William chuckled, then hid it in a cough.

"Buy us a drink, then?" the redhead said to him. "You'll be a hit at the pub."

"Sorry, we can't," said the youth. "We've got a plane to catch."

"Hold on, hold on," said William. "We've got time for a drink, haven't we?"

The young man met his gaze, frowning. William smiled. He had the fellow, and they both knew it.

A silent bargain passed between them: a drink at the pub in exchange for his cooperation. He'd get the drink, and then he'd see about the cooperation.

Turning to the redhead, William offered his arm. "Lead on, my dear."

A drink. A nice pint of bitters—it had been so long he could scarcely remember the taste.

"I'm Alma," said the redhead, "and that's Joanie."

"William," he said, and glanced at the youth.

"Festus," said the youth grudgingly.

Alma laughed, a little cascading sound. "What a funny name! Is it American?"

"It's short for Hephæstus."

"Like the Greek god," said Joanie, beaming up at him.

The youth said nothing, and didn't quite roll his eyes, though he looked away. Alma pulled William forward, and the other two followed. The coach, which neither of the girls had heeded, began a laborious turn in the street and eventually followed them.

The pub wasn't far. It was filled with people, mostly younger folk, chattering over loud rock music. A tiny dance floor in one corner was crammed with youngsters bouncing to the music. William had drifted in here once or twice, but it wasn't a good place for haunting. Too hard to get people's attention with all the noise and activity.

Alma led William up to the bar. The barkeep, a cheery fellow with the build of a prizefighter, looked up.

"Hallo, Alma," he said in a bluff voice that cut through the music. "Wotcha got here?"

"This is William," Alma shouted back. "Ain't he grand?"

The barkeep's brows rose. "How do, your lordship. What'll you have?"

"A pint of your best," said William loudly, "and whatever the ladies would like."

"Pint for me, too," said Alma.

"I'll have a GT," said Joanie. She looked at Festus, and the barkeep shifted his gaze to the youth.

"Just water for me," he said. "I'm driving."

An interesting lie, William thought. He watched as the barkeep fetched the drinks. Festus had better have the means to pay for them, because he wasn't wasting one of his guineas on a couple of pints.

The barkeep set a glass before him. William admired the dark, golden-brown color, then sipped and sighed. Good ale, sharp with hops, mellow underneath. Bliss.

"So what do you do, William?" Alma asked, leaning one arm against the bar and sipping at the ale in her other hand.

"Do? Nothing." He thought for a moment and added, "I'm retired."

"And you dress like this just for kicks?"

"That's right," he said with a glance at Festus beside him, who looked increasingly uncomfortable. "For kicks."

"You two should go dance," Alma said to Joanie and Festus.

Joanie looked shocked. "It's too crowded," she said, with a worried glance at Festus.

"I don't dance," Festus said flatly, and swallowed half his glass of water.

William took another sip of his ale. He was rather enjoying this. All the physical sensations were so strong. As a ghost, he'd barely had a whisper of them. He liked them better than he'd remembered.

He liked Alma particularly, she was soft and warm and smelled interesting. He wondered if she'd be willing to take a tumble with him. Women nowadays were much more open to that sort of thing, it wasn't nearly the disgrace it had been in his time. Perfectly respectable women slept with whomever they pleased, and called it dating.

"Are you at university?" he heard Joanie ask Festus.

"No," Festus said without elaboration.

William sighed and took another swallow of ale. The fellow was a fool. Here was a lovely young thing clearly enamored of him, and he was throwing it away.

"So, where's the plane taking you?" Alma asked.

"America. Want to come along?" William glanced sidelong at Festus, who looked fit to burst with annoyance.

Alma's cascading laugh rose above the music. "Yeah, sure. Can you get me home by morning? I've got to work."

"Call in sick," William suggested.

Alma laughed again. Festus, who had both elbows on the bar, stared sullenly at his glass. Beyond him, Joanie watched, a hopeless jumble of confusion and infatuation.

William finished his ale and ordered another. He flirted with Alma while he drank it, much to Festus's annoyance. Joanie tried a few more times to engage the fellow in conversation, then gave up and quietly sipped her drink. Poor girl. She wasn't having a bit of fun.

"'Nother round?" asked the barkeep, glancing at William's nearly-empty glass.

"Not for me," said Alma.

William finished his drink and set down the glass. He was feeling nicely mellow. "That'll do, I guess."

The barkeep waved a slip of paper. "Who gets the tab?"

William looked at Festus. The youth reached into the pocket of his driving coat and withdrew a twenty-pound note, which he dropped on the bar.

"Will that cover it?"

"More than. I'll get your change," said the barkeep.

"Keep it." Festus turned to William with a hard look. "Time to go."

William shrugged and offered an arm to Alma again. She finished her pint and slid her arm through his. Warm and soft.

Festus turned and began pushing his way through the crowd. William and Alma followed, with poor Joanie tagging behind. When they reached the street, Festus headed for the coach, and William noticed that he walked haltingly. That accounted for his not wanting to dance. Joanie followed him a couple of steps back, her arms crossed over her chest.

Festus stopped beside the coach, which was waiting at the curb. "It was nice meeting you both," he said to the girls, "but I'm afraid we have to say goodbye."

"Hang on a minute," Alma said, grinning at William. "You offered to take us along, right?"

"Sorry, we can't," Festus said shortly.

"In that case I'll stay here," William said. "You go on, my boy."

"I can't leave without you!" Festus sounded annoyed.

"Then you'll have to take us all," William said. "If you want me, you've got to bring Alma and Joanie."

Alma laughed. Joanie looked uncomfortable and murmured a protest, but her eyes were hopeful as she glanced up at Festus.

"I can't do that!" Festus said. "It's not allowed!"

"Why not? Private plane, isn't it? There's room, isn't there?" William was gambling on these assumptions, but from Festus's reaction it looked like he'd been right. He grinned.

"They're mundanes!" Festus said in exasperation.

"I *beg* your pardon!" Alma said, looking ready to clock him one.

"Mundanes aren't allowed in the Black Queen," Festus said, ignoring her. "Mr. Penstemon's very strict about it."

"Am I a mundane?" William asked.

Festus blinked. "Well—I guess you are—"

"So the rule doesn't apply on this occasion, does it?"

"You're an invited guest! They're not!"

Festus's brows were knit in an anxious frown, and color was rising in his cheeks. William felt a glow of calm triumph, an echo of his days as a solicitor. When one's opponent was flustered, one was on the verge of victory.

"Bring them along," he said in a kindly tone, "and I'll work it all out with Mr. Penstemon. You won't get in trouble. I'll explain to him."

Festus made a frustrated sound, like a strangled growl. "All right, all right," he said, yanking open the door of the coach. "Get in."

"Blimey, where did that come from?" said Alma. "It wasn't there a second ago!"

Joanie stepped toward the coach and reached out a hesitant hand to touch it. "Wow! It's gorgeous!"

"I wish you'd chosen some other vehicle," William said testily. "I have bad memories of my last carriage ride."

Festus waved an angry hand at the coach. A sudden wind came up, reminding William sharply of the maelstrom. The coach and pair transformed into a limousine, long, low, and black, engine purring. Joanie jumped back with a small shriek.

"Blimey!" Alma cried, then exchanged a wide-eyed look with her friend.

"It's time to leave," Festus said, standing by the open door. "Get in."

Alma looked at him with new respect. She took a deep breath, a little nervous but still game. "Can we just pop round to my flat, so I can get a few things?"

"No," Festus told her. "You can get whatever you need at the Black Queen. Now, Mr. Weare?"

William turned to Alma. "Coming, my dear?"

Alma drew herself up. "Yes." She stepped toward the car, and William offered a hand to help her in.

"Alma, you can't!" Joanie cried. "How will you get home?"

"I'm sure Mr. Penstemon can take care of that." William looked at Festus, who didn't answer.

Alma peered up from the car seat with a nervous smile. "Come on, Joanie. It's just a lark."

Joanie looked terrified. She glanced at Festus, who ignored her. Festus had turned into a bloody stiff-rumped footman. William couldn't understand why Joanie was still attracted to him, but attracted she must be. She took an unsteady step toward the limo and allowed William to hand her in next to Alma.

"I can't believe I'm doing this," Joanie moaned as William climbed in beside her.

The long bench seat had ample room for the three of them. The door closed with a snap, and a moment later Festus got into the front seat beside the invisible driver.

"I've always wanted to visit America," said Alma, a bit too cheerily. "Oh, look!"

She'd found a bar in the back of the front seat, fully stocked. William poured drinks all around as the limo eased away from the curb, glided through the village, and turned onto the A5.

"So, where are we going?" Alma asked him as the limo accelerated. "New York?"

William took a sip of his single-malt and leaned back, smiling. "I have no idea."

Joanie let out a small whimper. Alma laughed again, a note of hilarity in the bell-like cascade.

The car was changing, stretching out, and—William peered out the window beside him—yes, it was growing wings! Safety belts reached up out of the seat and buckled themselves around the three of them, causing Joanie to squeak again. Alma tossed back the rest of her drink and gave William a nervous smile as the coach-cum-limo-cum-plane roared, gaining speed, and lifted itself from the highway to fly off into the black October night.

~ James ~

Dave started up a drunken yodeling of "John Brown's Body" as a distraction while James carefully switched the hand he'd been dealt for the prestacked one in his pocket. He then picked up the cards and fanned them. Aces and eights, nine of diamonds. He'd argued that the queen of hearts should have been the kicker, but they had the nine up on the wall and weren't about to depart from long-standing tradition.

He downed the glass of whiskey at his elbow. The part he hated most was coming up. No matter how often he did the show, he couldn't get used to the gunfire. He could feel a spot between his shoulder blades tickling with tension. He *hated* sitting with his back to the door, even though he knew Joe's pistol was loaded with blanks, even though he knew all the saloon's employees were watching out for him.

God damn, it was a hell of a thing to be killed five times a day. Not all the whiskey in the world could set him up for it.

BLAM! BLAM, BLAM!

James jumped, as he always did, then pitched forward, taking care to spill his cards face up. The hullabaloo proceeded while the smell of gunpowder tickled his nostrils and he tried to keep from sneezing. They used far too much powder in the blank charges — liked a loud explosion, made the crowd jump. Unrealistic and wasteful, but this was a show, after all.

The fuss died down, and Dave and the girls came to carry him away. James kept his eyes closed and tried to stay limp, which wasn't ever easy. He felt his hat sliding off as they pulled him from the chair and restrained an impulse to grab at it. One of the gals picked it up and dropped it on his stomach as he was carried out of the room to a smattering of applause.

He was more successful at being dead than he'd ever been at

being alive. Ironic, but there you had it.

In the back room, which was half broom closet, half dressing room, they laid him down on the cot where he'd been sleeping nights. He sat up and then got to his feet, dusting off his clothes. Joe gave him a grin.

"Good show, James. Like always."

"Thanks."

They left him alone to change. There'd been some argument about that, James quite naturally wanting to continue wearing his own clothes. Mike, the manager, wouldn't have it. Said it would destroy the illusion of the show. As if the crowd actually believed they'd seen Wild Bill Hickok shot.

James snorted. Well, they had—better than they knew—but not even Mike was aware of that.

He'd gone about the town a little in the last couple of mornings, and been astonished at the numerous tributes to himself—statues, courtyards, memorials. It seemed that whole town existed for the sole purpose of glorifying his ignominious death in the dirty, scurrilous mining camp that it had once been.

He had honored Mike's desires and bought himself a pair of jeans and a modern shirt to wear between shows, and a coat for going outside. Not one of the puffy feather-mattress coats—those were expensive, he'd found out—just a nice heavy cloth coat to keep off the chill. He'd admired a sheepskin jacket at the clothing store, but that had cost even more than the featherbed ones.

He changed into the jeans and shirt and then put his own boots back on. He drew the line at pulling his hair into a braid or a pigtail like Mike wanted. All his life he'd worn it loose across his shoulders, and that wasn't about to change.

A knock fell on the door and it opened. Mike stepped in, closing it behind him. He was a big blustery fellow, kept a tight rein on operations at the saloon and enjoyed the hell out of stepping into the show if someone should happen to be absent. He grinned at James and held out a long, white envelope.

"Here you go, Jim. Good job tonight."

James ignored the misuse of his name and glanced through

the money in the envelope. Mike had wanted to pay him with a bank cheque, but James had convinced him to pay cash on account of he was working temporary.

"Goodly crowd tonight," James said, stuffing the money in the tight pocket of his jeans.

"Yeah, especially for a Thursday. It's the nice weather, brought some weekenders out for the end of the season."

James nodded. He'd figured out the crowds, even in just the couple of days he'd been working. In the afternoon it was mostly kids and their folks, in the evenings fellas with their gals, groups of boys looking for a game or a fight, and groups of gals looking for the boys. Tonight's crowd had been the biggest he'd seen.

He picked up his clothes, folded them, and put them along with his hat in the bag from the shop where he'd bought the new outfit, then put on his coat. "Good night, Mr. Shelley."

"Night then," said Mike, stepping backward and opening the door. "See you tomorrow."

"So you shall."

James walked out and headed straight for the bar. Jenny, the gal who'd given him a free whiskey on that first night, set a full glass before him without his asking. He put the money for it on the bar, but she pushed it back at him.

"Compliments of the lady," Jenny told him, nodding toward a woman sitting on a stool down the bar.

She was slender, dressed in a black shift and jeans with a satiny jacket like some of the sports fans affected. Hers was plain black. Her hair was black, too, dressed high on her head with a couple of curls dangling down beside her ears, and her eyes were green and almond-shaped. She smiled and nodded at him, and James felt a stirring of interest in his loins.

He nodded back and raised his glass to her. She slid from her stool and came over to sit on the one next to James. He had downed the whiskey by now and pushed the glass toward Jenny to be refilled. Jenny quirked an eyebrow at him as she poured, but didn't say a word.

"Evening, ma'am," James said to the stranger. "I hope you

enjoyed the show."

"It was very interesting," she said in a soft, low voice. "I confess I would never have expected to find you here. That's why it's taken me so long."

James felt a little chill run down his spine. He took a swallow of whiskey and gave her an appraising look. "Have we met?"

"No. You might have seen my—vehicle, though. At the cemetery two nights ago."

He knocked back the rest of his drink, set the empty glass on the bar, and frowned into it. She meant the black stagecoach. She couldn't have meant anything else.

He glanced at her and for a moment saw her dressed in a frilled and corseted gown from the 1880's, jet beads at her neck and a feather in her hair. He sucked a sharp breath and pushed the glass toward Jenny again.

"Jesus, James," Jenny said under her breath as she filled it. "Take it easy. She won't bite."

Much you know, he thought. There were nasty critters in the world, critters that could look human but weren't. He'd run into a few, on restless nights back at the graveyard. He didn't care to meet any more of them if he could help it.

"I'm Kitty," said the stranger, smiling. "I'm here to invite you to a poker game."

James frowned. "Poker?"

"Yes. You'd be an honored guest."

James frowned at her, uncertain. He'd been longing to get into a real game, not the play-acting they did in the show here. These boys weren't real poker players.

"And where is this game?" he asked.

"Atlantic City."

Bright sparks seemed to fly about the words as she said them. Fireflies again. James suppressed a shiver.

The money he'd been saving to travel east, the job reenacting his own death—all unnecessary, he realized. This woman would take him where he needed to go, where he was being called. Atlantic City.

"That's a rough town, I hear," Jenny said conversationally.

Kitty glanced at her. "Rough around the edges, yes." She looked back at James. "The game is at the Black Queen, the city's most exclusive casino."

"Why me?" James demanded. "Why come all this way to invite me?"

A slow smile parted Kitty's lips and glinted in her eyes. "You're legendary," she said.

Another kind of show, then. He was meant to be an attraction. Not his favorite line of work, but if he could play in an actual poker game and not get shot at, it would beat what he was doing now.

He thought about the black coach and decided he needed one more whiskey in order to face it. He pushed his glass back toward Jenny, then looked at Kitty.

"Buy you a drink, Miss Kitty?"

"No, thank you."

Jenny had filled his glass and stood frowning at him. He winked at her and lifted the whiskey to his lips, turning back to Kitty.

"I don't have much of a stake to put toward a game."

Kitty shifted on the bar stool. "That's all taken care of. It's—an exhibition game, sort of."

"But there's a prize purse?"

"There's a prize, yes."

James kicked back the rest of his drink and slapped the glass down on the bar. "I'm in."

Kitty stood up, and he noted she was tiny—the fluffy curls on top of her head just came to his shoulder. Jenny started wiping a rag in circles on the bar.

"Mike's gonna be pissed," she said conversationally.

"You'll explain to him, won't you darlin'? This just sounds too good to pass up."

"*Sounds* being the operative word."

James grinned at her and dropped a twenty on the bar beside his empty glass. He hurried to the back room to fetch his bag of clothes, then returned to Kitty. "Lead on."

She led him out of the bar and down the street a little ways to where a black sedan was parked. "Seeing that you're already acquainted with the modern world, I dispensed with the historic display," she said, opening the back door. "I hope you don't mind."

James grinned as he climbed in. "Got rid of the stagecoach, eh?"

"Actually, this is the same vehicle. It's just easier to park this way."

Kitty slid onto the seat beside him and closed the door. James tried to wrap his mind around the idea that this modern contraption—a car, as they called them—was the self-same coach he'd seen before. Couldn't do it, so he gave up and leaned back as the car pulled out into traffic.

"So tell me about this poker game."

"Mr. Penstemon will explain everything when we get there."

"Tell me about you, then."

"Me?" She turned surprised green eyes on him. "There isn't much to tell."

"Whereabouts are you from?"

She blinked. "I don't know. I've always been at the Black Queen."

That sounded a mite strange. Maybe she just didn't want to say. James raised an eyebrow. "Mr. Penstemon your boss?"

She tilted her head, frowning. "I live with him."

"Oh."

So much for the thought of getting a little closer to Miss Kitty, though that might be what this Penstemon fellow had intended, sending her along like this. James frowned. It wasn't right to use a young gal like that. He'd enjoyed many a lighthearted encounter in his day, certainly, but he liked to think it was the gal's free choice.

Anyway, he'd put that behind him. He'd been faithful to Agnes for the short time they were married. He wondered what she'd done after he was gone.

Thinking about her made him a little sad. He'd failed her, he supposed. Poor Agnes. She wasn't glamorous, but she had a good head on her shoulders and she was kind. And patient! She'd followed him all over creation, bringing her circus to the most God-forsaken places just to be near him. It had taken him a long time to realize she was the wife for him.

He missed her. His heart gave a sharp pang as he wondered again what had become of her. She'd trusted him to go to Deadwood looking to stake a claim, and he'd let her down.

Something was happening to the car. A loud flapping noise had started up overhead. James looked up, startled, as a harness strapped itself around him. Miss Kitty was strapped in, too. James's scalp prickled as the car began to rise slowly into the air.

"What's going on?" he demanded.

"Nothing to worry about. We're just taking a faster way to Atlantic City, is all. It would take a couple of days to drive."

It would take a couple of weeks, last he knew, and that was with riding the train. Things had changed beyond his comprehension. It was too late, though, to get out of the car now. It was flying.

James looked out the window and saw the tops of tall pines rushing away beneath them like grass alongside a railroad. Dizzy, he leaned back and closed his eyes. He could not get used to the way these modern people traveled. Always in such a damn hurry!

The car bucked a couple of times and seemed to stretch itself out, then the flapping was replaced by a steady roar. He dared another look out the window and saw a cluster of little specks of light far below.

"Holy Christ Almighty!"

"That's Deadwood," Kitty said. "Pretty, isn't it?"

"I'm gonna be sick."

"Put your head between your knees. There's a bag if you need it."

James followed her advice. With his eyes closed he tried to find something to distract his mind.

Deadwood was all he could think of, Deadwood falling away below him now. He'd promised Agnes he'd make his fortune there, and now he was leaving…

He woke to the pale blue glow of early dawn. Thought about risking a look toward the ground, then decided against it. The roar in his ears was descending, and the car was changing again. The flapping noise came back.

James looked at Kitty, who was sleeping with her feet tucked up under her, curled against the side of the car. He gasped as something big and dark flashed by the window beside her, and the sound woke her up.

She uncurled her legs and stretched luxuriously. Sure was a pretty little thing. She blinked at James, then sat up and looked out the window.

"Oh, good. We're here."

A blue glow drew James's attention to his window. Outside, a giant playing card floated past, its edges glowing blue. Queen of spades.

"No, it was the queen of hearts," he murmured.

"What?" said Kitty.

"Nothing."

The card passed from his view but the blue glow remained, as if the very air around them was on fire. The car slowly settled downward until it came to rest. Kitty opened the door beside her and beckoned to James.

"Keep your head down," she called over the flapping noise.

James grabbed his bag of clothes and followed her, crouching as she did, partly in a reaction against the noise. She scurried to a small, rectangular building outlined in glowing blue. Once there, James stood up straight and paused to look back.

The black car looked wildly different, bulbous and wheelless, with flashing lights and a giant propeller on top, madly spinning away. Beyond it was the queen of spades he'd seen, much bigger than he'd realized. It was as tall as the tallest building he'd ever seen, and above it hung glowing blue words, "The Black Queen."

"Welcome to Atlantic City," Kitty said.

He couldn't see anything of a city, though it was hard to notice anything but that gargantuan card. Beyond it was a blue haze that might have been the ocean or maybe just night air. James turned away from the sign and looked out to his right. The flat he was standing on, which he had thought was a field like to the black ones up in Deadwood, had an end to it he never expected. He gasped and flung himself against the little building, reassured by its solidity.

A scattering of lights spread out far below them, beyond the square edge of the place they were standing. He could see the shoreline now, with tiny waves curling over the darker blue of the ocean. Lights twinkled all golden like Deadwood had looked from the air, and nearer by there were many more lights and many more colors, moving and flashing, dizzy-making.

"You all right?" Kitty asked.

"W-where are we?" James managed to say.

"On the roof of the Black Queen. Would you like to go inside?"

"Yes, ma'am."

He managed to stand up and let go of the building, though he kept close to it as Kitty led him to a door in its side. Inside it was quieter, the noise of the car muted by thick walls and the heavy door that clanged shut behind them. Lights glowed on the wall and a thick blue carpet muffled their steps. Kitty led him to a pair of metal doors that slid open to reveal a small, windowless room. They stepped in and the doors closed again, then James's stomach tried to drop into his boots.

He clutched at a brass railing attached to the wall. Kitty gave him a curious look, then a smile that was probably meant to be reassuring but that just didn't have the punch required to soothe his jangled nerves. Glass of whiskey was what he needed for that, at this point.

The room bounced, then the doors slid open again, revealing a completely different hallway, this one much longer and more highly decorated. The walls were papered with a patterned design in shades of soft gold, and bore pictures, mirrors, and fancy lights all brass curly-cues and crystal drops. The carpet underfoot was thick and oriental in design, woven all in blue, black, and gold. It covered the whole of the floor, right up to the walls.

Kitty led James down the hall a ways and stopped at a door marked "4207." She pushed it open and gestured for him to go in.

"This is your suite."

The room was huge. It was set up as a parlor with sofa and chairs and a low table with a basket of fruit on it. To one side stood a small bar and a round table suitable for a game if one brought a couple more chairs to it. Doors led off into a bedroom and a washroom. Draperies of a soft gold covered the far wall. He had never stayed in so big and fine a place, not even in Buffalo on his honeymoon.

"You'd probably like to change clothes," Kitty said, strolling in after him. "There are shops on the ground floor where you can pick out some fresh outfits with Mr. Penstemon's compliments."

James lifted his bag. "If Mr. Penstemon don't mind, I'd just as soon wear my own duds."

"Of course."

She handed him a card, the queen of spades. It was too thick and heavy, and slippery, probably made out of the stuff they called plastic. Seemed like every little object he couldn't figure out was made out of plastic. He turned it over. The back was solid blue, with "The Black Queen" stamped on it in gold letters.

"That's your key. It slides into the slot on the outside of the door."

"Oh. Thanks."

Kitty tilted her head to look at him. "Did you learn how to use a phone in Deadwood?"

"Uh—I know you talk into them. Didn't have anyone to talk to, myself."

"Well, it's over here." She walked to a desk set against the wall and lifted the handle of a phone. "Press 2 for Room Service, order whatever you want to eat, and they'll bring it to you.

There's a menu here, and lots of other information. Don't worry about paying for anything, it's all on the house."

"Thank you kindly. When is the game?"

"It starts this evening." She smiled and headed toward the door. "You'll meet Mr. Penstemon in a couple of hours. If you need anything in the meantime, just use the phone."

James watched her go out, then carried his clothes into the bedroom and proceeded to bathe and dress. Feeling more comfortable, he braved the phone and asked for breakfast and a deck of cards.

"Certainly, sir," said the pleasant feminine voice that had answered. "Is there anything else we can get you?"

"I don't supposed you'd have some cartridges for a Colt .36 caliber pistol?"

"What year of manufacture?"

"1851."

"We'll send them right up."

Duly impressed, James put the phone back in its cradle. When the knock came at the door shortly afterward and he went to answer it, he about jumped out of his skin. The little rolling cart of food looked all right, but whoever was rolling it was invisible. If it hadn't been for the blue and black uniform, James wouldn't have known anyone was there.

He watched the critter put the food on the table and set a couple of sealed boxes of playing cards next to it, along with a box of cartridges for the pistols. It then started to roll the cart away again. Steeling himself to follow it to the door, James pulled a five dollar bill from his pocket and held it at arm's length.

"Here. Thank you for your trouble."

The critter paused, then an arm of the uniform raised up. James felt the bill twitched out of his fingers. A high-pitched whistle sounded, like the wind moaning through a cracked window. The bill floated into the critter's pocket.

"You're welcome."

The critter left with the cart, and James shut the door and

leaned against it. He supposed he ought not to be frightened of anything, having already been dead for a considerable long while. The truth was, though, that he was frightened of almost every new and strange thing he encountered. He always had been. The secret to his reputation was that he almost never let it show.

He went over to the table and loaded his guns, after which he felt better about things. He moved the dishes so he could sit facing the door. His breakfast was bacon, eggs, and beans, along with biscuits and jam and a whole pot of hot coffee, all excellent.

When he'd finished, he pushed the empty plates aside and picked up a packet of cards and broke it open. They were like the ones they'd used in the show at the No. 10, unnaturally slippery, coated with plastic. The backs were black with a blue diamond check pattern and "The Black Queen," again in gold.

He fiddled with the cards, dealing out poker hands a half dozen at a time to see which would win. If he won the tournament he could maybe go on to more games, live comfortably, enjoy a chance to sink gracefully into the old age of which he'd been robbed. It seemed strange to be given another shot at that. He wasn't sure it was what he wanted.

If he lost, maybe he could hire on with Mr. Penstemon to deal cards, or do some kind of show though he'd be the first to admit he was not the best of showmen. He'd have to meet Penstemon first and size him up before considering any such arrangement.

He set the deck aside and strolled over to the draperies. Daylight was seeping in around the edges, which implied they covered a window. He pulled one aside and immediately stumbled back, letting it fall again.

His room was floating in air. He stood staring at the gently swinging drape, breathing hard and fast, his breakfast churning in his stomach. Clenching his teeth together, he cautiously stepped toward the drape again and peeked out.

Far below him the beach spread out, white sand along the edge of a bright blue ocean. People were down there, crawling on the sand like so many ants. The whole wall in front of him, floor to ceiling, was glass. He put a hand against it and felt the warmth of the morning sun.

He could see a tower rising up into the sky a little way down the shore. A building, impossibly tall. Maybe he was in the same sort of building. The tallest he'd ever seen was in New York, six stories.

He swallowed. Different times, and he'd better adjust. He found a little rod attached to the drape and used it to push the curtain aside, then took a couple of steps back from the window 'til he felt safe. He saw no way to open the window, which was just as well because he had no desire to risk a fall.

"Magnificent view, isn't it?"

James spun around, hand to his guns and ready to draw. He hadn't heard the door open, but there was the fellow who'd spoken, a tall man with blond hair waving over his brow and falling thickly to brush the shoulders of his black jacket. He wore black trousers and shoes as well, and one of the modern neckties that looked so strange, of a blue so rich it seemed to glow. A tiny pin nestled in the middle of the tie, a diamond set in gold.

"Forgive me," the man said in the same melodious voice. "I didn't mean to startle you, Mr. Hickok. I'm Simon Penstemon."

He stepped forward, a small smile curving his lips as he offered a hand. James relaxed and shook hands, noting Penstemon's firm grip, his stance, his eyes that were clear and sharp, the sort of eyes that didn't miss much.

His skin was naturally fair but had a slight golden tint to it as if he'd spent some time in the sun. His mouth was pretty like a girl's, but the line of his jaw was firm and took away any hint of the effeminate.

"How do," said James, nodding. "Much obliged for the hospitality."

"I'm delighted you chose to join us. I hope the staff has given you everything you need?"

James nodded again, watching the fellow and trying to make up his mind what sort of man he was. Penstemon didn't seem like the showman type. That sort was usually full of bluster and bravado, not quiet like this man. He remembered Bill Cody, how he was constantly looking to display himself to advantage. Maybe Penstemon would act different in public, but just now he showed none of that inclination.

"Tell me about your poker game, Mr. Penstemon."

The smile tugged again at the corners of Penstemon's mouth. "I'd prefer to explain the terms to all of you at once. The final player should arrive around noon. If it's agreeable to you, we'll all have a late lunch together and I'll go over the rules then."

"Fair enough. Exhibition game, is it?"

The smile widened into a grin. "Indeed it is. I see nothing escapes you, Mr. Hickok."

"I like to think ahead. So was it you that raised me from the dead, so to speak?"

"Ah—yes, but we're getting into the explanation I'd like to make to all of you together. If you don't mind, I'll save that. Why don't we go down to the casino now, and I'll show you around?"

"All right." James got his hat and shrugged into his buckskin jacket.

"Do you have your key?" Penstemon asked.

James went back and found the queen of spades and slid her into his pocket, then followed Mr. Penstemon to the door. Penstemon led him down the long hall and back into the little hallway that gave onto the square windowless room. He pushed a little light on the wall, same as Kitty had done.

A flute started playing somewhere near. Penstemon took a little silver box out of his pocket and the music got louder. He glanced up at James.

"Please excuse me."

Penstemon poked the box with a finger and the music stopped as he held it up to his ear. "Yes? Yes, I know, Donovan told me. Well, find him! How hard can it be? Ask the people at the bus station." He frowned as he put the box back in his pocket, then noticed James watching him.

"Sorry about that. Administrative problem. Nothing to worry about."

James nodded agreeably. A bell chimed and the metal doors slid open. Penstemon stepped into the square room and invited James to follow.

"Is this a magical thing?" James asked as the doors closed and his stomach sank again.

Penstemon smiled. "No, it's technological. It's called an elevator. Carries us from floor to floor on long cables."

"I see."

James leaned against the wall, trying to look casual though he had a firm grip on the railing with one hand. The sensation did remind him of falling, now that he knew what it was, which wasn't a pleasant thought.

"You people sure have come up with a lot of ways to travel fast," he said.

Penstemon smiled again. It seemed a smile was constantly hovering at the edge of his mouth and only waiting for a reason to slide onto it.

"As a line from one of my favorite movies says, 'The world has got itself in a big damn hurry.'"

James raised an eyebrow. "Movies?"

"Moving pictures. Another technological innovation. A sequence of many photographs, taken very swiftly by a camera and then played back at the same speed by a projector. You'll see."

After a much longer ride than the first one, the elevator finally came to a stop with a gentle bounce and opened its doors. James saw an identical set of doors across from him, then Penstemon led him out and to the side into a gigantic blue-carpeted room.

A barrage of color and sound came at him and he paused to compose himself before following Penstemon out into it. There was music of a sort, though it had no melody and hung in the background, a constant ripple of sound.

Penstemon led him down a broad carpeted walkway in between rows of silver machines that seemed to be the source of the music. People were sitting in front of some of them, punching buttons that caused lights to flash.

"Slot machines," Penstemon said as they left the machines behind, continuing into the casino between a pair of roulette tables. "A game of chance, rather unimaginative. There's absolutely no skill involved. I don't care for them myself, but the customers expect them. Hello, Stan," he added, nodding to a croupier.

"Morning, Mr. Penstemon," said Stan, who had a black beard that covered his whole face nearly up to the eyes. It was neatly trimmed, granted, but still gave him something of a savage look, and didn't quite fit with his starched white shirt, blue brocade vest, and stiff, black bow tie. James just had time to notice that his ears were hairy as well, and then they were past, moving into a section of card tables.

The room was bigger than any ballroom he'd ever seen, more like the size of an arena where Bill Cody's Wild West Show might be performed. It was filled with tables for dice and cards and roulette, and more rows of the slot machines.

One young lady dealing beneath a sign that said "Omaha" caught James's eye—she had black hair hanging down her back like a dark waterfall, deep blue eyes, and skin a vibrant shade of violet. She glanced up at James as they passed and smiled, revealing silver teeth. He shivered, unable to avoid imagining those teeth fixing on some part of his anatomy.

"You've got some interesting folks working here," James said.

"I'm an equal opportunity employer," said Penstemon.

"How come none of those invisible critters are dealing?"

"The will-o-wisps? I had some of them dealing to begin with, but the customers tended to avoid their tables. They prefer to see what the dealer's hands are doing. This is the poker room," he added, leading James into a somewhat less gigantic room off the side of the big one, still big enough to hold a respectable crowd.

The tables here were bigger than the others and lower to the ground, so the players could sit in regular chairs instead of on stools—except for the one green fellow who was too big for a regular chair. He was sitting on a large crate at the short end of one of the tables. He was green from head to foot: green hair, green eyes, and he wore a dark green outfit, nicely tailored, which was about the only thing that kept him from looking like a big old troll.

Only two of the ten or so poker tables had games going. James watched the cards being dealt around at one of them and got a tingling feeling in the palms of his hands.

"Why's the dealer throwing cards face up in the middle?" he asked, staring at the table.

"It's Texas Hold'em," said Penstemon. "A variation on seven-card stud. You'll learn all about it, don't worry."

"What's the matter with draw?"

"Nothing, but this game is in fashion. It's the game used in all the big poker championships."

Two of the players were whispering together, staring at James. As he watched, the word went around the table like a brisk wind, and the players all began to steal glances at him.

"You know," James said in a musing tone, stroking his mustache with his left hand, "in the past I have been compensated for playing in public venues, over and above any winnings I have claimed."

The smile twitched onto Penstemon's lips. He answered just as quietly, still gazing at the poker game.

"That isn't quite appropriate in this case. You'll have everything you want now and while the game is going on, but trust me, after it's finished it really won't matter."

James misliked the sound of that. He wasn't about to trust Penstemon, though he wasn't about to annoy him either, if he could help it. He frowned, and the huge green fellow at the poker table hastily glanced away down at his cards, as if afraid of having angered James.

Penstemon turned to him. "Would you like a drink, Mr. Hickok?"

James's suspicions were instantly reduced, though not altogether eliminated, by this suggestion. "Don't mind if I do."

They strolled together to a saloon that opened off the big gambling room. It was dark and cozy inside, with furniture that looked like it was made of big pillows. Penstemon led him to a couple of chairs with a tiny round table between them. James sank into one with a sigh and wondered if he'd ever be able to get out of it again.

A pretty gal with legs a mile long that were covered with nothing but a wisp of black stocking came up to them. She had on a little blue satin shift that stretched tight over her bosom and didn't quite hide her very attractive bottom and that no self-respecting whore of James's time would be caught dead in. She noticed him staring and gave him a little smile. James felt himself coloring up to his scalp.

Penstemon glanced up at her. "Hello, Nichole. A martini for me, and I imagine Mr. Hickok would like bourbon."

"You imagine right," James managed to say. He couldn't take his eyes off Nichole until she passed out of his view. When she was gone he looked back at Penstemon, who seemed amused.

"If you'd like some feminine company, it can be arranged."

James cleared his throat. "I might could use a little."

A pang of guilt struck him but he tried to ignore it. Agnes was dead by now, surely, so the tumble he was contemplating would not violate his marriage vow.

Or had Mr. Penstemon raised her up, too? Surely he would have brought her round in that case. But even if he had done, death had most definitely parted her and James, so the promise was null and void.

James shifted uneasily in the chair. He never wanted to cause Agnes any pain. He feared he had done so, getting killed so stupidly. He wished vaguely that he could make it up to her somehow.

Nichole returned with the drinks. James stared at her lovely young body again, but the heart had gone out of him and he couldn't muster up any lustfulness. He thanked her for the glass she handed him and sipped at the generous helping of bourbon in it, then sighed.

"See that screen?" Penstemon said, pointing up toward the ceiling off to one side. James looked that way and saw a rectangle, something like a picture frame but filled with flickering colored light.

"Moving pictures," Penstemon said.

Moving awful fast. James at first couldn't make out what the pictures were of, then he realized it was people on broomsticks, flying madly about and dodging what looked like cannonballs. The speed of it all was too much for him. He looked away.

"Mighty impressive," he said, feeling some compliment was expected.

"Your poker game will be broadcast like that," Penstemon said.

James sipped the bourbon again, enjoying the glow beginning to light in his belly. "That a fact?"

"Yes. So millions of people will be watching."

"Millions, eh?"

James was a mite skeptical about that. There'd have to be one of those rectangles in every home in the country for millions to be able to see it, and how could you put the pictures on all those things at once?

Granted, there were a lot of things he didn't understand about the world nowadays. There seemed also to be a lot of magic in it, which there hadn't been in his day, or at least not in evidence. He was coping fairly well, he thought.

The familiar sound of a tootling flute made him glance toward Penstemon's pocket. Penstemon put down his drink and took out his little music box.

"Yes? Good, I'll be right there." He stood up and put the box back in his pocket. "I'm afraid you'll have to forgive me, there's a matter I must attend to. Lunch will be in about an hour. Would you like some company in the meantime?"

James sat up straighter. "Wouldn't mind it." He took a hit of the bourbon and added, "That little gal you had fetch me was a charmer. Or is she a special friend of yours?"

"Kitty?" Penstemon's brows rose. "She's ah—not available.

Let me find you someone similar."

He smiled, then, and went away, pausing to murmur something to Nichole, who was standing by the bar. James saw that the barkeeper was a big, handsome fellow, Mexican-looking, with two stubby horns sticking out of his forehead. El Diablo, James thought idly. Shaking his head, he finished the rest of his bourbon in a gulp, and the glow in his belly turned to fire.

"Would you like another?"

Nichole was standing over him. James followed those amazing legs up, continuing to her waist and her bosom and finally managing to look her in the eye.

"Sure," he said as he gawked like a farmboy.

She took the empty glass from his hand, her fingertips brushing warm against his, then added Penstemon's unfinished drink to her tray and sidled off toward the bar. James watched her all the way, only facing forward again when his neck started complaining.

He glanced at the moving picture frame. A cheery-looking woman with short, curly red hair was now talking at him while she put various things into a big, black, burbling kettle. Making soup, he guessed, except some of the things she was putting in there didn't look too appetizing. He thought he saw a lizard go by. She was easier to watch than the people on broomsticks, but since James couldn't hear what she was saying, he quickly lost interest.

Nichole returned with his drink, and he smiled up at her. He was starting to feel more relaxed.

"Here you go, Mr. Hickok," she said, handing him the glass. "And this is Shavonne."

She stepped aside to reveal a woman who reminded him more than a little of Kitty, except her eyes were dark brown instead of green, and her lips were fuller and painted a shade of red that in his day, at least, would have been a clear advertisement that her calling was to serve mankind, so to speak. She was dressed in a red shift almost as short as Nichole's that clung to every single line of her body, leaving little to the imagination. She sipped at a tall glass of something dark over ice, and smiled while James took her in.

"I've been dying to meet you," she said, "ever since I heard you were coming. May I join you?"

Nichole had gone away. James nodded, since he wasn't confident he could speak just at the moment. Shavonne folded herself into the chair Penstemon had sat in and set her drink on the little table between them.

"It's so exciting. I don't play poker myself, but I love to watch."

Poker was the farthest thing from James's mind, at the moment. He took a swallow of bourbon, coughed a little, then managed to find his voice.

"A pretty gal like you would be a mighty big distraction at a poker game."

She smiled. "Thank you, Mr. Hickok."

"You can call me James."

"Thank you, James."

She picked up her drink and sipped it again, her eyes watching him all the while. He thought he saw a flash of pointy teeth, but it could have been his imagination. James felt a stirring in his belly that had nothing to do with the liquor. He'd been a long time abstaining, not even counting while he was dead.

"I'd love to get better acquainted with you, James," she murmured. "Maybe we could go somewhere a little more private?"

"I got a room," he said hoarsely.

Her smile widened. "Let's go, then."

Boy, howdy, thought James as they both stood up, abandoning their drinks. She took his arm as they strolled out of the saloon, and he felt it start tingling all up and down, wrist to shoulder.

James glanced around the huge gambling room, knowing he'd be hopelessly lost trying to find his way through it. "You know where them ... elevators are?"

"Right this way."

She steered him past some of the slot machines, their music jangling in his ears. James knew he was sporting a huge, silly grin.

The day just kept getting better.

~ Clive ~

The casino bus was more crowded than the first. By the end of the journey, Clive could smell the sea. Excitement was growing in him. The bus deposited him in front of a gigantic building covered in flashing lights that made him dizzy. He followed the other passengers inside and stood in a queue with them, to be given a slip of paper when he showed his bus ticket. The others dispersed into the darkness of what must be the casino, a cavernous room filled with noise and more blinking lights. Clive wandered after them, watching.

There were rows of machines, which were the source of most of the noise. Some of his fellow passengers took seats in front of them and fed their slips of paper into the machines. Clive watched them push buttons, which caused the machines to make more noise. Mystified, he continued deeper into the room.

At length he came to an area where games of cards were being run. There was even a roulette wheel! This he could understand.

The people around these tables were betting round colored markers, vaguely coin-shaped. He watched, hoping to find a game he understood enough to play, but they were all strange and terribly fast, and his courage failed him.

The game at some of the tables was twenty-one, though here it was called "Blackjack," and again it was too fast and included variations he did not understand. It was being dealt by a uniformed individual, a formality of which he disapproved. It was common enough for faro, where the house often held the bank, but not for twenty-one and such. He saw no faro tables, though there were large tables for throwing dice.

Continuing to stroll, he saw a light growing stronger ahead of him. He quickened his stride and saw that he was approaching a row of glass doors through which daylight shone. Passing through them, he felt a rush of elation as he found himself on the Boardwalk.

Like the rest of the world, it had changed. The wooden walk itself was three or four times as wide as it had been in his day. Gone were the beachside bathing machines, the hotels and dance halls. In their place stood enormous buildings aglitter with moving electrical lights of every imaginable color, flashing and gleaming with amazing brilliance even at the height of day. With his newspapers tucked securely beneath his arm, Clive walked slowly along, staring in awe at each glimmering building he passed.

Some were taller than the Brooklyn Bridge, or so it seemed. These had fanciful names, and all seemed to be called "hotel and casino." Between them, smaller buildings were adorned with signs advertising all manner of attractions, food, and souvenirs.

In all, the place had a carnival air, though Clive sensed a sinister undertone. His skin prickled with anticipation, of what he knew not. As he trod the boardwalk, his sense of destiny grew.

Another of the large hotels caught his attention. Behind a wall of glass doors he saw more lights glimmering, and people moving about. A casino again; gathering his resolve, he went in and was again assailed with a glamour of light, sound, and color.

A glowing pink sign in the distance read "POKER," and he could not resist investigating. He made his way toward it.

The sign marked the entrance to a large room filled with a dozen or more card tables. Most were empty, but two hosted poker games, also with uniformed dealers. The players here, as at the other tables he'd seen, were betting colored markers instead of money. Clive frowned, misliking these changes. The markers might be backed with money—he would have to find out.

The uniformed dealers were worse. Not being allowed to deal robbed the professional gambler of certain advantages. Clive had personally, on one memorable occasion, dealt four aces to every player at a table, just to prove he could.

Poker had survived the years of his hiatus, however, and for that he could only be glad. He watched the game for a while, noticing changes. For one thing, the play went so quickly he could scarcely follow it. The dealer, a woman, spun the cards to each player with a speed and precision he could only admire, and managed multiple pots equally as fast. Confounded by what was happening at the table, Clive stood a little apart, watching intently.

The game seemed to be stud, with seven cards instead of five, and five of them shared cards on the board. There didn't appear to be much challenge in that, but Clive was willing to give it a try. His fingers tingled at the thought of playing again, but he knew he needed to understand the game first. Five shared cards changed the odds, and threw enormous importance on the two in each player's hand.

Fairly frequently a player would say, with a certain ceremony, "I'm all in," and push all his markers across a line drawn around the center of the table. This was what caused the multiple pots, if other players exceeded the bet. As Clive began to understand the flow of the play his admiration of the dealer grew. She kept track of which players had a stake in each pot, rapidly made change with different colored markers, and raked a percentage for the house, or so it appeared.

That meant the markers were indeed backed with money. Clive felt a rush of excitement and looked around for a cashier.

There was no sign advertising such, but a woman stood attentively behind a counter nearby. She was a dusky madame of indifferent years, handsome enough, wearing a close-fitting gown of black. Her face was painted, but this appeared to be commonplace, for most of the women he had seen wore paint. She smiled as Clive stepped up to her.

"Would you like to play?"

Clive returned the smile. "Yes, indeed."

"Twenty dollars to get in the game." The woman set two diminutive stacks of blue and white markers before her. "Dollar chips," she said. "Blinds are a dollar and two dollars. Minimum bet's two."

Clive brought his slip of paper out of his pocket and offered it to her.

"That's from the Taj Majal, honey. It's no good here. Go on back to the Taj and you can use it to play the slots."

Hiding his disappointment as well as his confusion, Clive mustered a last charming smile. "Thank you."

She raised an eyebrow, then put away the markers—the chips. Clive turned away, feeling a flush of color rise in his cheeks.

He thought briefly of offering to deal, but discarded the notion. He couldn't deal as swiftly as the uniformed dealers, nor calculate the pots. There was too much he didn't understand about this new version of poker. It would take time to learn, and he didn't have much time. He had enough for one meal in his pocket.

Suddenly he felt oppressed, overwhelmed by the lights and the noise, confined despite the size of the gaming hall. He hurried away, back to the boardwalk, and almost gasped with relief as he stepped outside into the brisk air.

Blinking at brightness, he crossed the boardwalk and found steps descending to the beach. He strode across the sand toward the ocean, wanting to be alone and away from all the noise and glitter behind him.

When he reached the hard surface of damp sand, he stopped and stood gazing at the sea, listening to the rumble of the surf. This was one thing man could not change, and it gave him a sense of stability. Far out on the ocean a storm was brewing, blue-gray clouds hanging low, dulling the water to a stormy greenish blue. It fit with Clive's mood.

Why had he come here? Following that small voice. Had it misled him, this time?

No. He had found what he wanted, a place to gamble, a place to make his fortune anew. That he must first exert a little effort was humbling, but he would not let it discourage him. It was right to be here, he knew it in his bones. He had been called here, and the call was ever stronger.

A chill shivered through him and he turned, surveying the boardwalk and the monstrous, glittering hotels that stood along it. Called here. He was certain of it. Not just here, to Atlantic City, but to a specific place here, a place he had yet to find. Frowning, he stared at each hotel in turn, trying to sense which of them might be the place he wanted.

Madness. Jones had knocked him on the head and addled his wits. Clive hoped the bastard was rotting in hell for his sins.

He closed his eyes, trying to silence his thoughts and let the small voice speak to him. He needed more guidance. A chill breeze ruffled his hair, and his stomach grumbled again. He ignored these distractions as best he could, waiting, waiting for the voice.

Something touched his right leg below the knee. He flinched, opening his eyes, and saw a pale hound beside him, looking up with hopeful eyes.

"I have no food to give you. Go away."

The hound took this for praise, apparently. It danced upon its feet, uttered a small whine, and licked its chops.

Clive relented and stroked the animal's head. The heat and the smoothness of the fur recalled to him how pleasurable the world could be.

The questions he'd been avoiding ached in his heart. Had he died? He rather thought he had, so why, then, had he been brought here? Who had done it?

Cold realization poured through him, the same as when he sensed he held a winning hand. Some*one* had brought him here, not just some chance. Who had the power to do that? God Almighty? He was not a devout man, but he did believe in things beyond man's knowledge.

His gaze was drawn once more to the boardwalk. The answer lay there, somewhere amid the carnival games and gambling halls. Time for him to search it out. Setting his shoulders, Clive strode across the beach toward it, his gait slowing as the softer, dry sand pulled at his feet and sifted its way into his shoes. The hound followed, dancing with joy about his legs, deceived in his intentions.

~ Ned ~

Ned sat in a booth in the back of a strip club that had opened since his supposed departure from the planet. The stage was lit with a lot of pink neon, with bits of apple green here and there for contrast. The music pumped and the dancers were cute, but he wasn't enjoying himself as much as he would like. The hundred Donny had loaned him wouldn't go very far, so he'd decided against getting a lap dance.

He admired this self-restraint very much, feeling only slightly grumpy about it. He was being careful. He'd only bought two drinks. He was just getting comfortable again, had to do that, but he was being conservative. He did, however, want a fix very badly, and a fix wouldn't cost near so much as a lap dance.

Fifty bucks ought to score him enough horse for several hits, enough to last a day or maybe two if he was careful. The next dancer that came over, he'd ask her who to talk to.

He ordered another tequila and watched the tits bouncing on the stage while he thought vaguely about all the things he had to do. Talk to the lawyer, score some horse, get some money. Buy a book and find out what the fuck had supposedly happened.

A pretty little Mexican girl slid into the seat across from him. She was wearing a low-cut black t-shirt and tight jeans. A heart-shaped pendant glittering with diamonds dangled into her cleavage.

"Hi," she said, smiling. "I've been looking for you."

Ned's blood froze, recognizing her face. The chica from the limo. "Yeah?"

"Yeah. I was supposed to give you a ride."

Ned felt his palms break out in a sweat. "Why do you want to give me a ride?"

"To the poker game."

"Poker game?"

She nodded. "Texas Hold'em."

He loved playing poker. He'd learned it at his father's knee before he was out of diapers, practically.

"I don't have the money for a game."

"You don't need any money," said the chica, shaking her head and making the diamonds wink in her cleavage.

"Why bother playing if there's no money?"

"Oh, there's money, you just don't need it to get into the game. You're invited." She smiled proudly.

Ned stared at her, then shot back the tequila. "Who are you?"

"I'm Corazon."

"That's nice, but I mean who sent you?"

"Mr. Penstemon."

"Never heard of him."

"It's his game, you see?"

Ned flagged down a waitress and ordered another drink. He glanced at Corazon but she shook her head. The waitress went away, and Ned leaned his elbows on the table so he could get a better view of Corazon's tits.

"No, I don't see. Why should I accept this invitation?"

Corazon blinked, as if thinking. "For the prize."

"And what is the prize? Money?"

She nodded. "And more. I'm supposed to let Mr. Penstemon explain."

"Uh-huh. Listen, honey, I never heard of this guy. There's no Mr. Penstemon running a Hold'em game in Vegas."

"No, not here. In Atlantic City."

Ned froze. This was definitely strange. He'd thought being kidnapped for fourteen years was weird, but now this chica was reading his mind.

Or maybe he'd been brainwashed, given hypnotic suggestions to go to Atlantic City. The whole thing smelled fishy.

The waitress arrived with his drink. He traded his empty shot glass for the full one, then took the tequila in his mouth and let it burn while he gazed at Corazon.

She was sure a cute little thing. That was probably why this Penstemon clown had sent her. Whoever he was, he knew what would appeal to Ned.

But Ned was too sharp to fall for it. Pleased with himself, he swallowed and gave a little shrug.

"I'm sorry, honey, but I'm not interested."

She pouted. "You can have anything you want."

"Sure. Got any smack?"

"We can get it."

"Black-tar?"

"Whatever you like. It's in the car."

Ned's interest perked up. "You got horse in the car?"

She looked a little puzzled, then nodded. "If you want it, you can get it in the car."

She must mean they could drive someplace and get it. Her English wasn't too good, though he'd heard a lot worse. He'd had lap dances from girls who knew only a dozen words of English. Want a dance, hunned bucks—

"Come on, let's go!" said Corazon, flashing another smile and bouncing in the seat.

This was looking more and more appealing. Maybe the invitation was legit. After all, why would the nut case who snatched him let him go, only to pick him up again?

He tried to imagine that he had valiantly escaped his abductor, but even he didn't buy it. He'd been dumped. They'd decided he wasn't useful now that his money was gone, and he wasn't dangerous enough to need killing. He sure as fuck had no clue who had grabbed him.

Little Corazon couldn't be working for the mob, either. Unless they were the fucks who'd abducted him—and he seriously doubted that, like Donny'd said, it wasn't their style— the mob thought he was dead like everybody else did.

So why not go with her, at least to score some horse? He could decide later about AC and the poker game. He needed some fun and relaxation, dammit.

He pulled out some money and dropped it by his empty shot

glass, then stood up and got out of the booth. He grinned as Corazon got up and he scoped her ass.

"OK, baby," he said. "Let's go see what's in the car."

~ William ~

"We're here."

From the tone of his voice, William deduced that Festus's mood had not improved. Pity. The boy would enjoy life so much more if he learned to relax.

William was enjoying life quite well, thank you. Aided by the coach-limo-plane's seemingly endless supply of champagne and a bit of back-seat shuffling, he and Alma had progressed to cuddling, though in deference to Joanie they'd gone no further. It seemed clear, though, that Alma was game for more.

Poor little Joanie had gone silent, quietly drinking herself into a stupor whilst gazing at the back of Festus's head. Wretched for her. William was sorry she'd come along, but he supposed Alma would know how to cheer her up. Get her away from Festus, find some fellow who wasn't oblivious to her plentiful charms. She was a sweet little thing, all she needed was a bit of appreciation.

The limo, for it had become that again shortly after landing, glided to a stop. Festus got out and pulled open the door beside William, who helped Alma out and then stood back, giving Festus one last chance to be gallant toward Joanie. Festus ignored it. With a sigh, William held out his hand and helped Joanie out of the car.

It was night, still. Possibly near dawn, though it was difficult to tell, for they were underneath a canopy in front of a hotel lobby. Blue neon lighting traced the edge of the building.

The car slipped quietly away, leaving them on a broad apron before a bank of glass doors. Through them came a tall blond man in a black suit, smiling in greeting.

"Mr. Weare, welcome..."

His smile drooped a bit as he took in Alma and Joanie. William offered an elbow to each of them, and they both clung.

The blond man shot a wry look at Festus.

"He insisted on bringing them," said the youth.

"I see." The man looked back at William. "Friends of yours?"

"Boon companions," William said, aware that the papers covering the trial for his murder had described John Thurtell as such.

The blond man was apparently also aware of that, for his eyes narrowed momentarily. William maintained his smile and waited for the other fellow to make the next move.

"Well," the man said, clasping his hands together and making a small bow. "Ladies. Mr. Weare. Welcome to the Black Queen. I'm Simon Penstemon, the owner. Please come in."

He led the way through the doors and into a spacious lobby. Walking quickly, he continued past the registration desk and down a hallway, then opened a door and ushered them into a small but nicely-appointed office. Festus, bringing up the rear, closed the door and took up a guard-like stance beside it, crossing his arms over his chest.

Penstemon invited them to sit. William and Alma shared a loveseat, while Joanie sat in a plush armchair and hugged herself.

"Coffee, anyone?" Penstemon offered.

"No, thank you," said William. Following his lead, Alma also declined. Joanie, who looked like she could use a pick-me-up, said nothing.

"Well, then." Penstemon sat behind a desk made of some dark wood and looked them over. "Mr. Weare, I trust Festus told you of my invitation?"

"A card game, as I understand it."

"A tournament, actually."

Alma perked up. "Oh, can I play? I love cards."

"Unfortunately, this is a special tournament," said Penstemon, glancing at her. "I'm sorry, but only five players have been invited, each of whom has—a special history with cards."

"Aww."

Alma looked disappointed. William patted her hand, and she

gave him a smile.

Special history, was it? William's special association with playing cards was that he'd been killed for it. He settled back into the loveseat, beginning to enjoy himself.

"So there are four other guests who share my . . . circumstances, shall we say?"

Penstemon fixed him with an appraising gaze. "Very good, Mr. Weare. Yes, there are four others."

"My, my. What an interesting gathering."

"I do hope so."

"What can be its purpose, I wonder?"

"Entertainment."

William raised an eyebrow. "Not just your own, surely."

"No, not just my own."

William well remembered the hullabaloo over his murder and Thurtell's trial. The press had gone on about it for months. Of course, that had been nearly two centuries ago, but it was just the sort of thing that could be made into an entertaining little human interest story nowadays.

Which meant that he had leverage on this Penstemon fellow. He could refuse to cooperate, spoiling the man's plans. The threat of such would gain him whatever he wanted, he imagined.

So, what did he want? To continue enjoying himself in company with Alma, of course. For Joanie—well, he was not so sure what might perk her up.

"We'll be having a luncheon with the other players," Penstemon continued. "I'll explain all the terms then. In the meantime, Mr. Weare, there's a suite at your disposal, and all the services of the hotel, of course."

"Shall the ladies join us at luncheon?"

Penstemon's face darkened. "I'm afraid not. It's a business meeting."

"They'll be watching the tourney, though, right?"

Penstemon's gaze locked onto William's. William allowed himself the ghost of a smile.

"I'll see what I can arrange."

Penstemon turned his attention to Alma and Joanie, looking at them with a troubled expression. Alma cleared her throat.

"Mind if I make a phone call? Me mum'll be worried."

Penstemon stood up, walked around the desk and handed her a cordless phone. Alma looked at it uncertainly.

"I guess it's an international call," she said.

"Just dial 'O' and the operator will help you," Penstemon said. "Mr. Weare, may I have a word with you?"

William got up and followed him out to the hallway while Alma placed her call. Penstemon pulled the door shut and fixed him with an unsmiling gaze.

"I'm afraid Festus must not have made clear to you that ordinary people are not usually admitted to this hotel."

William smiled and rocked back on his heels. "Oh, he made it clear. Mundanes, he called them. I'm one, too, aren't I?"

"Not really. You've been brought back from the dead."

"True. Clever trick, that."

"Thank you. Now, how can we resolve this, Mr. Weare? Our policy is for the good of all concerned, you see. If they remained here, your friends would see some things that might disturb them."

"Like invisible drivers and cars that turn into aeroplanes?"

The corner of Penstemon's mouth twitched. "Worse than that, I fear."

"Well, I'm not packing them off home, if that's what you're suggesting. They've only just arrived, all agog about visiting America! You wouldn't want to break their hearts, would you?"

Penstemon gave him a measuring look, then let out a small sigh. "No, of course not." His eyes narrowed in thought, then he took a cell phone from his pocket and tapped its face.

"Ramona? I need you to arrange an itinerary for two ladies, mundanes, friends of one of the players. Set up some tours for them—the lighthouse, sights on the mainland. Independence Hall would be good. Yes, exactly. And give them an escort, I don't want them wandering around by themselves, especially in the hotel. No, not Elvira, someone who looks more normal.

They're with me at the moment, in Dante's office. Thank you."

He pocketed the phone again and looked at William. "Believe me, Mr. Weare, the less time they spend in the hotel, the better."

"But they can stay with me in the suite?"

Penstemon pressed his lips together, but nodded. Pleased with himself, William smiled.

"You know, you might give your man Festus a hint about Joanie," he said. "She's dotty on him."

Penstemon's eyes widened. "Festus?"

"Yeah. Maybe he doesn't return the sentiment, but a little kindness would go a long way."

"She'd do better to forget about him," Penstemon said flatly.

"Try telling that to a girl in love."

The hotelier frowned. "You must understand, Mr. Weare, it isn't possible. Festus…isn't human."

"Well, that doesn't surprise me at all," said William testily, "but he could make a little effort, couldn't he? The poor girl's all in a mope over him!"

Penstemon closed his eyes. For a moment his calm demeanor slipped and he seemed a man beset by troubles. Drawing a deep breath, he composed himself, looked at William and smiled.

"Shall we go back in?"

William gave an agreeable shrug. As long as Penstemon wasn't trying to get rid of the girls altogether, as long as he took good care of them, William was satisfied.

When Penstemon pushed the door inward, it bumped into Festus. Alma was standing in the middle of the office facing him, hands on her hips. She shot an angry glance at Penstemon.

"He won't let us go to the loo!"

Festus said nothing, just stood with arms crossed and his jaw set stubbornly. Penstemon pinched the bridge of his own nose for a moment, then laid a hand on Festus's shoulder.

"Go on upstairs, Festus. You've done a good job. I'll see to it from here."

"I'm hungry," said Festus in a surly tone.

"Yes, all right. I'll be up in a minute."

Festus cleared out without even a glance at the girls. William sidled into the office and gave Alma a smile and a wink.

"Forgive me, ladies," said Penstemon. "Of course you want to freshen up after your trip. Why don't we all go up to Mr. Weare's suite, and you can make yourselves comfortable there?"

"A suite!" said Alma. "Coo!"

Penstemon led them back into the hall and out to the lobby, where he paused briefly at the reception desk and murmured to the young lady behind it. She smiled, revealing a row of needle-sharp teeth, and handed him some key cards. He rejoined William and the girls and led them to a bank of elevators.

The doors of one opened as they arrived, and a tall bald man in a floor-length blue-and-white striped robe came out. The robe billowed about his feet, and William realized with a start that he hadn't any—he had some kind of tentacles instead. He bobbed up and down slightly as he left the elevator, saying, "Good morning, Simon," in a squishy voice.

"Morning, Caractacus," said Penstemon, exchanging nods. "This way, ladies," he added brightly, catching Joanie by the elbow and shuffling her into the elevator, where she stood staring after Caractacus in horrified fascination.

"Out for a morning slither?" murmured William as he and Alma stepped into the elevator.

"Probably a breakfast swim," said Penstemon, punching a button. "The tide's in."

They saw no more interesting hotel guests. The elevator didn't stop until it reached the 42nd floor, on which Penstemon stepped out and led them down a long hall to a suite. He took a card out of the envelope and slid it into the door, then ushered the three of them in.

"Ocean view," he said, indicating the curtained window with a sweep of his arm. "Here's your key, Mr. Weare, and one for each of the ladies."

"Wow," breathed Joanie as her gaze traveled the sumptuous suite. She smiled a little for the first time since they'd left Elstree.

Alma headed straight for the wet bar. "Look! It's got

everything! Champers, single-malt, Guinness! Oh, but no Boodles!"

"Boodles?" said Penstemon.

"Boodles gin. Joanie likes it better than Tanqueray."

Penstemon rubbed the fingertips of one hand together absently. "I'm sure you'll find some. Look in the back."

She bent down again to rummage in the cupboard. "Oh, here it is!" Standing up, she held a square bottle up triumphantly. "Look, Joanie! Want a GT? We've got limes and everything."

"Maybe later," Joanie said, and with a blushing glance at William she headed off in search of the loo. Alma shot a smile at William and followed her.

"Luncheon will be at one, Mr. Weare," said Penstemon. "We're still waiting on one guest to arrive. You'd probably like a change of clothes in the meantime. There's a men's shop downstairs; call down and they'll send some things up."

"Good," said William, glancing down at his frock coat, "because I look a bit outlandish in this rig, even here."

"I hope you'll wear it for the tournament, though."

William raised an eyebrow, then strolled to the bar and helped himself to the scotch. "Color, eh? Well, I'll tell you what, Mr. Penstemon. I'll hear your terms at this luncheon, after which I'll give them due consideration."

Penstemon gave a quiet smile. "That's all I ask."

The girls returned from the nether regions, giggling. Joanie cast William a wide-eyed look.

"There's a tub big enough for all three of us!" she said.

"I think we should have a party in it," said Alma.

Joanie gave her a shove and blushed, laughing. Alma brandished a brochure.

"Mr. Penstemon, I see there's a spa here. Could we—?"

"By all means. I'll have Ramona set up an appointment for you both, then I'll send up a little brunch for you here, how does that sound?"

"Sounds all right," Alma said with an attempt at nonchalance that was betrayed by the glow in her eyes.

Penstemon turned to William. "Call room service if you need anything else. I'll see you at the luncheon."

William nodded and watched him go, then replenished his scotch and carried it over to the window. He pushed the drapes back and stood gazing out over the ocean. Down along the shore were lights, and another tall hotel stood nearby, a rectangle of light here and in its mostly-dark wall of glass. A pier jutted out into the dark sea, covered with carnival stands and more lights.

William looked for Caractacus down on the beach, but saw no sign of him. Already out to sea, he supposed.

Alma came and stood next to him. He put an arm around her shoulders.

"Well, Alma my dear, this is America," he said as if he'd planned it all himself exclusively for her entertainment. "Like it so far?"

She grinned and slid her arm around his waist. "I like it fine."

~ Clive ~

Clive walked with stooped shoulders and scuffing steps, wearily looking at each carnival stand, food stand, casino, and attraction he passed. He'd done this all the previous day and most of the night, chasing the ghost of the feeling that had brought him here.

He was meant to be here. He knew he was. He just had to find the way...had to find the way *in*.

The hound was still with him, testament to the endless optimism of its tribe. It paused now and then to investigate the distractions of abandoned food wrappers and other trash, but always returning to his heel.

The fifty dollars was almost gone. Bus tickets and the outrageous cost of food had swallowed it.

All along the boardwalk, the smells of fried potatoes, battered fish, saltwater taffy and candied apples mingled in the midday warmth to form a miasma that made his stomach growl. He'd spent a little on a frankfurter in a bread roll for last night's supper —he'd given the paper wrapper and part of the roll to the hound, who had cheerfully devoured both—but he had eaten nothing today, and it was now close to noon.

He'd gone all up and down the boardwalk and along the piers, looking at everything. Somehow he had missed what he was looking for. He could feel that it was near, but couldn't find it. He paused in front of a looming building called "Ripley's Believe it or Not."

Stupid name. Why, if one was told the place was called Ripley's, would one refuse to believe it?

As he stared at giant posters of carnival freaks, an ocean-born breeze blowing his hair into his eyes, he wondered if he might be considered a freak himself. After all, he was not where he belonged. Not in the least where he belonged. *When* he belonged.

He shuffled on, pausing to gaze for a moment at a round paper carton cheerfully labeled "POPCORN," perched in the top of a barrel of refuse. A handful or two of corn remained in the bottom of the carton. Clive was debating whether he was desperate enough to eat it when a pair of laughing young girls clad in next to nothing pushed their mustard-smeared trash on top of it, tipping the popcorn carton and spilling its contents. Clive stood listening to the corn rattling down inside the barrel as the girls walked away.

Perhaps he should go into one of the casinos and buy a deck of cards. He could sit on the pier and deal three card monte, make a little money that way, at least enough to buy a decent meal. He had thought of this some time ago but had resisted the idea. To stoop so low, when he had been a high-stakes riverboat gambler, would be a blow to his pride. He had not much pride left, however, and after all one must eat.

"There you are!" cried a young man's voice.

Clive looked up to see a youth—little more than a boy, really —hurrying toward him. Dressed in black trousers and shirt beneath a heavy black overcoat, the fellow was pale and slim. No threat, yet somehow Clive felt threatened. Large green eyes, wide and worried, fixed on Clive's face.

"Mr. Sebastian? It is you, isn't it?"

"Yes," Clive said slowly, frowning.

He had told no one in Atlantic City his name. He had told it only to the Dickersons, who were up in Trenton, he presumed.

"Thank the Goddess! I've been searching all over for you!"

"Who are you?" Clive demanded.

"My name's Shadow. I'm here to escort you to the Black Queen."

Clive sucked in a sharp breath. Shadow's name was unfamiliar, and also odd, but he now remembered he had seen the youth's face before. On the black riverboat, with flames reflecting in his eyes.

"Why should I go with you?" Clive said ungraciously,

shifting his feet to be ready to run.

Shadow looked hurt. "I'm very sorry, Mr. Sebastian. I was supposed to meet you in Bloomfield. I got there just as you were leaving."

So he had indeed been the man on the riverboat. Clive blinked, breathing nervously, shallowly. He had thought it was Charon on the boat, come to take him to the underworld. Charon, Shadow...

"You're invited to play in a poker tournament at the Black Queen," Shadow said. "Please, we're already late—"

"The Black Queen?"

"Yes. It's a casino and resort. It isn't far."

"I've been all up and down the boardwalk and saw no such place."

"It's a little tricky to get into," Shadow said, looking uncomfortable.

"And who is hosting this poker game? The king of the dead?"

Clive had spoken facetiously, but the youth's eyes opened wide with alarm. He had hit the truth, then, or come near it.

"Mr. Penstemon is hosting the game. The owner of the Black Queen," Shadow said. "Please, Mr. Sebastian, he'll explain it all when we get there."

Clive gazed narrowly at the youth's anxious face. There seemed to be no harm in him, but Clive didn't like the sound of Mr. Penstemon, his casino, or his game. Ironic, because it was with a desire to play poker that Clive had come here.

"I'm hungry," he said, and turned away.

There was a food stand nearby, advertising popcorn and corn dogs. Perhaps a corn dog would be good, he thought as he stepped up to it. He'd seen people eating them—they appeared to be breaded sausages served on little wooden sticks.

"Mr. Penstemon's ordered a luncheon for you and his other guests," Shadow said, skipping after him. "A banquet," he added as Clive glanced at him. "A feast."

"And what would this feast cost me?" Clive murmured.

"Nothing. You're a guest. An *honored* guest."

Clive thought of the underworld again, of Persephone, doomed to remain there half the year because she'd been tempted to eat a few pomegranate seeds. He looked at the fat, bored man in a paper hat gazing at him from the popcorn stand.

"A corn dog," Clive said.

"Four fifty," said the man.

Clive winced. It would leave him with little more than a dollar.

"I'll get it," said Shadow, producing a bill from his pocket.

"Keep your money," Clive snapped.

He paid, accepted the corn dog, pumped mustard onto it from a large jar at the front of the stand as he had seen others do, then turned to walk south, away from the majority of the casinos on the boardwalk. The hound danced beside him, and Shadow walked on his other side, silent now. Clive wished he would go away.

The corn dog was hot, salty, and delicious. Clive chewed each bite carefully, savoring it as slowly as he could bear to though hunger tempted him to gobble it. This might be his last meal for a while. He licked mustard from the corners of his mouth and gnawed the last of the crunchy batter from the stick, then handed it to the hound.

"Mr. Sebastian?"

Shadow had paused in front of a tiny carnival stand. A sign across the front said "The Black Queen," and underneath was a little gallery with a row of small, strange-looking rifles. Signs exhorted Clive to shoot a playing card and win a prize. Toy dragons, soft like a child's cuddle-toy and every color of the rainbow, hung from the ceiling of the stand. Clive frowned.

"You said it was a casino."

"This is the entrance," Shadow said. "Follow me."

He lifted a section of the counter and walked into the stand. The young woman who was running the game gave him a cursory glance, then went back to hanging fresh playing cards in the clips at the back of the booth. Like Shadow, she was dressed all in black, though her hair was an amazing bright blue.

Shadow held the counter panel up, waiting expectantly. Clive stayed where he was.

"Suppose I don't wish to be beholden to your Mr. Penstemon?"

Shadow blinked, opened his mouth, then shut it again. Clive glanced up at the dragons. An orange one hung right over him, looking down at him with a cross-eyed leer. Clive looked back at Shadow.

"What benefit to me is there in this game?"

"Mr. Penstemon will explain all that."

"And if I don't like his explanation? If I choose to leave?"

Shadow seemed unable to comprehend the possibility. "No one will stop you," he said at last, with a shrug.

"I'll hold you to that," Clive said.

Truth was, he was curious. He wanted a poker game, and here was one conveniently offered. Too much a coincidence, which might mean that Penstemon was responsible for his presence in this time. He suspected it was so.

He was aware, also, that the small quiet voice in the back of his mind that had urged him to come to Atlantic City was now whispering that he should go to the Black Queen. If nothing else, he might get an explanation of why he was here.

If Penstemon was indeed the king of the dead, Clive might be walking into a trap. He had no idea if Persephone's story constituted a cautionary guideline for entering the underworld. He would risk it, hoping that if he didn't eat any of Penstemon's feast he'd be under no obligation to remain. It was a gamble, but then, he was a gambler.

He stepped through the counter and into the booth. The hound followed, which caused an altercation with the blue-haired girl. Shadow hastened to intervene, saying with a glance at Clive that the hound could come, then led the way to a curtained doorway at the back of the booth. He pulled the curtain aside and held it as Clive stepped through.

Instead of a room, they were outside again, but in twilight. Clive caught his breath. It had been midday on the boardwalk, but here the sky was a glowing indigo. Before them a huge hotel rose into the sky, a tower of black glass with blue lights outlining its edges. On top was a gigantic playing card, the queen of spades, all made of light and brilliant against the indigo sky. Clive was certain he had not seen it before.

"You can't see it from the Boardwalk," Shadow explained, stepping up beside him. "You have to come through this entrance or drive in from the city side."

"Impressive," Clive said.

Shadow led him up a long pathway bordered with rosebushes and glimmering fountains. The roses were all in bloom, which was slightly unusual in late October. Fireflies twinkled among the bushes, also not a common sight this time of year.

A giant pool with seven fountains in it, all lit up so it glowed blue-white, lay in front of the hotel's entrance. Shadow led Clive onto one of three arched bridges that crossed it. Glancing down, he saw there were fish in the water, then realized that the fish were actually tiny mermaids. One of them smiled up at him, her hair a swish of auburn seaweed, her perfect breasts glowing like pearls above where her skin melded into green-gold scales. He nearly fell in.

The hound noticed them, too, and set up a barking that was only quelled by a sharp word from Shadow. The hound raised its hackles at him and growled. Shadow frowned back, then led them on toward the hotel.

The bridge ended on a broad space covered in blue carpet. A black velvet awning stretched out over the carpet, which extended into the hotel through a wall of glass double doors. Shadow led him through these and into the elegant darkness of the hotel.

The room they entered was spacious. In the distance Clive could hear the music machines that were in every casino, though here the music held a different note, as if the key were minor instead of major. Clive was not much of a musician, but he appreciated the art and could tell a sonata from a concerto.

A fair man dressed in a black suit with a pale shirt and blue cravat came striding toward them. Shadow paused, and Clive waited beside him, noting that the youth's anxiety seemed to have returned.

"Thank you, Shadow," said the man in black, nodding dismissal.

"I came as fast as I could," Shadow said. "He—"

"Yes, yes. Go on up, now."

Shadow glanced at Clive, his green eyes slightly resentful, then went away. The man in black smiled.

"Mr. Sebastian, I'm delighted to meet you. I'm Simon Penstemon."

He held out a hand. Clive hesitated, trying to think over all the old stories. Was it a bad idea to shake hands with the devil?

The hound, sensing his doubt, uttered two sharp barks. Penstemon's gaze shifted to the animal, then he bent toward it, reaching out to stroke its pale head.

"Hello. Are you Mr. Sebastian's friend?"

Another bark, accompanied by a wagging of the tail.

"I see. Just a moment."

Penstemon straightened, looked around, then waved to a young female in black to join them. "Please escort this gentleman up to Mr. Sebastian's suite, and see that his needs are cared for."

She smiled and scratched the hound's head. "Certainly. This way."

Clive stared after her, marveling, then was interrupted by Penstemon's voice.

"Don't worry, he'll be well looked after."

"He isn't mine."

"I know. And I apologize for all the confusion. When there's more time, I'll be glad to explain anything you wish, but I'm afraid we're running late."

Penstemon took Clive's elbow and gently steered him deeper into the hotel. "I do apologize for the misunderstanding about the boat. Shadow is inexperienced, and I failed to take that into consideration when I sent him to meet you. I hope your journey wasn't too uncomfortable."

Clive muttered something polite. He was having trouble thinking of Penstemon as dangerous. The devil had a thousand wiles, or so the preacher man would say. He must stay on his guard.

"If you don't mind, we'll go directly to the luncheon," Penstemon said, pausing in a small hallway and touching a glowing circle on the wall. "The others are all there."

"Others?"

"The other players," Penstemon said, smiling.

"I haven't agreed to play."

Penstemon gazed at him for a moment, and one fine, golden eyebrow twitched upward. "I see. Well, come and hear the details about the tournament, and then you can decide."

Doors slid sideways, heavy metal doors this time. Clive was still unused to doors that moved by themselves, though he had encountered them frequently in the last two days. He stepped into a small room with Penstemon and tried to swallow his nervousness as the doors shut them in. Penstemon touched another glowing circle, one of many in a panel on the front wall, and the room gave a lurch.

"Don't be startled," Penstemon told Clive, who had grabbed at the railing on the wall. "It's an elevator. I keep forgetting some of you aren't acquainted with them."

Clive listened to Penstemon's explanation while the corn dog in his stomach grumbled and threatened to part company. Before it could do so, the room lurched again and the doors opened, and Penstemon stepped out. Clive followed at once, preferring even the devil's company to remaining in the elevator.

Their footsteps hushed by thick carpet, they walked down a long, high-ceilinged hallway, paneled from floor to ceiling in dark wood. "I'm sorry you didn't have time to freshen up," Penstemon said. "There'll be time after lunch."

If I'm still here, thought Clive.

Penstemon stopped at a door and opened it, revealing an elegant dining room, also paneled in wood. A glowing chandelier hung over a long table set with fine linen, china, and crystal. Paintings in gilt frames hung on the walls, and at the table sat four men who all looked up at Clive as he followed Penstemon in.

One looked like a cowboy hero from some penny novel; the others wore clothing more like what Clive had seen the people of this present time wearing. One, a keen-eyed fellow who gave Clive an appraising glance, wore a black suit much like Penstemon's and had his receding hair oiled and combed into perfect order. The others appeared less formal, and less interested. The man with curling reddish hair who was dressed in black leather looked mildly curious. The pudgy fellow in rumpled shirtsleeves had already returned his attention to his drink.

"Thank you for your patience, gentlemen," Penstemon said. "I hope the staff have made you comfortable. Allow me to introduce Mr. Clive Sebastian, who is the least well-known of you all. In fact, if I had not happened to interview one Orson Jones recently, he would not have been invited—"

"You've seen Jones?" Clive demanded, turning toward Penstemon. "Where is he?!"

Penstemon made a placating gesture with his hands. "He's dead, Mr. Sebastian."

"Then he ought to fit right in with this crew," said a sarcastic voice from the table.

Clive glanced that way but could not tell who had spoken. The quick rush of anger he'd felt was already subsiding.

"Actually, he wouldn't," said Penstemon. "All of you were murdered because of your gambling, or for related reasons. Mr. Jones died of old age, I fear."

"The bastard," muttered Clive.

"He need not concern us," Penstemon said with airy dismissal. "Your future is of much greater interest than your past, at least to you. But let me finish the introductions. Mr. Sebastian, this is Mr. Arnold Rothstein. Murdered over a poker debt in New York, 1928."

The slick-haired gentleman grimaced, then nodded graciously to Clive. Clive returned the courtesy.

"And beside him is Mr. William Weare, who was killed in 1823 by a friend who accused him of cheating at cards."

"Not a word of truth in it," said Weare cheerily, lifting a hand in greeting. His accent proclaimed him an Englishman.

Penstemon gestured to the man at the far end of the table. "Mr. Hickok, of whom you have probably heard."

Clive looked at the cowboy, who sat unmoving, watching with wary eyes. "Wild Bill Hickok? Truly?"

Hickok gave a slight nod. Clive could not help smiling. "It's an honor, sir!"

"To Mr. Hickok's left is Ned Runyon, our most recent murder victim. He was killed in 1998. His father, Ronny Runyon, founded the Rabbit's Foot casino in Las Vegas and made a large fortune running poker tournaments. Ned was murdered for his share of that fortune."

"Fuckin' A," said Runyon without glancing up from his drink.

"Gentlemen, Mr. Sebastian here was robbed of his winnings and murdered by Orson Jones, a riverboat captain, who buried him in an unmarked grave that was never discovered. Please have a seat, Mr. Sebastian, and we'll get down to business."

Clive took the place indicated by Mr. Penstemon, to the right of his own seat at the head of the table. On the wall behind Penstemon hung a portrait of a woman dressed all in black, her pointed hat reminiscent of those worn by the queens in a deck of cards. She gazed unsmiling out of the portrait, her eyes seeming to look directly at Clive.

Glancing away, he noticed a crystal goblet filled with water by his place. He reached for it, then drew his hand back as if stung, remembering his determination to let nothing pass his lips at this table. He sat back in the chair and clasped his hands tightly in his lap.

Two invisible waiters in starched white shirts and black trousers set plates of salad before each of the men at the table.

Clive looked down at his, wondering why salad was being served before the meal instead of after the main course. Change of custom, he supposed. It didn't matter anyway, for he was not going to eat it, however appetizing it looked.

The others showed no such reserve. Rothstein ate slowly, each movement careful and precise. Hickok ate carefully, Weare with hearty abandon, and Runyon at Clive's right shoveled food into his mouth with an occasional pig-like grunt. Penstemon chewed a bite of salad thoughtfully, watching Clive. Clive picked up his fork and stirred the greens about on his plate. The smell of vinegar and garlic made his mouth water a bit and he swallowed.

"First off, gentlemen," said Penstemon after dabbing his mouth with a snowy linen napkin, "allow me to apologize for any awkwardness that may have attended your journeys here. I'm afraid I should have made the invitation more clear from the beginning. This is the first time I have organized such a gathering, and the envoys I sent, while they are all trusted associates, are a little inexperienced, I fear."

"But nonetheless charming," murmured Rothstein, his half-lidded eyes regarding Penstemon.

Clive felt a sudden chill, as if sensing dark intent beneath Rothstein's smooth demeanor. He shook himself, looking away. He must not let imagination run away with him.

Penstemon smiled blithely at Rothstein, then sipped from his water goblet. "Now that we are all together, allow me to explain the terms of the game I propose. It will be a poker tournament, winner take all, for the prize of one million dollars and the continued use of your body."

"Come again?" said Hickok, frowning from the foot of the table.

Penstemon cleared his throat delicately. "You have been resurrected at considerable trouble and expense. The bodies you inhabit are temporary; making them permanent would be even more costly. I will do so for one of you—the winner of the poker tournament. The others will return to their previous state."

Silence fell around the table. Even Runyon stopped scraping his fork across his plate and stared at Penstemon.

Clive was thinking furiously. It would seem that this was a Temptation, and he hadn't the religious background to know how to react appropriately. Penstemon was sounding less like Hades and more like a confidence man. Clive frowned.

"Why?" he asked. "Why have you done this?"

"Yes," said Rothstein in a smooth, quiet voice. "Why go to such trouble?"

Penstemon smiled. "You're all celebrities. Yes, even you, Mr. Sebastian; your story endures though no one knows your name as yet. That will all be changed by the tournament. There will be a live audience, all of whom have paid premium prices to witness this event. It will also be broadcast on the Occult Network."

"And you stand to make millions," Rothstein said, nodding. "Very clever."

Penstemon turned his head to regard Rothstein. After a moment he nodded. "Thank you." He looked all around the table, beaming. "There's a good deal of excitement about you, gentlemen. The hotel is booked solid with guests from all over the world."

"You promoted this, using our names without our consent?" said Wild Bill Hickok, glowering across the table.

Penstemon looked faintly surprised. "Well, yes. Perhaps it was optimistic of me, but I assumed you'd all agree. Am I wrong? Is there anyone here who does not want to keep his new body?"

Again, silence reigned. Clive kept his mouth shut and his hands clamped together. He disliked being manipulated, but there was no denying he'd prefer to stay alive than to go back to the endless nightmares in Bloomfield.

So he had to play for his life. They all did.

He looked around the table again, now measuring each of his opponents. Rothstein looked the most formidable, but looks could be deceiving. The fellow beside Clive, Runyon, looked the least in control of himself, but that did not mean he would not be a good card player.

Clive was distracted by his salad plate, which had floated up into the air. The invisible waiters were clearing the plates. Clive bit his lip to keep from protesting as his salad was borne away. He supposed it was all right to eat, now that he knew what Penstemon was up to. Glancing at his host, Clive tried to detect any deceit in his demeanor, but saw none.

"Now, then," said Penstemon cheerfully, "about the tournament itself. The game will be no-limit Texas Hold'em. We'll have a practice session after lunch so those of you who haven't played it can get used to the game. Mr. Weare, I believe you're the only one who hasn't played poker at all."

Weare looked up from the pint of beer he was sipping. "Oh, no worries, I've watched it on telly dozens of times. It's all the rage, you know," he added to Rothstein, who returned a flat, cold stare.

"Texas Hold'em is the best fucking game on earth," said Runyon, suddenly showing an interest in the discussion. He pointed an accusing finger at Penstemon. "You're just coattailing on the World Series of Poker!"

Penstemon's smile broadened. "Indeed I am. I won't deny it. Nor am I the only one. There's the World Poker Tour, Heads-Up Poker Championship, Celebrity Poker, of which this is a variation. The world's in love with poker. Why shouldn't we all benefit?"

"You've chosen a rather unusual market," said Rothstein.

"Yes," said Penstemon. "The magical community is a subculture, an underworld of sorts. I believe you're familiar with the concept."

Rothstein's eyes sharpened for a moment, then a cold smile crossed his lips. "And you're in control of this underworld?" he said softly.

Penstemon chuckled. "Hardly. I'm merely a businessman, seeking to increase my profits as all good businessmen must."

Rothstein made no answer, but continued to regard Penstemon with a measuring stare. Clive imagined a silent contest being conducted between them, a challenge of wills. Who was this Rothstein? he wondered. Penstemon had mentioned only that he'd been killed over a poker debt.

The tension was broken by the return of the waiters, bearing plates of prime rib with roasted potatoes and vegetables. Clive's mouth began to water the moment his plate hit the table and the smell of the roast meat wafted up to him, and he was hard pressed not to begin eating before his host.

"Bon appetit, gentlemen," said Penstemon, picking up his fork. He glanced at Clive. "Would you like something to drink with that? Glass of wine, or a beer? Whiskey?"

"Wine," said Clive. "Thank you."

One of the waiters was instantly at his elbow, pouring red wine into a glass that hadn't been at his place a moment before. Clive hastily looked away from the bottle that appeared to be floating in midair.

"That's quite an elegant portrait behind you, Mr. Penstemon. Is it the Black Queen?"

Penstemon went still for a moment, his gaze distant. He did not glance over his shoulder. With great care, he picked up his wine glass. "One of many."

"Anne Boleyn," added Weare from down the table, stabbing his fork into a large chunk of beef and waving it in the air. "They said she was a witch, y'know."

Clive took a deep breath, cut off a bite of his beef, and chewed it worshipfully. Hell, he was probably damned anyway. Might as well enjoy himself. Underworld or not, this was a damn sight better than Bloomfield.

~ Arnold ~

Texas Hold'em is a variation of seven-card stud," announced Penstemon, standing beside the dealer's chair where sat a young lady who would have been lovely except that she was purple. Arnold kept finding his gaze drawn to her. Distracting, and not in a good way. He gave his head a small shake and returned his attention to Penstemon.

"Each player gets two cards face down in the hole, followed by a round of betting. The remaining five cards are shared, and are dealt face up three, one, and one, with a round of betting after each deal."

Mutterings arose around the table and echoed in the large ballroom that had already been set up for the tournament. For the moment they were alone, watched by empty stands of bleachers.

Multitudinous lights and strange machines surrounded the tournament table. The five players and the dealer were seated around it, an oval covered in blue felt with the Black Queen's logo in the middle. Around the edge of the table was a strip that glowed with white light, and padded railings in which Penstemon had said tiny cameras were placed to peek at the player's cards as they looked at them. Some of the big machines were cameras, too, according to Penstemon.

"That makes chance a bigger factor in the game," Arnold said. "Puts a lot of weight on those two hole cards."

"Yes," Penstemon said, "and there's also the possibility of several different hands making with the same five board cards."

"Tell you what," said Weare in a chipper voice, peering through a pair of spectacles at the list of poker hand precedence that Penstemon had provided him, "why don't we just play piquet instead?"

No one laughed. Runyon, who had consumed at least half a

dozen drinks at lunch, leaned red-faced across the table and bellowed at Weare.

"Texas Hold'em is the best goddamn card game ever invented!"

Weare gave him a pitying look. "Yes, yes, dear boy, we all know how you feel about it."

"Let's go ahead and deal a few hands," said Penstemon. "You'll get a better feel for it by playing than by talking."

"What's the ante?" asked Hickok.

"No ante at first. There are always two blind bets, and they rotate with the dealer button." Penstemon picked up a white disc marked "DEALER" and set it before Runyon. "Dealer's left is the small blind, starting at fifty. Player to small blind's left is the big blind, starting at a hundred. So fifty from you, Mr. Hickok, and a hundred from Mr. Weare."

Hickok pushed a chip across the line on the felt, and Weare tossed two into the center of the table. "Behind before I begin," Weare said, laughing.

"It all evens out," said Penstemon. "Go ahead, Amber."

The dealer reached for the cards that were spread face-up in an arc before her, and expertly lifted one end of the row to flip them face down. She then messed them about with her hands and gathered them up, proceeding to shuffle, cut the deck onto a blank card, and deal.

Arnold watched the other players before looking at his own hole cards. Weare on his right picked up his cards and took no care about hiding them; Arnold glimpsed a heart, probably an eight or nine. Beyond Weare at one short end of the table sat Hickok, who also picked up his cards and held them.

"You don't do it like that," said Runyon crossly from the seat opposite to Hickok's. "You look at 'em like this, then put 'em down again."

He demonstrated, pulling his two cards toward him onto the white light panel and lifting just the corners, showing them to the small black rectangle that was the camera. He then let the cards drop to the table. To Arnold's surprise, he was unable to read whether Runyon liked the cards or not. The man might be a fool, but apparently he could play poker.

Sebastian, the riverboat gambler, was seated on Arnold's left. He hadn't said much, and seemed to wear a slight, perpetual frown of confusion. He now lifted the corner of his cards as Runyon had done, set them down again, and blinked once.

Arnold looked at his hand. Seven and jack of clubs. Hard to tell if it was a good hand. He was unused to evaluating only two cards. In normal seven-card stud you got three before the first round of betting.

"All right, so now you bet on those cards," said Penstemon, "starting with the player to the left of the big blind. You either match the blind, raise, or fold."

Arnold glanced at Weare, then at Hickok. His inclination was to fold out of a game he didn't understand and suspected he wouldn't like, but he called the bet instead. He had to play this game, so he'd better get a grasp on it now, while there was no real cost.

He glanced at Penstemon as the others put in their chips. What he really wanted was to figure out how to muscle in on Penstemon's operation. Proceeds from this ghoulish tournament aside, the Black Queen must make a tidy profit. It would be a good starting point.

Sebastian and Runyon had called the bet. This was practice, people wouldn't be playing as cautiously as they would in a real game. The dealer looked at Hickok.

"Fifty to call," she said.

Hickok raised an eyebrow, then pushed another chip across the line. The dealer turned her blue eyes on Weare.

"You have the option to raise," she said.

"Do I? Well, thank you, my dear, but I think I'll decline."

She thumped the table and swept the chips into a pile, then shoved the top card from the deck beneath it, dealt three cards face down before her, and flipped them over. Eight of hearts, ten of clubs, ace of spades.

"This is the flop," said Penstemon. "Now you bet again,

starting with dealer's left. Minimum bet is a hundred."

The ten gave Arnold three clubs, so he needed two more for a flush. Could even be a straight flush, seven through the jack, though it was unlikely that the next two cards would be eight and nine clubs. Any nine would give him a straight, though, as would any queen and king. Not a bad hand.

Hickok looked at his cards, then put two chips on the felt. Weare did likewise, and Arnold called the bet. Sebastian frowned at the board for a moment, then called as well.

"I'm all in," said Runyon, and pushed his entire stack of chips across the line.

The others protested. "He can't do that, can he?" demanded Weare.

"Yes, he can," Penstemon said. "There's no limit on the bets."

"So we have to risk everything we have in order to call him?" asked Sebastian.

"At this point, yes. It's a little unusual for someone to go all in on the first hand," he added, glancing at Runyon.

Runyon's face gave away nothing. Arnold revised his opinion of the fellow from complete idiot to self-indulgent fool. Apparently he could keep himself together at the poker table, at least for a short while.

"I'll call," said Hickok, pushing his own stack across.

Weare had his cards in one hand and the list of poker hands in the other, and looked back and forth between them and the board. "I believe I'll pass," he said.

"So you fold your cards," said Penstemon. "Push them across the line."

Weare put down the list and then ceremoniously placed his cards across the line. The dealer swept them aside.

Arnold looked at Runyon again. Probably he had paired the ace. If Arnold made either the straight or the flush, he'd beat the aces.

"I'll call."

He moved his own chips across the line. Sebastian pushed his cards over the line, shaking his head.

"Three players," said the dealer, adding Sebastian's discards to Weare's. "Turn 'em up."

Arnold glanced at Penstemon, who nodded. "You've all bet all you can, so we show the hands at this point."

Hickok turned over his cards, a ten and a six, giving him a pair of tens. The dealer drew them toward the cards on the board, arranging them together pointing toward Hickok. Arnold showed his two clubs, and Runyon turned over the ace and king of hearts.

Arnold watched Runyon's face intently. Now that the cards were up, he smirked like a gloating kid. His pair of aces was winning for the moment.

The dealer arranged their hands by the board as well, then pushed another card under the first round of bets and turned up the ace of clubs. Hickok made an unhappy sound. Three aces would beat two pair, so Hickok could only win if a third ten came up to give him a full house.

"That's the turn card," said Penstemon. "Now comes the river."

"We used to call it fourth street and fifth street," Arnold said.

Penstemon nodded. "Those are still used, too."

The dealer burned another card and turned up the final card. Nine of clubs.

Arnold kept his face still, though a rush of victory buzzed through his veins. The dealer put down the deck and pushed the three clubs on the board toward Arnold's hand.

"Flush," she said.

"Fuck!" yelled Runyon.

Weare tilted his head and looked at Penstemon. "Your tournament won't last long at this rate," he said as the dealer pushed Runyon's and Hickok's chips to Arnold.

"As I said, all-ins on the first hand are unusual. I'm glad it was demonstrated here. You should all remember to play cautiously. Let's redistribute the chips, since we're here for practice. Well played, Mr. Rothstein," he added, glancing at Arnold.

Arnold acknowledged the compliment with a nod, and watched in silence as the dealer returned their stacks to Hickok and Runyon. He knew he could easily have lost the hand, and it was unlikely he'd take such a risk during the actual tournament. Too much was at stake.

He had no intention of losing, and every intention of keeping this body. The instincts of a lifetime were back full force, and he intended to gain control not only of Penstemon's operation, but of all Atlantic City. There were a dozen or more big hotels here, all with casinos. Too sweet a setup to resist. He wanted to own it, and he would.

The tournament was almost a minor distraction, in comparison. There was just one point about it—he needed to win it in order to keep his body.

Unless he could get some kind of leverage on Penstemon and force him to perform whatever mumbo-jumbo it would take to make his body permanent. He'd have to find Mishka, get her alone, find out what she knew about Penstemon.

He leaned back and gazed at their host while the dealer shuffled the cards again. Penstemon was the most powerful warlock in the country, the tailor had said. Exactly what kind of power did he mean? Mystic powers, or was he influential as well? Arnold had to assume both. The magic had to be pretty good to bring five guys back from the dead.

Arnold wondered if magic was something one could acquire. He'd have to look into it.

~ Ned ~

"Donny, it's Ned. No, I'm not in jail, I'm in Atlantic City. No shit."

Ned shifted in the armchair and looked out the window of his suite at the tall hotel shadows slanting down onto the shore in the late afternoon light. After playing cards all afternoon, they were taking a break before dinner and the start of the tournament.

"Yeah, I'll tell you all about it later, but listen, I need a favor. Tom White's idiot receptionist won't put me through to him. Keeps hanging up on me. Will you call Tom, tell him I'm alive and I want to talk to him?"

There was a short silence over the phone line, then he heard Donny sigh. "OK, Ned. What's the number?"

Ned gave it to him, then thanked him and chatted just long enough to be social before saying goodbye. He was anxious to get in touch with Tom White immediately. He'd give Donny a few minutes to make the call, then he'd try again himself. He wanted to make sure his money had all gone to Connie.

It was a sense of doom that drove him. He'd felt it before, the day before he died. He'd called Tom then, too, and told him to change the will. Turned out it was already too late—he'd died before he could sign the papers.

He leaned back in the armchair and looked out at the ocean while he waited. Nice view. That was one thing this town had over Vegas, an ocean to look at. It was mesmerizing to a desert rat like Ned, but though he could zone out staring at it, it still didn't make him feel calm.

He'd played all right today, but he'd never really been a tournament player. He liked to play for fun and had never worried about the money. There'd always been plenty of money.

Now the stakes were different. If he couldn't play well enough to beat these four other clowns, he'd lose this body, he'd lose being alive again. He was worried about it. Of course he wanted to win—you always wanted to win—but he'd never *needed* to win before. It felt bad.

He glanced at the tin foil and the lighter, the little package of black tar on the table next to him. Corazon had disappeared after they arrived at the hotel, but the staff of creepy invisible guys seemed willing and able to provide whatever he wanted, including girls. There was one sleeping in the bed right now, a cute little redhead. No blondes. He hadn't been interested in blonde.

"Fucking Randy," he muttered, then picked up the phone again and dialed Tom White's number.

If he won this fucker he'd get Randy. He didn't know how, because the million dollar prize was chicken feed, but he'd do it. How she and Tabbet had managed to walk he had no idea; probably they'd paid off the judge.

"Hello? I'd like to speak to Tom White, please. This is Ned Runyon."

He waited for the hang-up, but instead there was a click and the purr of the phone ringing. After two rings White picked up.

"OK, who are you?"

"Tom, it's Ned. Honest. Didn't Donny tell you?"

"Donny told me a bunch of crap. Ned Runyon is dead."

"Yeah, well, I don't have time to explain it all right now, but I'm not dead. I'm alive, and I just want you to tell me what happened to my money. Did Connie get it?"

"I'm not going to discuss that over the phone."

"Shit, Tom, I just want to make sure Connie's going to be all right. My money should have gone into her trust fund. Please tell me fucking Randy didn't get any of it. I heard they let her out of jail."

"Yeah, they let her out. Everyone knows that."

"So tell me she didn't get anything. Please."

There was a pause. "She's suing Connie for ten million."

"Shit! Fuck!"

Ned jumped up from the chair and stomped around cussing for a minute. When he wound down, he cleared his throat and apologized.

"You do sound like Ned," said the lawyer, sounding amused.

"I am." Ned sighed, collapsing back into the chair. "I fucking am."

"The lawsuit is public knowledge," Tom said.

"How do we block it?"

"We don't. There's nothing we can do but ride it out."

"What about me telling you to change the will? I told you to fucking change the will!"

"And I'll bring that up with the judge, but the fact is the will was not legally changed, and Randy inherits a portion of the estate."

"Shit. Bribe the fucking judge!"

"I didn't hear that. I don't know who you are, but I'm not discussing this further with you."

"Tom, wait—"

"Even if you were Ned Runyon, I wouldn't discuss it. Ned Runyon is legally dead and I no longer work for him. So quit calling me, OK?"

Ned heard the disconnect and let the phone slide from his hand. He leaned his head back and stared at the ceiling, wishing Randy was dead.

He could try to put out a hit on her with the prize money, but he didn't like the idea. Hits could backfire, and anyway he'd need the money. He'd have to invest the million if he won it, and live frugally off the interest. That sucked, basically, but he still had hopes of seeing Connie. Maybe she'd give him back a few million. With ten or twenty mil in the bank, he could get by.

But Randy had to go. No way was she going to get her claws on any of Connie's money, goddamn it!

Ned frowned at the ocean, then at the heroin beside him. He wanted a hit, but he didn't want to get distracted before he'd settled what to do about Randy. He'd been fucked up on horse when she came to his place with Tabbet, that much he remembered. Maybe if he'd been straight he would have been able to deal with them.

The phone started beeping loudly. He punched the disconnect, then fished the receiver off the floor. Holding it to his ear, he dialed "O."

"Black Queen," said a throaty woman's voice.

"I want to talk to Mr. Penstemon."

"I'm sorry, sir, he's unavailable."

"This is Ned Runyon," he said. "I'm in the tournament tonight. I want to talk to Penstemon. Now."

"One moment, sir."

Music came over the line, weird music. She'd put him on hold. Ned got up and paced around.

"What can I do for you, Mr. Runyon?" said a voice behind him.

Ned whirled, still holding the phone to his ear. Penstemon was standing a few feet from him. His heart racing from surprise, Ned hung up the phone and stared at his host.

"That was quick."

"I don't have time to waste," Penstemon said, quirking an eyebrow. "You wanted to talk?"

"I want you to help me. I've got to do something about Randy Griffy. You know who she is?"

"Oh, yes." Penstemon nodded and a grim smile flitted across his lips.

"Fucking bitch is suing my daughter for ten million."

Penstemon didn't comment. Ned started pacing again.

"No way is she getting a penny of my money from Connie. I want her dead." Ned stopped and turned to face Penstemon. "You can do it."

"Kill her for you? No."

"She fucking killed me!"

"The court says she didn't."

"The court's full of shit!" Ned took an angry step toward Penstemon. "Listen, you brought me here. You want me to play in your tournament? I'll do it, but only if you keep Randy Griffy from touching my money!"

Penstemon tilted his head, giving Ned a skeptical look. "How much did Connie inherit from you?"

"I don't know. About sixty million."

"So losing ten of it wouldn't really be a hardship."

"That's not the point!"

"What you really want is vengeance, isn't it?"

Penstemon strolled to the wet bar, poured himself a drink, and brought it to the sofa next to Ned's chair. He sat down, sipped, and looked up at Ned as if inviting him to sit for a cozy chat.

Ned stayed on his feet. He was shaking with rage. "I don't want that bitch to get a cent of my money."

"Why? Because you want her to suffer?"

"Because she's got no right to it!"

"Ah. Well, Mr. Runyon, unfortunately you gave it to her, so she does have a right to it."

"I changed my fucking mind, OK?"

"Too late." Penstemon sipped his drink again, then set it down and crossed his legs. "You really should let her go, Mr. Runyon. That chapter of your life is closed. It would be better to concentrate on your future."

"Why won't you help me?" Ned demanded. "You're supposed to have all kinds of magic powers. You fucking brought me back to life, goddammit! That's gotta be way harder than killing somebody."

Penstemon chuckled. "Yes."

"Then why won't you do me a favor? Not like it would cost you much."

"Oh, but it would." Penstemon shifted on the sofa to face Ned more directly. "You see, there's a thing called the Law of Magical Repercussion. Varian's Law, it's called, after the witch who theorized it. It states that any deliberate act of magical origin that harms a living being generates reciprocal harm to the person who originated it."

Ned stared at Penstemon. The man was spouting gibberish.

"I don't expect you to understand it, Mr. Runyon," said Penstemon with a small smile. "You spent a lifetime pretty much ignoring the consequences of your actions. I, however, cannot afford to ignore consequences. I'm sorry to disappoint you, but I won't attack Randy Griffy for you, either physically or financially."

Ned balled his hands into fists. "Then I won't play."

A small crease formed on Penstemon's forehead as he frowned. "I hope you'll change your mind about that. If you're not at the table when the tournament begins, you'll forfeit your chance at keeping that body."

"Meaning what? I'll die?"

Penstemon stood up. "Yes, Mr. Runyon. You'll die. Again."

Terror stabbed Ned as he watched Penstemon walk toward the door. A part of his brain wondered idly why Penstemon bothered, since he hadn't used the door to come in. The rest was gibbering at him to play the fucking tournament, for chrissake, he had to win it, he had to stay alive. He had to protect Connie. He had to get back on Randy.

Penstemon opened the door and turned back to look at Ned. "See you at seven o'clock," he said cheerfully, then left.

~ James ~

James pushed his plate away and leaned back in his chair, sated. The others were still eating. After a second day of practice, Penstemon had provided an elaborate dinner for the players in the exclusive private dining room of the Black Queen's fanciest restaurant, the Diamond Grill.

The room was all done up in sapphire blue, with crystal chandeliers over the table. James enjoyed looking at the pictures on the far wall and being able to see their fine details, thanks to the contact lenses Mr. Penstemon's optician had provided him. He wasn't quite certain if they were magical or merely modern, but he liked them. Amazing how much his mood was elevated simply by being able to see clearly.

Many of the pictures were of women. One that struck him particularly looked a bit like a playing card, but the woman on it held a sword and wore a fearsome expression.

The waiters silently brought and removed plates, filled wine and water glasses, and saw to the guests' every need so efficiently they almost seemed invisible. Well, entirely invisible. James glanced at the white-shirted faceless form standing against the wall behind his left shoulder. He was still slightly unnerved by the critters, and he never liked having anyone behind him.

He returned his attention to the table. Mr. Weare was the life of the party, keeping up a merry flow of conversation that was entirely without consequence. James took no part in it, merely listening and watching the men against whom he'd shortly be playing.

Sated in every way, he was. There was not one indulgence he had craved that had not been satisfied that day, and he now floated in a warm sense of well-being, untroubled by any concern save for a small, tickling sense of unworthiness that had been with him since before he'd died. It was a shadow of guilt, of loneliness for Agnes, whom he'd left behind in Cincinnati. The shadow of his failure toward her.

She had such courage. Courage to walk a high wire, to do circus tricks on horseback, and to take a chance on one James Hickok.

He had to put that out of his mind. He had to put all distractions out of his mind and concentrate only on the cards if he was to win this tournament.

The prize, while attractive, was not what made him want to win. He supposed it would be nice to continue living, especially in this body that was in rather better health than he'd enjoyed just prior to his demise. But it was the victory itself that he craved. He always had.

He'd never got enough, and that was why, he now realized, he had never gotten around to much serious prospecting in Deadwood Gulch. He'd been chasing a victory that was perhaps impossible to seize, a success so overwhelming it would sate his desire to play on. To bust every card player in a town flowing with gold.

Was this the echo of that hopeless attempt, he wondered? He knew little about Atlantic City, but it seemed to flow with its own kind of gold. If he won the tournament and lived to play on, could he capture all the wealth in this city, or at least find a second fame in the attempt? The thought appealed.

He would first have to beat the four men seated with him at Penstemon's table, however. They were all competent card players, as evidenced by the afternoon's play. Weare had quickly caught on to poker, and James knew that little escaped the Englishman's sharp gaze, despite his inconsequent chatter.

Runyon understood the game of Hold'em best of any of them and had a brutal instinct. Rothstein was as silent as a snake and twice as deadly; he could take your chips from under your nose without your knowing, it seemed. Sebastian—well, James had yet to figure Sebastian out.

The riverboat gambler had been quiet all day, but James

didn't figure him for the quiet type generally. Something was eating at him. Could be just the strangeness of it all, or could be the way he was murdered. James had the satisfaction of knowing his own murderer had been hanged for his crime, but Sebastian's had gotten away scot free.

He watched Sebastian, who was seated on his left, take the last of the red wine in his glass and swish it around his mouth before swallowing. The waiter behind them darted forward to fill the glass again the instant Sebastian set it down.

James's own red wineglass was still half full, as were the champagne glass and the glass of white wine he'd been served with earlier courses. Similar ranks of glasses stood around each place at the table. The ones above Rothstein's plate were empty except the water glass—he'd declined all the wine. Many of the other glasses on the table—from the earlier courses—were empty or partially so. Candlelight flickered in them all like ghost shadows.

Time to begin, soon. The others were about done eating. James waited, feeling a strange sense of calm about it.

There was excitement, too, curling around in his gut, but it wasn't the desperate excitement he'd often known in his prior life. Maybe death had mellowed him.

At last Penstemon set his napkin aside and stood up, signaling the end of the meal. No brandy and cigars tonight. No dainty little desserts. That might come later, in a victory celebration. For four of them it might not come at all.

James stood up as well and the others quickly followed suit. Penstemon led them out through the Diamond Grill, where every table was filled with diners who openly gawked at the five resurrected gamblers. Someone started up a cheer and then the whole place was applauding. James bit his lower lip, trying to pay no mind despite being pleased by the attention.

Out through the wide, carpeted corridors, past the casino and up a fancy grand staircase to the mezzanine floor. Penstemon paused and had them all stand along the balcony railing, waving to the cheering crowd down in the casino. Big moving picture screens hung from the ceiling at intervals throughout the giant room, each at present showing a signboard proclaiming the Black Queen Poker Championship.

The casino was packed with people, some odd, but most normal-looking. James found himself searching for Kitty. He didn't see her, but he spotted Shavonne on the arm of a big fellow at a roulette table. With a half-smile of remembrance for the morning's pleasures, he turned to follow Penstemon down the vast hallway to the ballroom where the tournament was to be held.

It had changed considerably since their practice session that afternoon. Then it had been quiet and echoing with emptiness. Now it was crowded with light and color and the noise of the five hundred people who crammed the bleachers around the poker table.

Unlike downstairs, there were quite a few strange folks in the audience: green folks or hairy folks or folks with horns or tails or other non-human appendages. One of the green ones looked like he had leaves instead of hair. A gal in a white dress with silver around her brow looked pretty until James realized she had three eyes, one in between the usual two, up above the silver band. All of the audience looked excited. Their chatter fell away at first as Penstemon led the players in, then it turned into a roar of applause.

James stepped into the blazing light in the middle of the room and went to his seat on the dealer's right. They'd drawn cards for seats at the end of the practice, and James had pulled the ace of hearts, so he had the "button," the nominal dealer's seat. Best starting place you could have, according to Runyon, who'd drawn the deuce of diamonds.

Runyon seemed in a bitter mood, and James didn't think it was just on account of having the big blind. Everyone was tense, he supposed. Some just showed it more than others.

Penstemon stood in front of the table to address the crowd. "Welcome to the Black Queen's first Poker Championship," he said in a loud voice, and paused for the renewed cheering to subside. "We hope it will be the first of many. Tonight we are privileged to watch five legendary gamblers compete for the prize of a lifetime—literally. Plus a million dollars for the necessities of starting fresh."

James glanced down at the stack of chips in front of him, hiding a laugh. Two hundred thousand dollars in chips, same as each of the others had. Two hundred grand was far more than he'd ever had in his lifetime, but it didn't seem like so much now.

"Five men who were robbed of their right to a peaceful old age by the foulest of murders are now competing for the chance to win it back. Gaeline here is your hostess for the evening, she'll explain the details of the tournament," Penstemon added as he was joined by a tall blonde in a long, tight, blue dress that sparkled and shimmered in the bright lights.

James had met her that afternoon, when she'd interviewed each of the players in front of one of the big, mysterious machines Penstemon called television cameras. The interviews had been captured by some mystical means James didn't understand, and would be shown on the motion picture screens at intervals during the tournament.

As Gaeline addressed the crowd, getting them even more riled up, Penstemon stepped to the poker table. "Good luck, gentlemen," he said quietly, smiling and shaking hands briefly with each of them.

With the remembered warmth of Penstemon's fingers still tingling in his right hand, James glanced around the table and took a deep breath, trying to relax. The glare of the lights was disconcerting, and the two cameras that were being managed by two large fellows dressed head to toe in black now moved in closer, making him feel claustrophobic. There was another camera hanging above the table like a chandelier, to take pictures of the cards as they hit the board. James swallowed, trying to put all of it, and the crowd who were now cheering again, out of his mind.

The dealer, Amber again, shuffled the deck and dealt the first hand. James watched her purple hands swiftly spin the cards through the air to land precisely before each player. He pulled up the corner of his two cards and spread them just enough to see the marks in the corners—five of clubs and the two of hearts. Not much he could do with that. He folded them and watched while the hand played out.

Weare had folded, too, and Sebastian folded after the flop, which was nine-nine-jack. Runyon and Rothstein stayed in. A ten and a five hit the table on the turn and the river. Rothstein took a modest pot of eleven thousand with three nines, and the play went on.

Everyone was playing cautious, so there wasn't much excitement in the game at first. Runyon lost half his stack to Weare on a reckless bet, then won it back again a couple of hands later. Weare gave a jolly laugh as the dealer pushed his bet over to Runyon, but James saw a hostile glint in the Englishman's eye.

A haze was gathering up toward the ceiling, fed by the tiny gray trail of smoke from the cigarillo sitting by Runyon's elbow. James glanced up, sure that one little smoke couldn't have made the cloud hanging over the table. Sure enough, it hadn't. He could see something moving up there.

A chill ran down his spine. He looked at the cards Amber had just dealt him—a ten and a three—and folded them, then leaned back and tried to be inconspicuous as he stared into the fog overhead that was surely not natural.

He thought he saw a face. Mesmerized, he could not take his eyes from the roiling gray mist, though a sense of dread accompanied his observations. There were arms and legs and things moving in the shadows—he saw a familiar looking boot. What the hell was going on up there?

"Your action, Mr. Hickok."

James glanced at Amber, who was looking at him expectantly. Two cards lay in front of him. He hadn't even noticed the new hand being dealt.

"Beg pardon," he said, and glanced at the cards. Two hearts, ace and jack. "I'll call," he said, pushing in some chips. He kept his head level so the brim of his hat would block the smoky chaos overhead from his view.

Sebastian called as well, and Runyon raised five thousand. Rothstein fixed his dark, liquid eyes on Runyon for a moment, then folded the small blind. Weare folded as well, leaving three players when James and Sebastian both called. Amber swept up the bets and dealt five and six of hearts and the queen of clubs.

James needed one card for the flush, two for a high straight. He put in two thousand. Sebastian called, and Runyon raised five thousand. James and Sebastian called him.

Next card was the deuce of spades. No help to anybody, unless someone had a three and four for a straight. Runyon might stay in with that kind of hand, but Sebastian probably wouldn't. James decided to ignore the possibility of a low straight and pushed a stack of five thousand across the line.

Sebastian, on the other side of the dealer, gave him a long, narrow-eyed look and then matched the bet. Runyon immediately did the same. James watched him while the last card was being dealt, wondering if he had the thirty-four after all. Runyon showed no glee, no flash of victory in his eye. He didn't move at all.

James looked down at the river card. Three of hearts.

He held the winning hand, the nuts as Runyon liked to say. No way any hand made with three of the cards on the board could beat his ace-high flush. The money on the table was his, the only question was whether he could get Sebastian and Runyon to add to it.

"Two thousand," he said, selecting the chips from his stack. He set them down across the line and looked at Sebastian.

"Call," said the riverboat gambler.

"Raise," said Runyon at once. "Five thousand."

"Total of seven," Amber said.

James fixed his gaze on Runyon and counted to five so as to look a bit hesitational. He counted another five thousand in chips, then set two identical stacks it next to it and pushed them all forward.

"Raise ten more."

Sebastian's gaze flicked from James to Runyon. "Fold," he said, tossing his cards into the middle with a scowl.

Runyon pulled ten thousand from his stack and spilled them across the blue felt. "Call," he said, fixing a hostile look on James's face.

James smiled as he turned over the ace-jack. The crowd roared in approval. Runyon flung two queens into the center, cussing, then reached for his cigarillo and puffed angrily at it while Amber pushed the pot over to James.

"And that brings us to our first break," said Gaeline, glittering as she stepped in front of the nearest camera. "Stay tuned for more exciting action in the Black Queen Poker Championship!"

The red lights on the cameras went off, and the audience turned its attention to the big motion picture screens suspended from the ceiling as the first of the interviews started. Weare's jolly face appeared on the screen, and Gaeline's voice came out of nowhere, introducing him.

The players stood up and stretched. Rothstein headed off toward the gentleman's privy.

"Good show," said Weare, winking at James.

James nodded acknowledgment, then saw Sebastian approaching. The riverboat man offered a hand, and James shook it.

"Well done," said Sebastian. "I had the flush to the king."

"You got out cheap, then," said James.

"I did indeed. Not cheap enough."

He flashed a smile, gone as quick as it came, and stepped away to say something to one of the invisible critters who were waiting around to bring the players whatever they wanted. James thought he might enjoy a whiskey himself, but then he remembered the gray cloud overhead and decided he'd had enough to drink for the moment.

He tilted his head and peered up at the ceiling. The cloud had grown, and had more arms, legs, and faces to it. He saw a lady's big fancy hat with a lot of curling plumes spilling over the brim, and a topper, and a battered scout's hat with an eagle feather stuck into it.

"Jane!" he said in surprise.

"Howdy, Bill," called the grinning face beneath the feather.

He knew that face. It surged forward out of the cloud, separating itself into a single, battered figure that drifted down to stand before him. The initial surprise having worn off, James now wished he hadn't said anything. Calamity Jane wasn't his favorite person on earth, or off it.

"What the hell are you doing here?" he demanded.

"Watching you win this damned card game," Jane said. "That was a fucking great hand you just played!"

James glanced at the bleachers, where most of the audience sat ignoring the moving pictures of Weare and Gaeline, staring at him and Jane instead. "Watch your mouth, Jane," he muttered. "There's ladies present. This ain't Deadwood."

"It sure as hell ain't!" she replied cheerfully. "Damn, Bill, I never thought to see you in a high-stakes game like this'un!"

"Yeah, well, me neither," said James, watching as Penstemon descended on them like a bull.

"Excuse me," Penstemon said, stepping up to Jane with a nod toward James. "I'm afraid you can't stay here. Only paid ticketholders are permitted to watch the live tournament. You'll have to leave."

Jane's eyes flashed. "Oh, yeah? You just try and make me!"

The polite smile vanished from Penstemon's face. He took a step back and raised his hands. Blue lightning crackled back and forth between them.

"Hold on," said James. "She ain't the only one."

He glanced significantly toward the ceiling. Penstemon followed his gaze and let out an exasperated sigh. The next second he bent his knees, hopped into the air and sailed on up to the cloud. Upon his arrival, it arranged itself more orderly like, becoming a gaggle of forms more or less identifiable as people.

Ghosts, must be. James stared at them out of curiosity. So that's what he had looked like? All gray and floaty?

Penstemon looked like he was talking to a bunch of folks all dusted with chalk. He was the only bit of color up there, standing in the middle of the air by the ceiling. James could see the soles of his shoes, good leather, slightly scuffed.

"Word's got around," said Jane. "Everbody's all het up over the big tournament."

James looked at her. Same old Jane in the same old battered buckskins, colorful despite being colorless.

"Yeah?" he said.

"Sure thing! I tried to get old Charlie to come along, but he was feeling shy on account of you're more famous now than when you was alive."

"Charlie Utter, shy?"

"Yeah, funny ain't it?"

James nodded, musing. He wondered why he'd never seen Charlie, or Jane or anyone he knew for that matter, during all the time he'd been dead. Maybe because he'd hung around Deadwood, instead of moving along. He glanced at Jane, who looked happy enough that he doubted she'd been in hell all this time, though she surely couldn't have gone to heaven.

Well, neither had he. He hadn't been to hell or heaven either. He'd just sort of drifted. Seemed a waste of time, but then time didn't run the way you'd expect when you were dead.

Movement overhead drew his gaze upward again. The ghosts were filing off toward the bleachers. The people and critters in the audience gawped at them, pointing and whispering. Penstemon floated back down and landed lightly before James and Jane.

"This here's Calamity Jane," James hastened to say. "She's a famous old Deadwooder, too. Jane, this is Mr. Penstemon. He owns the Black Queen."

"How do," said Jane stiffly.

"I'm honored to meet you," said Penstemon with a little bow. "Please accept my apologies. You're welcome to watch the tournament from the—ah—gallery over there."

He waved a hand toward where the ghosts were arranging

themselves back of the bleachers, up by the ceiling out of the way. The audience down below were craning their necks, staring at the gray assemblage.

"Nice of you to be so accommodatin'," said Jane with an edge of sullenness to her voice.

"Calamity Jane?" said Sebastian, stepping up between James and Penstemon. His eyes were lit with interest. "Pardon my interrupting, but I just had to say I'm a great admirer of yours, ma'am."

"Well, thankee," said Jane, unbending a little. She flashed Sebastian a smile and a coy glance.

"You were a fair hand at cards yourself, if I recollect aright," Sebastian went on.

"Aw, pshaw," said Jane, waving away the compliment. "I was just a piker. Liked to play, but never won much." She looked pleased, nonetheless. Her cheeks got a little brighter gray.

"Perhaps we'll set up an all-girl match down the road," Penstemon said.

"Hell, I'd rather play with the boys," said Jane. "Always did."

One of the camera men waved a hand to get Penstemon's attention and held up five fingers. Penstemon nodded, then turned to the group again.

"I'm afraid it's time for you gentlemen to resume your places. Miss Jane," he added, bowing again before going off to talk to Gaeline.

"Well, Jane," said James, "it's good to see you."

"Give 'em hell, Bill! You, too," she said to Sebastian with a wink, then she pushed off the floor and floated on up to join the others in the gray gallery.

Sebastian had a wistful look on his face, watching her go. He noticed James's gaze and gave a lopsided smile.

"I always wanted to be famous. I was going to go play the Mississippi riverboats when I'd built up enough of a stake."

He glanced down, then turned away without another word and walked toward the poker table. James watched him go, thinking to himself that being famous wasn't all the fun it was cracked up to be.

Being famous meant every cocksure young buck with something to prove tried to provoke you into a fight. Being famous had got him killed.

A stab of resentment hit him, he didn't quite know why. Shaking off the thoughts like a dog shedding water, James strolled back to the table and took his seat.

CUE INTERVIEW 1:

"So, Mr. Weare, you've never played poker before, is that right?"

"That's right, love."

"How do you like it?"

"Well…it grows on one. A game that's designed for liars is refreshing, I find. You have to know your opponent in any card game, but it seems especially important in this one."

"And what is your opinion of your opponents in the Black Queen Tourney?"

"Able players all, m'dear. Able players all."

"Do you think you're going to win the tourney?"

"I have every intention of doing so. Care to help me celebrate my victory?"

"Ha, ha—"

"Hey! Hands off, you! He's mine!"

Alma, seated in the front row of the bleachers with the other most honored guests, came storming toward William, who happened to be chatting with Gaeline. The startled hostess took a backward step before the onslaught of the righteous redhead clad in clinging forest green velvet and wearing heels that could be considered a deadly weapon.

William grinned and intercepted her, catching her in his arms. "It's just for show, love. You know that."

Alma shot an angry glance at the hostess. "Yeah, well, I meant it! Keep your mitts off!"

"You're adorable when you're in a jealous rage." William chuckled and kissed the tip of Alma's nose.

She melted a bit at that and cast him a shy, meek look, comically at odds with her wrath of the moment before. William glanced up at the screen where his interview played on.

"You're missing the best bit," he said, and guided her back toward the stands where Joanie, with an expression of determined cheerfulness, sat waiting.

"What do you plan to do if you win the tournament, Mr. Weare?"

"I expect I'll stay in Atlantic City. Perhaps visit Las Vegas—well, I rather think I must. But this is closer to England, you know."

"Will you be going back to England eventually?"

"I really don't know. I haven't a home there any more. I think I might like to settle down, marry and have a family. I never wanted to do that before, but you know...dying changes one's perspective."

"Indeed. Thank you, Mr. William Weare. Best of luck to you in the game."

"Ah, thank you, my dear."

"And now, back to the tournament!"

~ Round 1 ~

Thank you," Clive said to the waiter who brought him a glass of bourbon. He couldn't help staring at the drink floating toward his hand, and as he accepted it he felt a brush of something cold and tingly. Suppressing a shiver, he looked up at where the waiter's face should be and tried to smile, then turned away and took a large swallow of the drink.

This left him facing the stands where the audience sat chattering and fidgeting, waiting for the game to resume. They were an amazing and peculiar sight, but Clive found his gaze drawn above them to where the ghostly ranks drifted, no less restlessly than the live audience, near the ceiling.

He searched the gray faces for anyone familiar. There were a lot of women, but none he recognized other than Calamity Jane, who was plucking at the clothes of an old man in a round-topped hat. They were arguing, it appeared.

"See anyone you know up there?"

Clive glanced at Rothstein, who had come up beside him without his noticing. "No," he said, and took another sip of bourbon.

"Me neither. Looks like just a bunch of gawkers."

The slight sneer in his voice caught Clive's attention. Rothstein was a pretty quiet man, and meticulously polite. His dark brown eyes were full of intelligence and speculation, but just now they also held a hint of revulsion.

Rothstein turned his head to meet Clive's gaze. "Thought I might see Mishka here. You met her?"

"Mishka? No."

"She's the one who brought me here. Who brought you?"

Clive blinked, trying to remember the name of the youth who had escorted him to the Black Queen's boardwalk entrance. "Fidgety fellow," he said. "Shadow, that was his name."

"Shadow? Nickname, eh?"

"He didn't give any other. Penstemon called him Shadow."

"Hm. What was he like?"

"Young," said Clive, feeling strangely old as he thought about it. He'd been thirty-two when he was killed, and had never felt as old as he did now.

"Time to sit down, gentlemen," said Penstemon's voice behind them.

Clive turned around. Rothstein was already walking toward the table. Penstemon gave him a brief smile, then did the same.

Clive had a feeling of wanting to ask the man something, but he didn't know what. Frowning, he returned to his seat.

He looked at his somewhat depleted stack of brightly colored chips with dissatisfaction. They represented money, he knew, but it was hard to think of them as valuable. He had always played for cash, for bank notes or preferably good, solid gold or silver coin. Chink of coins in his pocket—he missed it.

He glanced up at the ghosts again. Someone up there bothered him, made him uncomfortable. He looked from face to face, trying to discern who. It wasn't Calamity Jane—or was it?

"Blinds, please."

The dealer had changed, a dark-complected young man whom Clive had not previously seen now sat in the chair to his right. Clive glanced at the table and put in the small blind.

He played conservatively, still feeling his way into the game. It was strange not to hold his cards in his hand. He wanted the comfort of feeling those little bits of paper in his grasp.

The dealer was looking at him. He hadn't even checked his cards. He glanced at them and folded, watching the dealer sweep his blind bet into the pot.

Why was he here? Perhaps that was what he had wanted to ask Penstemon. The others were all famous in one way or another. Weare hadn't been famous until after his death, but he seemed perfectly comfortable about that and about all of this. Clive was not comfortable at all.

He watched Weare scoop up a tidy pot, ruffled cuffs dangling out of his sleeves and a large emerald winking on one finger. The Englishman looked at home in his quaint attire. Clive, though the clothes he wore were his own, felt awkward.

He was not famous. He had no wish to be famous, not in this way. He had wanted to make a name playing on the riverboats, but that opportunity was long gone.

There were riverboats still, he had learned, but they were now only tourist attractions, antiquities, curiosities. If he played cards on one, it would be as a carnival freak, as bad as all the hucksters down on the boardwalk.

A curiosity. That's what he was.

"Your action, sir."

Another hand had started. Clive pushed his cards across the line without looking at them. He was scarcely paying attention to the game at all. He shouldn't be playing in such a mood. If he kept this up, he would inevitably lose.

He picked up a half-dozen chips, riffling the stack against the table as he mused. Runyon, across the way, was splitting a rather larger stack in two and shuffling them together one-handed. Very showy. Clive supposed he could teach himself such a trick —he was nimble-fingered, after all—but it wasn't the sort of thing one practiced in public.

He sighed. There was no way to adjust this game to his benefit, not that he could see. Too risky to try to palm a card for later, for the dealer would surely notice the missing card when there were only two to a hand. He could try to get a matching deck, but the deck had changed with the dealer, and how was he to anticipate what the next deck would be? He'd have to have cards stashed all over his person. No good.

He tried to imagine himself winning the tournament on skill alone. He could do it, he thought, but the vision of victory gave no comfort. It wasn't just money he wanted, and the realization came to him accompanied by a wash of cold. It was *his* money.

His money, stolen from him by that rogue, Jones. What had the bastard done with it, he wondered? Bought a new piano for the *Slipper?* The one that had graced its shabby saloon had been ghastly.

Clive closed his eyes, thinking of all the patient toil he had invested whilst a passenger on that cursed boat. All the hours he had spent gently fleecing the sheep who came to the card table, attracted by the riffling sound of the cards as he had shuffled them. Like lambs to the shepherd's call they had come, and he had made them feel at home. Bought them bourbon, complimented their play, commiserated with them on their bad luck, and encouraged them to hope for fortune's turn.

He glanced around the table. These men were no sheep. No fleecing to be done at this table, unless by sheer arrogant bluffing. That was more Runyon's style than Clive's. To win here, he'd have to rely on his wits, observation, and luck.

On the next deal he received an ace of spades and a queen of diamonds. He was sorely tempted to palm the ace, but knew it was not worth the risk. There were cameras taking photographs of every movement at the table. If he were not caught at the moment of palming, he might well be observed in the pictures later on.

He called the blinds after Hickok folded. Runyon called as well, and Rothstein put in chips to match the big blind. The dealer gathered the bets and dealt the flop: two of hearts, king of clubs, jack of spades.

Clive watched the others. Rothstein tossed in his cards with a frown of disgust. Weare put in the minimum bet, and Clive called it. Two cards yet to be dealt, and if either was a ten, he'd have a straight to the ace.

"Raise five thousand," said Runyon, pushing a stack of chips forward.

Clive looked at him. Little bloodshot pig eyes stared sullenly back. Back in his day, such a fellow was generally an ugly customer and Clive had preferred not to play with them. He had no choice about it now.

From the cards on the table, he must assume that Runyon had either paired the king or held a pocket pair. The straight, if he made it, would beat that hand. Or he might pair the ace and beat it that way, unless Runyon held an ace, in which case they might split the pot.

"Call," Clive said after Weare folded. He pushed five thousand chips across the line and watched the dealer sweep them into the pot.

The next card was another deuce. Clive watched Runyon closely for any sign of gleeful reaction that might mean he held a third deuce in his hand. Seeing none, he checked to Runyon, who bet ten thousand. Clive called this as well and waited for the river card.

Queen of spades. The black queen. It gave him a pair, but kings would beat it. Disappointed, Clive gazed narrowly at Runyon.

"Check," he said.

"Fifty thousand," Runyon said instantly, and pushed two large stacks of chips onto the table, then leaned on his elbows, staring mulishly at Clive.

It could be a bluff. Runyon was arrogant in that way. With a pair of deuces on the board, Clive's queens would stand against anything except a pair of kings or pocket aces. If Runyon had held aces he'd have gone all in, Clive decided. Probably would have gone all in on the kings, come to think of it.

"Call."

Clive counted fifty thousand and pushed them across the line. It was the largest bet he had made so far, leaving him with less than a hundred thousand.

Runyon turned over his cards. King seven.

Clive stared angrily at them. He'd lost. Dammit to hell.

Applause from the audience for Runyon's play. The pig was grinning now, blowing kisses to someone in the stands. Clive watched the dealer push his chips over to the bastard, and for a moment saw Jones's face instead of Runyon's.

His hands clenched with the urge to throttle as his blood

surged with rage. Jones's image flashed so clearly in his mind and he realized it was the image of his killer—he saw Jones as he had looked bending over him, saw the cap topple off his head, revealing the thinning hair Jones always tried to hide, saw the foul grin as the bastard went through his pockets and then picked up Clive's beaver hat, putting it on his head as he backed away.

Clive was breathing like a steam engine, short explosive breaths through his nose. Blinking away the foul vision, he shook his head to clear it, then downed the rest of the bourbon in the glass at his elbow.

A waiter came forward and lifted the glass in its invisible hand, making a wordless squeal of inquiry. Clive gave a single nod.

"More," he said, and the waiter left.

The next hand had been dealt. Clive called the blind on a pair of threes, hoping for a third in the flop. When none came, he folded. The next two hands he paid the big and small blinds and folded the garbage he was dealt. Rothstein took one pot, Runyon the other.

Clive played his next cards, a jack nine that made two pair on a flop of nine, jack, six. Rothstein took the pot with three sixes, leaving Clive another fifteen thousand poorer. When the second break was called a few hands later, he had little over sixty thousand left. He stood up, finished the rest of his drink, and headed for the door. Overhead, Miss Gaeline's voice announced his name.

Penstemon intercepted him, affecting a cheerful smile but with watchful eyes. "Where are you going?"

"I need a breath of air."

"You don't have time to go downstairs, I'm afraid."

Clive thrust his chin forward. "What will you do? Kill me?"

Penstemon chuckled, then took Clive's elbow. "Step over here, Mr. Sebastian."

Clive had half a mind to refuse, but he allowed Penstemon to guide him between the bleachers toward a curtained wall at the back of the room. Penstemon drew back the edge of a drape with one hand, revealing a small, dark passage which he invited Clive to enter with a gesture.

"After you," said Clive.

Penstemon shrugged, then stepped into the passage, holding the drape open for Clive to follow. He then led the way down toward a patch of blue at the end of the passage. This proved to be a glass door, which Penstemon opened.

A sharp breeze smote Clive's face, smelling of ocean and corn dogs. He stepped out onto a small balcony, and Penstemon joined him.

Dark had fallen. The neighboring hotel, the boardwalk below and the pier off to the left gleamed with light, flashing, flickering, ever restless. Clive leaned his elbows on the cold iron railing and looked away from the lights, peering instead into the darkness that was the ocean, trying to see the breakers beyond the city's glare.

"Why me?" he murmured.

"Beg pardon?" said Penstemon.

He had meant nothing specific, but now Clive turned to face the hotelier. "Why did you choose me for your game? I can bring no advantage to you, being unknown."

Penstemon cleared his throat. "Your story is romantic. And you were here in New Jersey, close at hand. Your wrongful death may not be widely known, but it's certainly known to the locals. You're quite effective at haunting, you know."

Clive hadn't known, mostly because he hadn't understood that he was haunting, or even that he was dead. He had been caught in a nightmare confusion. At least Penstemon's whim had saved him from that.

"Will I remember all this, when I go back to being dead?"

"Come, come, Mr. Sebastian. You have a chance of winning."

Clive stared into the darkness, trying to imagine victory. What would he do in that case? Take up residence in Penstemon's hotel? Pursue a life of gambling, or take up some other occupation?

He wasn't fit for any other occupation that he cared to follow. He infinitely preferred gambling to any sort of physical labor, though today the game held no enjoyment for him.

Jones had robbed him of pleasure as well as gold. Robbed him of peace. Clive closed his eyes, holding in the surge of remembered anger.

"What happened to Jones?" he demanded, turning to Penstemon.

"As I told you, he died of old age."

"When? Where was he buried?"

"Do you intend to haunt him now?" A wry smile came across Penstemon's face. "It won't do you any good."

"That's for me to judge," said Clive, more forcefully than necessary. "Where is Jones now?"

Penstemon's blue eyes flickered, though his face remained guileless. Clive knew from long-honed instinct that the man's next words were false.

"I have no idea, Mr. Sebastian. And I'm afraid it's time we went back in."

Clive turned toward the ocean again and took a last, deep breath of fresh air, then followed Penstemon down the corridor and back into the ballroom. He heard his own voice as he entered, and glanced up at the nearest of the large screens. His face, five feet across, looked cheerful, excited. Nothing like his feelings now. A cloud of gloom had been growing over him ever since the tournament began.

He paced around the room, stretching his legs, pausing only when one of the other players or the staff talked to him. Weare and Runyon were standing together, laughing with a couple of women from the audience. Clive made to pass them, but Weare reached out and caught his arm.

"Clive, dear boy, come and meet my young friends. Clive Sebastian, this is Alma Winter and Joanie McCordle."

The comely redhead who had her arm snaked through Weare's nodded and smiled at Clive. The other girl, a brunette, thinner and rather pale, took a step away from the hovering

Runyon and smiled tremulously.

"How do you do?" she said with an English accent. "I'm so sorry about how you were killed. It's tragic, really!"

She looked uncomfortable in a spangly gold dress that clung tightly to her spindly form. Her large brown eyes gazed up at Clive, inviting him to gather her in. Why he hesitated he had no idea, but instead of warming to her, he merely gave a curt nod.

"Pleased to meet you."

The shadowy form of Calamity Jane drifted past overhead, making a beeline for where Hickok stood chatting with Rothstein. In her wake floated the little old man in the round hat. He was dressed rather like Rothstein, though it all looked gray, of course. Beneath his jacket he wore a vest with a gleaming watch chain across it.

Clive frowned. Something about the old man troubled him.

"Have you been to Atlantic City before, Clive?"

He glanced down at the brunette, who was standing a little closer, looking up at him with bright, anxious eyes. Behind her, Runyon glowered. Clive understood what she wanted, and ignoring the wreckage of his mood, gallantly offered her an arm.

"Yes, but it was over a hundred years ago. Things have changed considerably."

"Town changed a lot in just the past thirty years," put in Runyon.

Clive and the brunette both stared at him, saying nothing. The brunette turned her head away and looked up at Clive again. Her hands were small and fine-fingered, warm as they clung to his arm.

"Alma and I are going on a tour tomorrow. Would you...would you care to come with us? William is," she added, gazing up at Clive with an agitated blink.

"I—don't know, really. I'll consider it."

"It should be great fun. There's a lighthouse, though I gather it isn't by the shore any more. And we're going to see Philadelphia—"

"Sorry, gentlemen," said Penstemon, coming up to them.

"Time to get back to the table."

He looked straight at Runyon, who shot a sullen glare at Clive and then took himself off. Weare heaved an exaggerated sigh.

"Back to the salt mines. So sorry, my dear," he said to the redhead. "Allow me to escort you to your seat."

Clive followed with the brunette and handed her up the steps to the bleachers. She smiled at him as she and her friend sat down. Weare then took Clive's elbow and strolled with him toward the poker table.

"Nice girl, Joanie. Absolutely desperate to fall in love." Weare glanced sidelong at Clive, who frowned.

"She should pick someone who has better than a one in five chance of surviving the game."

Weare gave a jolly laugh. "Chin up, lad. You've got as good a chance as anyone."

Not true, thought Clive, remembering his depleted stake. He said nothing, though. No point in complaining. Bad luck was a fact of life, as much as good luck.

His decision to play on the *Silver Slipper* had put him in bad luck's way. No way of knowing it, unless he had bothered to look into Jones's background before boarding his ship, a preposterous idea. Even if he'd done so, he likely would not have learned anything to deter him. If Jones had committed crimes other than his murder, he apparently had not paid for them.

They passed Hickok, who was urging Calamity Jane to return to the gallery. Clive's sleeve brushed that of the old man in the round hat. He felt a sudden chill at the contact, and the old man looked up.

Dread seized Clive's heart. He knew the eyes that glanced up into his. The ghost quickly looked away and then flew straight toward the ceiling, sailing over the heads of the audience to disappear among the other spirits.

Orson Jones. That little man, so small and insignificant, was all that remained of the steamboat captain who had murdered Clive.

"Come along, dear boy," said Weare's voice. "What's got into you? Seen a ghost, ha ha?"

Clive remained rooted to the floor, staring at the gray ranks into which Jones had disappeared. His feelings were in turmoil: anger foremost, but also astonishment that the looming figure of his nightmares was now a frail-looking, dowdy old man.

He wanted to pursue Jones, but knew he couldn't. Apart from being unable to fly, he probably wouldn't find the bastard. Jones had vanished into the throng, might even have left, knowing Clive was aware of his presence.

God damn him, Clive thought. He was shaking, he realized. Shaking with anger.

"You all right, Clive?"

Weare's concerned face imposed itself in front of him. Beyond, Clive saw Calamity Jane returning to the audience, shouting for her drinking buddy. He tore his gaze away from the gray ranks, and it fell on the brunette, Joanie.

Her face brightened in a smile and she waved at him. Clive turned away, sliding his arm from Weare's grasp, and stalked to his seat at the table, listening to his recorded voice express hope for the future.

CUE INTERVIEW 2:

"I don't really know. Perhaps I'll be a riverboat gambler again—I understand there are still riverboats."

"Yes, there are."

"Well, you know, that's a nice life. It's peaceful, drifting along the river all day. Tranquil. You get the feeling you haven't got a trouble in all the world."

"And going back to that environment wouldn't bother you, even though it's where you were murdered?"

"Oh, I wasn't murdered on a boat, no, no. I was murdered in Bloomfield. I surely won't go back there, ha ha."

"I see."

"But on a boat you can forget such unpleasantness. On a boat there are no obligations, really, beyond paying one's fare. It's a pleasant life."

"What about family?"

"Well, any family I had are long gone. And I didn't really have any such ties to speak of. I never married."

"Will you marry now, if you win the tournament?"

"I don't know. I think probably not. I like my freedom."

Seated once more at the table, Clive frowned. The bustle of the camera crew getting ready to record Gaeline's next "welcome back" speech distracted him. He noticed a full glass of bourbon at his elbow. Thoughtful of some invisible waiter. He picked it up and drank a large swallow, glancing up as the purple girl sat down again in the dealer's chair.

Penstemon was with her, bending down to murmur in her ear. She nodded, and as Penstemon stood up Clive caught his eye.

"Is Jones still here?"

"Beg pardon?" Penstemon raised an eyebrow slightly, but Clive would not be put off.

"I know you can tell. Is he still up there?"

Clive jerked his head toward the ghosts. There seemed to be more of them than before. He saw a large white cowboy hat among the crowd, and something that looked like a set of foot-long spikes but that he suspected was the wearer's hair.

Penstemon followed his glance, then gave a small sigh. "Yes, he's there."

"Can you keep him from leaving?"

"Why?"

Clive ground his teeth, then picked up the bourbon again. "Unfinished business."

"Not wise."

"That's my affair. If you don't keep him here, I'll walk out."

A slight frown creased Penstemon's brow. "Give up, you mean? Forfeit the game?"

"To hell with the game."

Clive stood up and made as if to step away from the table. Penstemon put a hand on his shoulder.

"Easy, there. Please sit down, Mr. Sebastian. The tournament's about to begin again."

"I tell you I don't care!" He pushed Penstemon's hand away, glaring at him, daring him to fight.

"I'll keep him here," said the sorcerer quietly. "Now sit down and play."

Half-disappointed, Clive sank back into his seat. The others were staring at him. He didn't care. All he cared about was wringing Jones's ethereal neck, or at least making the attempt.

"What do you think of the twenty-first century?"

"Well, I've only had a glimpse of it, you know. I was thinking today about the first time I came to Atlantic City. Very different from all this, of course. It was a spa, then—a place to restore one's health and good spirits. When I first came here, the boardwalk was only about eight feet wide."

"It's very different today."

"Yes, very different—and yet in some ways, just the same. Even back in the 1880s, it had a...carnival atmosphere."

"Salt water taffy, sideshow tents."

"Exactly. The spirit of the place is still the same. There's more gambling, of course, but even then you could get up a card game if you wished."

"A poker game?"

"Certainly a poker game. Or twenty-one, or dice."

"So things really haven't changed all that much."

"No, I suppose they haven't. I suppose not."

~ Arnold ~

Arnold gazed coolly across the table at the riverboat gambler, Sebastian. The man was in the grip of fury, that was certain. Bound to play carelessly. Arnold wrote him off and turned his attention to the others.

Weare was grinning at the cozy redhead who was making eyes at him from the stands. Distracted by a female, not a good idea, but Arnold wasn't ready to discount Weare yet. The man had brains, and he could play cards. Better than Hickok, Arnold thought, though he hadn't yet seen enough to be sure. Hickok could be impulsive, though not as much as Runyon.

Runyon seemed more jovial than before. He was enjoying all the attention, enjoying the limelight. Arnold avoided it himself, but then he had more important considerations.

He'd talked to a number of people—camera men, the other players, Gaeline—and none of them knew who Mishka was or where she might be. Why wasn't she here, watching the big to-do? Penstemon had her locked up, maybe. Odd.

Maybe she knew too much, or maybe Penstemon just didn't want to expose her to the riffraff. Arnold had taken Carolyn to the races, but not to fights or poker games or other less savory pursuits. Though there really wasn't anything unsavory about this game, except for maybe a few of the people in the audience.

There was a thought. Maybe somebody in the audience would know about Mishka.

The camera lights came on, and the dealer started tossing the cards. Arnold watched the other players settle in and turn their attention to the game. He waited until they'd all looked at their cards before glancing at his own.

Hickok liked his hand. Runyon didn't like his. Weare was unreadable, and Sebastian was on tilt, as Runyon liked to say:

angry, unpredictable. Arnold folded his middling hand and watched.

The others all called the blinds, and Weare folded when Runyon bet hard after the flop. Hickok stayed in and Sebastian doubled the bet. The others matched it.

The turn made a pair of aces on the board. The river card was a king. Runyon bet hard again, and Sebastian and Hickok both called. Runyon turned up a third ace, Sebastian a straight, and Hickok showed ace-king for a full house. The crowd roared as the dealer pushed the huge heap of chips over to Hickok.

Runyon cussed as he lit up a fresh cigarette. He'd lost his temper again. Two players on tilt. Wonderful.

Arnold chuckled softly. He was actually enjoying this game. Runyon and Sebastian were their own worst enemies, but it was poker. Anything could happen.

Arnold folded out of a few more hands, sometimes paying for a look at the flop, more often just throwing in his cards. On an ace-jack of clubs he stayed in, calling bets, biding his time. The flop was queen-ten-six, every suit but clubs. That killed the flush, but a king would give him a straight to the ace.

Sebastian led the betting this time, putting in a third of his stack when the turn card came up a nine. Arnold called him and the others dropped out.

River card. King of Diamonds. Arnold checked and looked at Sebastian, waiting. The man's eyes were still dark with anger. He returned Arnold's gaze, then with an impatient gesture he said, "All in."

Arnold calmly waited for the dealer to count Sebastian's chips, then called the bet. Sebastian turned up a pair of kings. Arnold suppressed a smile as he turned over his cards.

"Straight," said the dealer, pushing the queen, ten, nine, and king toward Arnold's cards.

Sebastian stood up, nearly kicking over his chair. He was staring angrily at the cards. He met Arnold's gaze, then looked startled as if he felt a sudden cramp.

He began to grow fuzzy around the edges. A hissing sound

accompanied what had to be the dissolution of his magical body; a cloud of dust grew and swelled around him, then dissipated in a wave of sparkling motes that expanded around the table.

Arnold shivered and instinctively held his breath as the cloud surrounded him. Fortunately, it dispersed almost at once.

Something remained, though. Sebastian was still there, only now he was all silvery, like the ghosts up there watching the game. He opened his mouth, let out a howl of rage, and shot up toward the ceiling.

The audience gasped and shrieked and barked in dismay. Arnold stood and turned around, trying to see where Sebastian had gone. He'd vanished into the thick swath of gray, which was roiling like a thundercloud getting ready to spill.

"Player down," said the dealer.

"Go to a break," Arnold heard Penstemon urge the hostess in blue, who stepped in front of a camera and started talking, smiling brightly.

Penstemon strode toward the stands, staring up at the ghosts like everyone else. The gray bank suddenly divided itself, pulling away right and left, leaving in the center a tumbling mess that looked to be Sebastian trying to beat the tar out of some old man.

"You leave my buddy 'lone!" yelled a woman's voice, and a third figure, improbably dressed in buckskins and an Injun-style hat, darted into the fray.

Penstemon raised his hands. Blue electric fire flashed from them toward the grappling ghosts, surrounding them in a globe of glowing blue. Their motions slowed like a movie when a projector went bad, and gradually came to a halt.

Arnold could see now that Sebastian had both hands around the old man's throat, and the woman in the outlandish buckskin outfit was on Sebastian's shoulders, hand raised as if to clobber him. Penstemon shifted his hands and the whole mess, ghosts and globe all together, floated slowly toward the sorcerer.

A smattering of applause started up from the audience. Penstemon paid it no heed. Arnold saw that his brow was furrowed in concentration, and a tiny bead of sweat had trickled down one temple.

The blue globe drifted gently to the floor between the stands and the poker table. Penstemon lowered his hands and the globe dissolved.

"Gentlemen," the sorcerer called before the fight could get rolling again. "And Miss Jane. Please listen a moment."

They all three stared at Penstemon for a second, then the woman hopped down off Sebastian's shoulders.

"Just tryin' to defend the weak," she said, hitching up her trousers.

"Admirable," Penstemon acknowledged. "However, I think there's an easier way. Mr. Jones, I believe you have something to say?"

Jones replied with a gagging sound. Sebastian reluctantly let go of his throat. The little man coughed a couple of times, then straightened up and squared his shoulders, turning to face Sebastian, who still radiated hostility.

"Mr. Sebastian, I came to apologize and to ask your forgiveness."

"Apologize?" shouted Sebastian, looking apoplectic. "Apologize? You took away everything I had! You took my life!"

"Yes, I know. I do beg your pardon."

"You bastard! You sonofabitch!"

"I am those things, and worse. I was careless and spendthrift. I now see how wrong it was."

"I want my money back, you murdering bastard!"

"If I could give it to you I would. Alas, I lost it at the faro table the next day."

"God *damn* you!"

"Oh, I am damned," said the old man in a choked voice. "I truly am. I cannot move on until you forgive me. I am trapped, as trapped as you are yourself."

Sebastian gaped at him in amazement. The audience, ghosts and living alike, set up a murmur of speculation.

"What do you mean, trapped?" demanded Sebastian. "I'm

not trapped!"

Penstemon stepped toward him. "What was it you've been doing the past hundred years?"

Sebastian turned on him, enraged. The sorcerer stood his ground, merely gazing steadily back, and Sebastian's anger seeped away like air from a punctured tire as a look of confusion came onto his face.

"You were caught in a negative loop," Penstemon said in answer to his own question. "It's common. Both of you were caught that way, in slightly different manifestations. The only way out is to address the conflict that set up the loop."

Runyon shifted in his seat at the table. "Sounds like a fucking shrink," he muttered.

Arnold glanced at him, then returned his attention to Penstemon. Had he set this up deliberately?

"You mean every restless soul that walks the earth is caught in some kind of loop?" Sebastian asked.

"Not every one," said Penstemon. "Miss Jane here stays because she likes doing good deeds for the living. Right, Miss Jane?"

The woman in the buckskins hemmed and hawed, looking embarrassed. "Hell, I done enough bad deeds in my day I got plenty to make up for. Besides, I like the little'uns. They sure do smile when you make silly faces at 'em after they've had a bad dream or such like."

The old man, Jones, stepped forward. "I am most humbly sorry, Mr. Sebastian," he said with a quaint little bow. "If I had known what it would cost, I would never have assaulted you so. I wish I could return your money, even though it would do you little good in the spirit world. Alas, I cannot return it, but I can give you this."

He unhooked the watch chain from his vest and drew out a pocket watch. The big, round disc was like a silver moon, glowing at the end of the chain that winked and glinted as Jones held it out toward Sebastian.

"My watch," said Sebastian in a broken voice. His hand came

up to receive it, and the chain spilled across his fingers as Jones let it go. "My watch."

Arnold heard a restless movement behind him and glanced over his shoulder to see Hickok and Weare standing nearby.

"That watch ain't real, though, is it?" Hickok murmured.

Weare answered as quietly, "Perhaps it is the essence of the watch that was taken."

Sebastian stared down at the watch and chain in his hand, touching them as tenderly as one might touch a lover, crooning over them in a low, pitiable moan. At last he looked up at Jones.

"Thank you," he said unsteadily.

Jones nodded, then stood with his hands folded before him. Sebastian straightened up a little.

"You sonofabitch," he added.

The old man nodded again. "I deserve that. Shall we talk about it some?"

He gestured toward the aisle that ran between the stands. After a second, Sebastian gave a curt nod and slowly walked away with him. The woman in the buckskins followed.

"I'll just go 'long, make sure it stays peaceful-like," she said to Penstemon.

"Thank you, Miss Jane." The sorcerer smiled, then turned toward the poker table. "Now, then. We have another round to play before the evening's over. Gentlemen, if you would?"

Arnold returned to his seat, as did the others. He kept an eye on Penstemon, watching him confer with the cameramen and the glimmering hostess.

Was this guy one of those compassionate do-gooders, out to save the world? That might be a way to get to him. Arnold watched him narrowly, a feeling of reminiscence accompanying the familiar routine of staking out a mark.

"Fascinating," said Weare, shaking out the ruffles of his sleeves as he made himself comfortable at the table. "Positively engrossing. Could it be that Mr. Penstemon here selected us all in order to rescue us from eternal misery?"

"You mean are all of us in one of them loop things?" said

Hickok.

"That is my meaning, yes."

"How about it, Mr. Penstemon?" said Arnold in a quiet voice, drawling out the words a little. "That the story?"

Penstemon, standing nearby, raised an eyebrow. "You are each in some kind of loop, certainly. That's what gave me access to you. As for straightening them out, that's really none of my concern. My interest in you has to do with playing cards. Which it's time to get back to. Raoul?"

The dark dealer was back. Had a spic name, which fit, Arnold thought. He dealt deftly, never said anything.

Arnold won a little, lost a little as the game went on. All the while he was thinking about Penstemon. How to get a handle on the guy. Chances of doing it through Mishka seemed to be diminishing, since she was more invisible than the damn waiters. He'd have to find another way.

By the end of the round, nothing spectacular had happened. Runyon had the lead over Arnold by close to a hundred grand. Ninety-three thousand and five hundred, Arnold concluded, staring at the chips stacked carelessly in front of Runyon's seat. Hickok had the fewest chips, but he wasn't in desperate trouble.

The hostess made a wrap-up speech, then the cameras were turned off and people began to amble away. A few diehards in the audience remained, including some of the ghosts. Hoping to chat with the players, Arnold assumed. Weare and Runyon were happy to oblige, both going over to the stands to flirt with the women.

Arnold preferred to get away from the light and noise. He looked at Hickok.

"Care to find someplace for a quiet drink?"

Hickok gazed at him, a flat, dull, gunfighter's stare. "Don't mind if I do," he said after a moment.

Arnold led the way toward the exit, making sure to pass close to Penstemon. "Care to join us for a drink, Mr. Penstemon?"

"Perhaps I'll catch up with you," said the sorcerer, nodding. "I have a few matters to tend to."

Arnold gave him a friendly smile, then went out with Hickok down the wide, carpeted hallway to the elevators. "Do you mind if we don't take the stairs?" he asked Hickok. "I'm a little tired of being stared at."

"You and me both," said Hickok. "Had enough of it when I was alive."

The elevator glided gently down to the ground floor, where Arnold looked around. The music of the slot machines—marvelous inventions, he had to get hold of some—hovered in the background.

"I guess we could try the Diamond Grill," he said.

"I know another place," said Hickok, and started off through the vast casino.

Arnold followed him through the ranks of slots, card tables, craps tables, roulette tables, and tables for games he'd never heard of. Amazing, this casino, and from what he'd learned talking to people throughout the day, this place was not unusual except for its clientele. He'd never seen such an efficient operation for separating marks from their money. He practically salivated at the idea of owning it.

Hickok led him to a lounge that was dark and out of the way, just the sort of place Arnold liked. They sat in large chairs that threatened to swallow them. Arnold gave a small sigh as he relaxed. A waitress, dressed to leave little to the imagination, came over and smiled at them.

"Good evening, gentlemen. What can I get you?"

"Whiskey," said Hickok.

"Tonic with lime," said Arnold.

Hickok trained his gunfighter gaze on Arnold as she strolled away. "Thought you wanted a drink."

"I do, I just don't want booze. I like to keep a clear head."

"Game's done until tomorrow."

"I know."

Arnold shifted a little in his chair so he could see out into the casino. The distant rippling sound of the slots still reached him, underlying the soft jazz that was playing in the lounge.

It was time to start building his bankroll. He still had the pitiful haul from his visit to the pawnshop, but that wasn't enough to get him very far. He needed a chunk of cash, and then a game in which to build it.

The poker tables seemed like the best bet. The house took a percentage, but otherwise it was the players competing against each other. In most of the other games the house had a big advantage, including craps.

Arnold suppressed a sigh. He loved craps, but only if he was running the game.

"I'd like to try my hand at some of those games," he mused. "Wonder if Penstemon would give me some chips."

"I've got some money if you need it."

Arnold turned his head to gaze at Hickok. Friendly, guileless. Willing to lend cash to a stranger. Must be that folks were more trusting in the old west.

"That's good of you," Arnold said cautiously. He didn't want to commit to anything, especially if the cowboy wanted to be paid back with interest. That was a game Arnold ran, not one he ever played himself.

Hickok shrugged. "I was saving up 'cause I thought I'd need to pay my way out here, then it turned out I didn't."

"How did you get here? Came from out west, right?"

Hickok nodded. "Deadwood. I was fixing to travel by bus, then this gal showed up and invited me to Penstemon's game, took me with her in a flying machine."

"What was her name?" Arnold said quickly.

"Kitty."

Not Mishka. Damn.

"Wait a minute—you said you were planning to come here before she invited you?"

"Yeah, well, I didn't know about this place here, but I had an urge to come back east. I was thinking I'd head to Cincinnati, actually."

"We were called," Arnold said, remembering his own urge to come to Atlantic City.

"I reckon so," said Hickok, nodding.

Arnold frowned. He didn't like being under anyone else's control, not in any way. That Penstemon could inspire him with a desire to come to Atlantic City bothered him, and made him want even more to get the upper hand. It was starting to look like he'd need some magic of his own to do that.

The waitress arrived with the drinks. Hickok offered to pay, but she shook her head.

"On the house," she said, smiling. "I caught part of the tournament tonight. You guys are awesome."

"Well, thanks, Miss," said Hickok. "Here, this is for you."

He dug a small wad of bills out of his pocket and handed her a five. She palmed it, smiled broadly, then strolled away. Arnold sipped his tonic and watched Hickok take a hearty belt of the whiskey. Unlike Runyon and the unfortunate Sebastian, Hickok hadn't drunk during the game.

"Ahh," said Hickok, leaning his head back. "Been dying for that." He sat up after a moment and glanced at the entrance, then took another, much smaller, sip of his drink.

"I'll take you up on that loan," Arnold said after a minute. "How much can you spare?"

Hickok took out his roll and peeled off five twenties. "Hundred do you?"

"It's a start. Thanks," Arnold said, slipping the cash into his own pocket. "Pay you back of course."

Hickok waved a hand in dismissal. Didn't care much about money, then. More fool him.

Arnold sipped his drink and chatted with Hickok for a while, discussing the game, going back over some of the hands. Hickok said Runyon was "a good, tough player but too reckless," an assessment that closely matched Arnold's own and made him revise his opinion of the cowboy. Hickok was a fair judge of character, it seemed, even if he didn't respect the power of money.

"Now, that fellow Weare," continued Hickok, "I can't figure him out. Seems like a gladhand, but I think he's really sharper than that."

"Speak of the devil," murmured Arnold as he watched Weare stroll in, his two lady-friends on either arm.

Hickok rose immediately to his feet, eyes on the ladies. Arnold stood as well. The Englishman had changed out of his fancy Thomas Jefferson outfit into clothes like the modern folks wore: black pants, purple shirt, black leather jacket.

"He was a lawyer, you know," Arnold added.

"Oh, a lawyer," said Hickok. "That explains it, I guess."

Weare's face lit with a smile as he saw them, and he made a beeline for where they stood. He handed the ladies into the two chairs across from Arnold and Hickok, then dragged up a straight-backed chair for himself.

"Evening, gentlemen," he said as he sat. "Relaxing after the game, I see. Mind if we join you?"

"Looks like you already have," said Hickok, resuming his seat.

The redhead giggled. Weare exchanged a grin with her.

"To be honest, we're escaping from Mr. Runyon."

"Neddy," put in the redhead, making a face.

"He wanted us to go with him to something called a disco bar and drink tequila shooters," added Weare.

"Ugh," said the redhead. "Disgusting. I *loathe* tequila."

"Well, you can have a nice G and T, how does that sound?"

Arnold began to think about leaving. He wasn't much in the mood for feminine company, and between the redhead's chatter and the sad demeanor of the brunette, there didn't seem much to like.

"Have you gentlemen met Alma and Joanie?" Weare said, indicating the ladies in turn.

"Don't believe so," said Hickok. "How do?"

"How do you do, Mr. Hickok," said Alma, the redhead. "Very pleased to meet you." She glanced at Arnold with an uncertain smile. "You, too, Mr. Rothberg."

"Rothstein," said Arnold quietly.

"Oh, sorry." She giggled nervously.

"I've read about you," said Joanie, suddenly breaking silence. "You were one of the founders of organized crime in America."

Arnold blinked. "Is that what they say?"

She nodded, warming to the subject. "You laid the foundations for the great gangsters who followed you—Meyer Lansky, Bugsy Siegel, Al Capone—"

"You'll have to forgive her," put in Weare. "She's a student of history."

"Siegel, a great gangster?" said Arnold in surprise. "When I knew him he was just a thug. A good thug, did his job right, but he was nothing special."

"Bugsy Siegel built the Flamingo Hotel in Las Vegas," said Joanie with a touch of pride. "He was the one who had a vision of Vegas as a gambling resort, a place people would come to from all over."

"That so?" said Arnold, wondering where the hell Las Vegas was. He'd heard it referred to frequently since he'd come to the Black Queen.

"Yes. And in fact, he was murdered, too," said Joanie, musing. "I wonder why he wasn't invited to play in the tournament."

Arnold sipped his tonic. "He wasn't much of a card player when I knew him. More interested in women."

"Was he murdered at or over a card game?" asked Weare.

Joanie shook her head. "No, he was killed by the mob because he'd spent too much money on the Flamingo. He never actually got to see his dreams for Las Vegas come to fruition, but he's the one who created it."

Arnold finished the last of his tonic and set down the glass, then sat back and looked Joanie over. The arrival of the waitress to take drink orders provided a distraction that allowed him to observe her closely.

She was pretty enough, neat, quiet. Had big, hungry brown eyes. One of those smart girls who read too much and thought too much. Not the sort he'd usually want to spend much time with, but in his current situation she might prove to be very useful. He needed information, and she was the sort of girl who could get it. She might be able to get into places he couldn't, too.

"You ever played roulette, Joanie?" he asked her, giving her a beguiling smile.

She shook her head, eyes wide. "No. I've never gambled at all, except for bingo."

"I was thinking I might try out the tables here. Care to come along and bring me luck?"

He could spare a little cash to blow with her. He'd use the pawn money, save Hickok's for the poker tables where he could start building a bankroll.

She looked hesitant. Alma gave her a nudge.

"Sounds like fun! Maybe we should all have a go." She looked at Weare, who gave a shrug and a resigned smile.

Arnold smiled, too, though he'd rather not have company. If Joanie felt better with her girlfriend along, he'd put up with it. The key to wooing a shy girl was to make sure she always felt comfortable.

He waited until the drinks arrived, then proposed they head out to the casino. Everyone agreed except Hickok.

"Think I'll be turning in soon," the cowboy said, saluting them with his second glass of whiskey.

"See you tomorrow, then," said Weare, standing up and offering to help Alma out of her chair.

Arnold got up, too, and held out a hand to Joanie, accompanying it with a smile. She blinked a couple of times, then smiled back and let him help her up. He slid her hand into his elbow and started to lead her out to the casino.

"So Joanie," he murmured. "Tell me more about Las Vegas."

~ Break ~

Ned sat in bleary dissatisfaction, staring at the gyrating hips of the dancer in front of him. She was like nothing he'd seen before, and he'd seen a lot of dancers. None with a tail though—a real, twitching cat tail, leopard-spotted.

The novelty had worn off a bit after an hour or so. Only so much you could do with a tail, he guessed.

He glanced around the bar and realized there weren't a whole lot of customers. A couple of other guys sitting at the edge of the stage. One had horns—a horny guy, ha ha—and a guy on the other side of him was skinny and completely hairless, his skull a knobbly, lumpy mess with purple veins running all over it. Back in the corner, two gray-faced old dudes in long black robes like you'd wear to graduation were talking over a drink, oblivious to the cuties on the stage. Why did they even come here?

"'Nother drink?"

Ned glanced up at the waitress and grinned. She had really big tits and a really wide mouth. If he wasn't so tanked, he'd see if he could slip her one. Sad fact was he wasn't as young as he used to be. Lately he'd settled more often for the pleasant buzz of tequila and smack, and forget about the sex.

"Sure," he said, and tried to cop a feel as she turned away. She was too quick for him, though. Slid out of reach before he could grab.

Oh, well. Next time.

Something soft brushed his face. He glanced up and saw it was the dancer's tail. She tickled his neck with it, then pulled it away just as he tried to catch it. Damn, his reflexes were too slow.

He grinned at her as she shimmied in front of him, her big bare breasts jiggling. He pulled another twenty out of his pocket and leaned forward to tuck it in her g-string, managing to get a pinch at the same time. She slapped his hand and danced away to the horny guy.

The waitress came back with tequila. He shot it back and then got up, leaving her a tip. He didn't know how much money he had left—not enough, though. Oughta get some more. Demand some from Penstemon, maybe.

A vague idea was swimming around in his head about money. Something to the effect he didn't need any, but that was bullshit. Sure, everything he ate and drank in the Black Queen was free, but what if he wanted to go down the boardwalk and see the sights? What if he wanted to buy a drink at the fucking Taj? He needed some money for that.

He left the bar and headed for the elevator. Penstemon would have the penthouse, he assumed, so he punched the button for the top floor. The doors opened on a hallway that looked like any of the others—blue oriental carpet, blue walls, chandeliers. The only difference he could see was that the hall was shorter and the chandeliers had real candles in them, and on the walls there were torches instead of the little stained glass sconces like on Ned's floor. The smell of candle-wax hung in the air—plain wax, not those damn perfumed things fucking Randy always liked to burn.

All that fire. Had to be against code. Ned could threaten to contact the city about it, if Penstemon was slow about coughing up the dough.

He headed toward the door at the end of the short corridor, sure that it would lead to Penstemon's suite. It was unmarked and had a peephole in it, like any hotel room. Discreet little doorbell button at the side. Ned ignored it and pounded on the door with a fist, waited a few seconds, and pounded again.

The door was answered by a woman so pale that for a second Ned thought she was one of the ghosts. Her white hair was pulled tightly back into a bun, and she wore a cream-colored dress. Her eyes were pale blue and frosty as they gazed at Ned.

"It's past midnight," she said.

"I want to talk to Penstemon," said Ned.

"He isn't here."

"Bullshit. Let me in."

"No," she said in a thoughtful tone of voice, as if it was almost a question.

Behind her, he could see down a short hallway into what looked like a living room full of dark, wooden furniture. Everything in there was lit with more candles and torches.

Ned looked back at the woman. "Listen, Granny, I'm one of the tournament players. I have something very important to discuss with Penstemon and it can't wait."

"I know who you are." She seemed totally unimpressed.

A black cat trotted up, looked up at Ned and let out a meow. It had a small heart-shaped patch of white on its throat that disappeared from sight when the cat started rubbing against the woman's legs.

"I'll tell Mr. Penstemon you want to speak to him," she said. "He'll contact you in your suite."

"I'm not going to my fucking suite! I got business."

She raised an eyebrow, reminding him strongly of Mrs. Roach, his third grade teacher. Another cat, a gray one, came stumping toward the door, walking like it had a bum hip. Ned stared at it, remembering a dog he had once that had walked like that after getting hit by a car.

"I'm sorry," said the woman, "I can't help you. Mr. Penstemon can't be disturbed."

"Like hell."

Ned moved to push his way past her into the penthouse. A bolt of lightning struck him between the eyes and the next he knew he was lying on his back, looking up at a chandelier.

A drip of wax was sliding down one of the candles, fixing to land on his face. He tried to move, but his arms and legs weren't working too good. In a flash of panic he remembered being like this in his house, lying on the floor, with Randy and Tabbet leering over him —

"It's all right, Marie," he heard Penstemon's voice say. "I'll talk to him."

Hands gripped Ned's shoulders, strong and gentle, helping him sit up. It was Penstemon, but he wasn't wearing the suit he'd had on earlier. He was dressed in a velvet graduation robe like the goony old guys in the titty bar, except his was blue. Around his neck was a heavy gold chain with a star hanging from it.

"Sorry about that, Mr. Runyon. Marie can be a little overprotective at times. Won't you come in?"

Penstemon helped Ned off the floor. Ned brushed at his suit, then followed Penstemon into the penthouse past the glowering woman. The room they entered took up the whole width of the hotel, with floor-to-ceiling windows on either side giving a spectacular view of the boardwalk and the ocean far below. The far wall had four doors and was split by another hallway, and was painted a dark blue that glowed like the sky after sunset.

Penstemon invited Ned to sit on a black leather sofa. A black cat jumped up next to him, but Penstemon snatched it up.

"No, kitty," he said, putting it down on the floor again. "Go on."

The cat mewed, then strolled away. Penstemon sat in a leather armchair next to the couch.

"What can I do for you, Mr. Runyon?"

"I need some cash."

"Pardon me for asking, but why?"

Ned turned on the couch to face him square on and leaned forward. "Listen, you owe me! Guys who play in televised tournaments get paid a bundle."

"You're receiving all the hotel's services on a complimentary basis—"

"Yeah, well, I should be getting paid on top of that! Don't think you can cheat me!"

"I have no intention of cheating you, Mr. Runyon, but really, what do you need money for?"

"I've been spending my own cash tipping your waitresses and your dancers. I need more, OK?"

Penstemon was silent, sitting and gazing at Ned like he was looking at some kind of freak. It pissed Ned off.

"I want ten thousand," he said. "Think of it as an advance on the million."

"But if you don't win the tournament, how will I get it back?" asked Penstemon reasonably.

"Give me ten grand or I won't play in the fucking tournament!"

Penstemon shifted in his seat, crossing his legs beneath the robe and leaning his head on one hand. "You saw what happened to Mr. Sebastian this evening. If you fail to appear at the tournament table tomorrow night, the same thing will happen to you."

A cold twist grabbed at Ned's stomach. He swallowed but kept his face still. Penstemon wasn't going to see him afraid, goddammit!

"Ten grand's gotta be peanuts to you," he said. "What are you so worried about?"

"I'm worried about what damage you might do with it."

"Damage? What the fuck? I just want to have a good time!"

"Exactly."

The pale woman butted in, setting a tray down on the coffee table between them. "Tea," she said in a voice dripping with disapproval. She picked up the teapot and poured two cups, handed them to Ned and Penstemon, then left.

Ned stared in disbelief at the dainty china cup in his hands. Fucking tea, for Christ's sake! He put it on the table with a clatter and a slop over the rim.

Penstemon sipped his. "I'll tell you what, Mr. Runyon. I'll give you a thousand. That should be enough for one day, shouldn't it? Then if you need more tomorrow night, I'll give you another grand."

Implying maybe Ned wouldn't be around after tomorrow night, the son of a bitch. Ned frowned and thought about protesting, then gave a nod instead. He didn't want to sound like a whiner. If he ran out of dough, he'd wake Penstemon up for more, and serve him right for being a stingy asshole.

He'd wanted enough to put out a hit on Randy. A grand

wouldn't do it, but maybe he could build it up at the poker tables. Worth a try, and in the meantime it would keep him going.

Penstemon finished his tea, set his cup down, and reached into his billowing sleeve, coming up with a roll of twenties. He handed this over to Ned, then stood.

"Don't do anything I wouldn't do."

"Ha, ha," said Ned, following him to the door.

Penstemon opened it and stood watching him with a quizzical smile. "Good night, Mr. Runyon."

"Yeah, g'night."

Ned went out, riffling the twenties as he walked down the hall. He stuffed them in his pocket, then took the elevator down to the casino.

The burbling music of the slots greeted him and he sighed with pleasure. The slots sounded weird here, but they were still the familiar background music of his life. He'd grown up in the Rabbit's Foot, knew the odds of every game in the house. Knowing the odds, he made a beeline for the poker room.

There were three tables going. One was all black-haired young women—barely older than teenagers—wearing tight black outfits and red, red lipstick, like a whole table of nubile Morticias. He was sorely tempted to sit down at it, but he spotted Arnold Rothstein and William Weare at another table and chose that one instead.

It was just a two-dollar five-dollar game, small change, but Rothstein had a big stack of blue dollar chips and an even bigger one of pink five dollar chips in front of him. Had to be close to two grand sitting there.

Weare had a more modest stack and was flanked by his two girlfriends. Alma had a few chips and was gaily losing them as fast as she could. Joanie, the geeky brunette, sandwiched between Weare and Rothstein, wasn't playing.

Ned bought two hundred in chips and sat between the redhead and a guy who had scales instead of skin. The guy flickered a forked tongue at him. Ned turned the other way.

"Hiya, Alma. How's it going?"

"Jolly," she said curtly. "Look how much Arnold's won!"

"Nice stack."

Rothstein glanced at him and gave a nod of acknowledgment, then went back to the game. Ned paid the blind to get in and looked at his hand. Five-two off. Garbage. He threw it in.

"So, Alma, guess what? I was just up in Penstemon's penthouse."

"Really? What's it like?"

"Like a fucking Halloween funhouse, if you want to know. Complete with a witch."

"There are a lot of witches around here," said a player across the table with hint of annoyance. Ned met his gaze, surprised. Guy looked totally ordinary in a button-down shirt and gold wire glasses. A stockbroker type, the sort who came to Vegas to go wild for a weekend and then went home to his nice, orderly life.

"So there was a woman there," said Rothstein, casually matching the bet. "Did you catch her name?"

"Uh—something with an M," said Ned. "Not Mary—"

"Mishka?"

"No. Marie, that was it. She was a fucking bitch, too."

"Oh, a bitch witch," said Alma with a brittle laugh.

"What else did you see in the penthouse?"

Rothstein's voice was casual—too casual. He kept his gaze down, looking at the cards. Ned watched him, wondering why he was so interested in Penstemon's digs.

"A mess of cats," Ned said. "Black cats, and one gray one."

"Oh, I love cats!" piped up Joanie.

Everyone looked at her for a second, then went back to the game. Rothstein took the pot with two pair, tens and sevens. Next deal, Ned caught a pair of jacks. He raised the blinds.

"So I'm thinking of taking a stroll down the boardwalk, maybe checking out a couple of the other casinos," he said. "Anyone want to come with me?"

"I'm fine here," said Rothstein, calling Ned's raise.

The flop was ace queen four. Ned grimaced, then bet twenty bucks. Rothstein called him.

"Alma and I saw the boardwalk this afternoon," Joanie said. "We rode all the way up and back in one of those chairs."

"William hasn't seen it, though," said Alma, rubbing her arm against Weare's.

"A delight I shall have to continue to anticipate," Weare said, throwing in four pink chips. "Call."

The turn card was another queen. Everyone but Ned, Rothstein and Weare dropped out. When the river card came up a jack, Ned went all in. Weare folded and Rothstein called.

"Full house, buddy," said Ned, showing his jacks.

"Nice, but mine's better," said Rothstein. He turned up ace queen.

"Queens full of aces," said the dealer, pushing the pot to Rothstein.

"Shit," said Ned. He glanced up and waved the pit boss over. "Bring me another rack."

He played a while longer, lost half his rack to Rothstein, won a couple of pots to bring him even again, and couldn't convince any of them to go cruising with him. He stuck some five dollar chips in his pocket and tossed one to the dealer.

"Seeya mañana," he said, getting up.

They all murmured unenthusiastic goodbyes. Fuck 'em, then.

He cashed in his chips, then went out to the lobby and left the hotel on the boardwalk side. One of the doormen squealed at him. Ned gave him/her/it a look, which was hard to do when there wasn't a face to look at.

"Yeah, you too," he said.

He could see other hotels around and a dim glow of light from the boardwalk, but it was all blocked by a lot of trees. A huge garden surrounded the hotel, and the only clear way through it was a path leading toward the ocean. Ned followed it, walking fast until he got out of breath and had to slow down. Fuck, he hated getting old.

He played with the chips in his pocket as he walked. God, it felt good to be playing again, even in this weird-ass place. The strange people and the invisible workers were getting to him, though. He wanted to be in a normal casino for a while. Find some cute girls to hang out with who didn't have tails or fangs.

The path dead-ended at the back of a cheesy little sideshow shack. Ned looked around, frowning, but he didn't see any other way to go, so he tried the door.

It was unlocked. He pushed it open and stepped into a storeroom full of stuffed toys. He picked one up, a pink dragon with orange spikes along its back and googly eyes. A smile crawled onto his face as he thought about how Connie would love a tacky toy like this. Even though she was in college, she still liked kid stuff sometimes.

Jesus, Connie. He still had to do something about her money. He didn't want Randy touching it. To be honest, he didn't want to have to ask his daughter for money, but he missed her. He wanted to talk to her.

He almost turned around right then, but he realized it was too late to call, even though it was two hours earlier in Colorado. Nah, better wait. He'd call tomorrow.

A curtain was pulled back and light spilled in from the front of the booth. A kid dressed in black with tattoos on his bare arms and all the way up his neck looked in.

"Can I help you?"

Not, "What the fuck are you doing here." Interesting.

Ned put the dragon back in the waist-high cardboard bin he'd taken it from. "I just came from the hotel."

The kid nodded. "Going out? It's this way."

He gestured toward the curtain. Ned blinked, then stepped forward.

"Thanks."

"Not a problem."

The kid held the curtain aside for him. Ned walked through and found himself in a carny booth, a dart game. Hit the ace, win a prize. The darts would be crummy and badly weighted, the pips on the cards too small to hit easily. Usual scam. Standing at the counter were a couple of people waiting anxiously to lose their money. The kid lifted a section of the counter and Ned walked through.

He strolled north, toward where the Taj was. The air smelled like a carnival, with popcorn and grease and sugar and darker, less clean smells, all overlying a whisper of salt and the strange, heavy humidity from the ocean.

He glanced back and was startled to find he couldn't see the hotel. There was the Tropicana, and farther down the Hilton, but no Black Queen.

Ned stopped and stood frowning. How the fuck do you hide an entire hotel? He hadn't walked that far. He could still see the little carny booth with the dragons. The sign across the top of that said "The Black Queen," but there was no sign of the hotel behind it.

Fucking weird. This place was freaking him out. Witches and goblins and black fucking cats. He needed some normal.

Turning north again, he walked until he was tired, then got into a rolling chair and told the driver he wanted to go to the Taj. A pang of homesickness struck him. Stupid, but he missed Vegas. Everything here was an imitation of his town. The Sands, Tropicana, Caesar's—all pale shadows of the real things in Vegas. The clientele was a bit different. Atlantic City had six million people living within a short drive, not even counting NYC, so there were lots of little old grayhairs with their oxygen on wheels, feeding their Social Security into the slots.

In Vegas there were regulars too, but there were a lot more tourists, come for a weekend of decadence, happy to unload a heap of cash they'd been saving up for it. The shows were better, the casinos were better, and the mob didn't have its teeth in a deathgrip on the whole fucking town, like they did here.

"Taj Mahal," said the driver as the chair glided to a stop.

Ned paid him and headed for the casino entrance. Lots of pretty neon and no weirdos. Everyone looked normal. The grayhairs had mostly gone home to bed by now, so it was down to hardcore regulars and a few restless tourists. Ned kept his hand on his roll of cash as he made his way to the bar.

He needed to do some serious partying. He called the bartender over with a wave. It was a big guy, older, salt-and-pepper hair and glasses, looked like you wouldn't want to mess with him. He also had no horns, no claws, and his skin was a normal tan, slightly weathered.

Ned bought a drink, then pushed a twenty toward the bartender. "Can you recommend a good strip joint?"

"Bare Exposure's all nude but it's BYOB."

"Ah, fuck that. Where's a place with a good bar?"

"Delilah's Den."

"Thanks."

He caught a cab to Delilah's Den and felt at home the minute he walked in. Loud music thumped, lights flashed in rhythm, and girls were gyrating on several round platform stages and on the floor. On the nearest stage was an all-American gal with long legs and a cute little cowgirl outfit and bouncy blonde curls. For a second Ned thought it was Randy, and an unpleasant jolt of adrenaline went through him.

He found a table near another stage where an amazon with green eyes and red hair curling down her back was performing feats of gymnastic agility that made him seriously envy her pole. Sitting down with his back to the cowgirl, he ordered tequila and settled in.

A couple of girls joined him before long. One was Hispanic, probably Puerto Rican in this part of the country. The other was white, no tan which was unusual, with brown hair brushed up into a spiky mess and little silver rings through her ears, her nostril, her lip, one eyebrow and her navel.

"Hi, I'm Angela," said the chica. "This is Red."

There was nothing red about her that he could see, but whatever. He bought them drinks and stared at Red's black leather halter top, trying to discern the shape of whatever was pierced through her nipples.

Angela chattered and giggled, asking his name, was this his

first visit to AC, was he all alone. Standard extraction of key information, he'd been through it before. The alone part hurt, though. Back home, the girls had crawled all over him; they all knew who he was, knew he was a mover and a party guy. Here nobody knew him. Nobody gave a fuck.

"So, Neddy, you wannna lap dance?" said Angela, leaning close and displaying her ample and ill-concealed bosom.

Ned grinned and slid a finger under her bra strap, trying for a feel of her nipple. "Boy, howdy!"

Red slunk a long, pale arm around his shoulders and tickled his ear with her tongue. "Both of us. Private dances, a hundred apiece."

"Sure, baby," said Ned, wishing he'd brought some smack with him, or even some coke. "You lead the way."

Their second round of drinks had just arrived, and they carried them back to a cramped hallway of booths the size of K-Mart dressing rooms, with no doors. Music boomed from overhead speakers. Red led Ned to the very back, pushed him onto the booth's vinyl seat and straddled him.

"Pay up, Neddy," she crooned.

With slight difficulty, Ned extracted his money from his pocket and peeled off two hundred. The cash disappeared with lightning speed, Angela's into her little sequined purse, Red's into her stiletto-heeled boot. Red got off Ned's lap and stepped back, and as the Doors' "Break On Through" started up over the speakers, heavy on the bass, she reached for Angela's top.

Ned slammed his drink and leaned back while the girls went to town. Angela was cushy in all the right places, tan everywhere. She'd got all the tan Red missed out on. No silicone either—it was all the real thing.

Turned out to be rings in Red's nipples, half-inch silver rings with little silver crosses dangling from them. Ned tried to catch one with his teeth as they brushed by, but she was too good and knew to stay just out of reach.

He got his money's worth, though. His lap was danced upon with a vengeance. Both girls ran their shapely gams repeatedly across his crotch, and to his surprise he actually got a hard on, something that wasn't so easy any more. The girls were a little rough, which he didn't mind, so he just ordered another round of drinks and when Red asked if he wanted more lap dances, he peeled off another two bills.

He called it quits when they offered to get him a lay. Why pay for that when he could get it for free back at Penstemon's place? He'd had a good time here, but he was ready to move on, so he kissed Red and Angela sloppily, tucked an extra twenty into each one's bra, and stumbled out to a taxicab.

"Black Queen," he said, sliding down in the back seat.

"Where's that? Never heard of it," said the driver, a black guy who craned his head around to stare at Ned like he was nuts.

"Huh? Oh, shit. Crap. OK, just take me to the Plaza."

"Got it."

At Trump Plaza, Ned got out and went through the casino out to the boardwalk. He was too drunk for poker and kind of tired, too. It was colder now, and he shivered as he walked carefully down the boardwalk. Finally he reached the little Black Queen carny booth.

The tattooed guy raised an eyebrow as Ned leaned on the counter. "Long night?"

"Yeah." Ned stood blinking, peering groggily at the dinosaurs. Dragons. Whatever the fuck they were.

The guy opened the counter for him. "Come on in."

Ned walked stiffly through and into the back of the booth while the guy held the curtain for him. He paused to look at the stuffed toys again, picked up the pink and orange dragon.

"I want this," he said. He fumbled in his pocket, came up with a five dollar chip.

The tattooed guy waved a hand. "Take it. Have a good night, Mr. Runyon."

Mr. Runyon. That was nice. Respectful. Ned gave the guy a smile, hoping it wasn't too loopy looking.

"Thanks." He waved the dragon, then went out the back door into the chilly night.

There it was, big as the fucking Empire State Building. All the edges of the Black Queen were lit with blue neon. Ned stared up at it, wondering what kind of David Copperfield mirror trick Penstemon had used to hide it from sight from the boardwalk, then remembered Penstemon could probably do Copperfield one better.

He started forward, clutching his stuffed dragon, following the winding path to the hotel. It seemed like he'd been walking for miles by the time he finally reached the entrance. He went straight to the elevator, straight up to his suite.

The hallway was deserted. Even with the carpet muffling them, his steps seemed to echo. Maybe that was just his head. He found his door, rummaged in his pockets for the key card, and finally got in. Staggering over to the couch, he sank onto it and closed his eyes.

Head spinning a little. He waited for it to settle down, then opened his eyes and saw that he was holding the pink dragon on his lap.

Connie. He'd wanted it for her. He'd send it to her, but he wanted to talk to her first, let her know it was coming. Let her know he still loved her.

A sob surprised him. He stifled it, even though no one was there. God, how'd he get so down? He needed a hit, settle his nerves.

He scooted sideways on the couch until he could reach the end table where he'd left his supply of horse. Beautiful black tar, a big gooey lump of it. He put the dragon down next to it, smeared a hit on the tin foil, and picked up the lighter.

Took a couple of tries but couldn't get the flame going—his hand was shaking. Annoyed, he took a firmer grip on the lighter and gave it a hard stroke, then held the flame under the foil until the smoke began to rise and curl. He sucked it in and felt it spread out through his head like maple syrup, and with it the bliss he craved.

He sighed with pleasure. The pink dragon watched him with its googly eyes. He giggled. Chasing the dragon.

When there was no more smoke he put the foil and lighter down and leaned back on the couch, drifting pleasantly. After a while, he sat up and reached for the phone. Had to call Connie. Tell her the dragon was coming.

It rang a long time before she picked up. Oops, he'd forgotten to check what time it was. Oh, well.

"Yes?" she said in a sleepy voice. "Who is it?"

"Bunny, it's your daddy. Don't hang up."

"Daddy? Daddy's dead."

"Yeah, well. Haven't you ever heard of ghost phone calls?" He laughed awkwardly. "It's really me, Bunny. I just called to tell you I miss you and I love you."

She was silent for a long minute. "Where are you?"

"I ah—well, you probably won't believe it. I'm in Atlantic City."

"Not heaven, huh?"

"Nope. Closer to hell."

She laughed, and the sound rained through him and washed him clean of fear. He put his hand on the pink dragon, soft and fuzzy, then closed his eyes.

"I love you, Bunny. I wish I could come see you."

"Oh, Daddy."

"Listen, you watch out for that Griffy bitch, all right? Get a good lawyer."

"I'll be OK, Daddy. Really. You don't have to worry."

"I'm sending you a present. It's nothing big, just a little reminder so you'll know this wasn't just a dream."

"What is it?"

"A little pink dragon. A magic one."

"Magic?"

"Well, maybe. Maybe's it's just a toy."

He was fuzzy. Not making sense, he knew. Better shut up before he made a fool of himself with his daughter.

"I'll let you go, Bunny. Sorry I woke you up."

"It's OK. It's…good to hear your voice."

Ned's throat tightened and he felt a tear threatening, rubbed at his eye to get rid of it. "I miss you," he said again. His voice was getting ragged.

"Miss you, too."

"Maybe I'll come see you in a few days."

She didn't say anything. That was too much, probably. A phone call was one thing, but to have your dead dad come walking in the door...

"OK, bye," he said. "Love you, Bunny."

"Bye, Daddy."

He didn't hang up. Instead he listened until he heard the click of her disconnecting, then sat with the receiver in his hand, staring numbly at Atlantic City glittering outside the picture window.

~ Arnold ~

Arnold sat at the bar, a glass of soda in front of him, and watched the news on the television hanging overhead. It was witch news, everything you wanted to know about what was happening in the magical underworld. Advertisements for the Black Queen Poker Challenge were interspersed with the news stories. Arnold hid a smirk.

Quite a machine Penstemon had here. The Black Queen was a golden goose.

He waited until he was the only one in the bar, which took a good hour or more even though it was quite late. He had been at the poker table for several hours after ditching Weare and the girls, long enough to win the stake he'd decided he'd need.

Finally, when there was no one else in the place, he beckoned the bartender over.

"Another drink?"

"No. I have a question." Arnold laid a hundred dollar chip on the bar between them. "I need someone highly skilled at magic. I imagine that sort comes in here now and again."

The bartender snorted. "Try finding a customer here who isn't."

"I'm not." Arnold caught his gaze and held it. "This person must also be discreet."

"I wouldn't try to cheat, if I were you. Penstemon is no fool."

"I'm aware of that." Arnold smiled. "I'm no fool either. No, this is a…side bet. Nothing to do with the game."

Arnold laid a second chip beside the first, then a third. The bartender gazed at them and licked his lips.

"I can find you someone. Hang on."

Arnold finished his drink while the man was on the phone. A short while later, a tall, gangly woman entered the lounge and came over to him. She was hook-nosed, with long, ratty hair that looked black until it caught the light, when it glinted with dark green highlights. She wore black trousers that hung limp from her bony hips and a frilly red blouse that clashed with her hair. A dozen mismatched bangle bracelets jangled on one wrist. She carried an enormous patchwork purse. Arnold resisted the inclination to sneer.

She sat on the stool next to Arnold's and gave him an appraising glance. "You look taller on TV."

He ignored this. "I understand you're an expert?"

"I'm the best. And I ain't cheap."

Arnold stood and left another chip on the bar. "Let's walk."

~ James ~

James woke up on the sofa, where he'd spent most of the night drinking his way through a bottle of Johnnie Walker Black Label from the bar in his suite. He sat up stiffly, blinking, wondering what time of day it might be. The suite was so quiet. No sounds reached it from outside, only the hum of various machines.

His glance fell on the curtained windows and his stomach turned uneasily at the mere thought of looking out. He did not want to be reminded of how preposterously high in the air this room was, or to go near the edge of that precipitous drop with only a bit of glass between him and it.

There was light glowing through the curtains, so he guessed it was daytime. He glanced at the electric light on the table nearby. Always the same, night or day. He wasn't sure he liked this modern world.

Stumbling into the bathroom to relieve himself, his attention caught on the shower. He stripped off his clothes and stepped into the tub, turned the water on to pour warm and steamy over him, used the miniature bar of soap to scrub himself and his hair. His head was throbbing a bit, and the hot water eased it some, pouring on his scalp in an endless waterfall.

Some modern things were good, he conceded. Endless hot water at your fingertips, without any lighting fires or filling kettles, was one of them.

Much refreshed, he got dressed again and went out to use the phone to order breakfast. There was a heap of written information on the desk and it took him a while to find the room service menu and then the directions for using the phone. Finally he managed to place a call and order eggs and bacon, sausage and pancakes, and a pot of coffee.

There was a motion picture box in the room. Out of curiosity and to pass the time waiting for his breakfast, he played with the control box until he got the picture box to work, but he soon shut it off again. It was too loud, and the pictures moved too fast. Made him dizzy.

Strange that he should feel so out of place today, when yesterday he'd been happy to indulge himself in every way that offered. He thought about the gal who'd come here with him— Charlene? He couldn't even remember her name, and though he'd enjoyed every minute he'd spent with her he had no desire to do it again.

He felt lonely. He wanted his own kind. The other players weren't like him. No one here was of a like mind with him. Sebastian had been the closest thing to it, probably, but they hadn't really had a chance to get acquainted, and now the riverboat gambler was gone.

Breakfast arrived and James ate it in silent solitude, feeling better afterward. He decided he'd better get out of the suite, or else he'd end up moping here all day and putting himself in a foul mood. Not good if he wanted to win this tournament.

A stroll outside might do him good. Walk in the fresh air, stand by the ocean a whiles. The sea had always been a marvel and a mystery to him.

He left the suite, being careful to remember the little playing card that was his key. Queen of spades. He toyed with it while he waited for the elevator, flipping it through his fingers as one might a coin. He dropped it and was stooping to pick it up when the bell rang and the elevator doors opened.

Penstemon was standing in the elevator, dressed casually in what they called jeans and a long-sleeved white shirt. He nodded to James.

"Afternoon, Mr. Hickok. Going out?"

"Thought I might get some air."

"My plan exactly. I'm going for a walk on the beach. Care to join me?"

"Right kind of you."

James got in the elevator. He was getting used to it now, but he still took a good hold on the rails as it hummed along.

"You can do magic," he said, looking at his host. "Why do you bother with this contraption? Can't you just put yourself where you want to be?"

Penstemon chuckled. "I could, but it requires expending more energy. This is easier in the long run."

"So you save up your magic for the big things, that it?"

"That's it."

The elevator stopped to let some more people on, two young gals with hair like corn silk, dressed in long green gowns that clung to their tender bodies in a most appealing way. They couldn't decide whether to stare at Penstemon or at James, so they looked back and forth between them and stifled giggles whenever they glanced at each other. That put a stop to any chance of conversation for the duration of the ride.

At the ground floor they all left, the girls going into the casino and Penstemon motioning James toward a wall of glass doors. A burst of giggling made the sorcerer pause and glance back.

"Dryads," he said to James as they continued out through the doors held for them by invisible critters in uniform. "This is their first visit to the city. We've got a lot of first-timers this week."

"That so?" said James, glancing up at the sky as they left the hotel and walked along a garden path. Must be later in the day than he'd thought. The sky was a deep, glowing blue. The air had a touch of chill to it—water nearby and a hint of the coming winter.

"Thanks to you," Penstemon added. "And the others, of course, but I think it's mostly you. You're the headliner, Mr. Hickok. I hope I've made it clear how much I appreciate your being here."

James reached out toward a bush covered with bright red roses, touching one to see if it felt real. It did, and he caught a whiff of its scent. He pulled a petal off and held it to his nose, soft and velvety.

"Kind of an odd thing to say, since I didn't have much choice about it."

"True. I apologize for inconveniencing you. I assumed the chance of a new life would be welcome."

"I suppose it is."

Agnes would like these roses, James thought. She'd like this garden. She liked good things and civilized places, even though she'd traveled all over with her circus and seen some pretty mean little towns, like Abilene where they'd met.

"You ever been to Abilene, Mr. Penstemon?"

"Abilene, Kansas? No, I haven't."

"I was wondering what it's like nowadays."

"You were marshal there, correct?"

"For a while."

Penstemon rubbed at the back of his neck. "Well, it still exists, but I don't know much about it myself. The concierge could help you if you want to find out more."

James waved a hand. "Just passing curious. Wondering if it was bigger now, with paved roads and all."

"I'm sure it is."

They were getting closer to the boardwalk. James could hear carnival music coming from somewhere ahead, and the smell of frying food hung in the air. Penstemon led him up to the back of a shack and through a door into it. As they passed from a dingy back room into a booth glaring with light James glimpsed a man aiming a pistol.

Without thought, he brought up his own weapon. Penstemon shouted. The other man dropped his gun, eyes wide with terror in the instant before he disappeared behind the counter at the front of the booth.

Penstemon's hands were on James's arm, pushing it down. "It's just a game, just a game! Sorry, I should have told you. Didn't think we'd catch anyone playing."

James now saw the playing cards pinned to the back wall. A blonde girl was in the booth with them, skinny in black jeans and a black shift with "The Black Queen" tricked out on it in flashing paste jewels. She shot James a reproachful glance and went to coax her customer up from the ground. James holstered his gun and took a deep breath, waiting for the thunder in his heart to slow down.

The man got up and dusted himself off, eyes still wide, looking embarrassed and angry at once. He was maybe thirty, wore the usual jeans and t-shirt and a light jacket over them. James walked over and offered a hand.

"Sorry," he said. "Misunderstanding. Thought you were drawing down on me."

"Who the hell are *you?*" said the man indignantly. "You look like frigging Buffalo Bill Cody!"

James just smiled, and since the fellow didn't want to shake hands, he lowered his. Penstemon joined them, pulling a little slip of colorful paper from his pocket which he held out to the man.

"Here. Two free drinks at the Tropicana. Sorry about the confusion. Pick a dragon, too. On the house."

The fellow took the slip and appeared to relax a little. "Thanks." He glanced at the blonde girl, then pointed up at the colorful mass overhead. "I'll take that green one."

Penstemon led James out of the booth as the girl fetched down the toy dragon. James blinked at the brightness, realizing belatedly that the sun was out. It hadn't been when they were walking in the garden. He looked back and didn't see the hotel where he expected. It should have been rising up behind the carnival booth, but there was nothing.

"That's a mighty good trick, Mr. Penstemon."

Penstemon glanced back, then grinned as he led the way across the boardwalk toward the beach. "Thank you. It's necessary. I don't want just anyone coming into the Black Queen."

"Why not?"

"Because I built it for my people."

"Magic people?"

"Yes—the magical community. There are a lot of us all over

the world, but we're largely underground. Some of us are literally underground, in fact."

James nodded. He'd seen a fellow looked like he was made out of rock in the casino. Wouldn't surprise him if that fellow lived in a cave or some such.

"Wouldn't you make more money if you opened the place up to everyone?"

"Perhaps, but I'm not in it just for the money."

They'd reached the side of the boardwalk where a short set of wooden steps led down to the sand. Penstemon went down it first.

"You see," Penstemon went on as they walked across the sand, feet sinking in the softness with every step, "I wanted to make a resort for *my* people, a place where they could come and play and be themselves, not have to worry about being harassed about the way they look or their habits or their beliefs."

"And you make enough profit from your own kind?"

"Oh, yes." Penstemon smiled. "I'm also a businessman. I wouldn't keep the Black Queen open if it wasn't successful."

"So this whole tournament thing was also a business decision," said James.

Penstemon shot him a guarded glance. "Primarily, yes."

They had reached the firm, damp sand near the water now. The smells of food and candy and grease and other less savory things fell away before the great salt dampness of the ocean. Penstemon walked straight toward the water with his arms spread wide and his blond hair streaming back in the breeze, breathing deep. James followed, watching him, curious.

Penstemon's brow was furrowed. Almost looked like grief.

"There's another reason," James said without thinking.

The wizard's throat moved in a swallow. "Yes."

For a moment they were both still, wrapped in silence. Then a wave broke, its rushing sound filling the emptiness.

The man had power. James had seen it himself. Penstemon clearly knew what the world was about, but at the same time he had an air of innocence to him.

James realized that was what drew him to Penstemon, what kept him from being angry at the way Penstemon had brought him here. There was profit in it, of course, but there seemed to be an underlying kindness in it, too.

"How much is it costing you to keep us alive?" he asked, shouting his words over the roar of the surf.

Penstemon had been standing with his eyes closed. Now he turned to face James with a wry smile.

"A little less than it did yesterday."

James felt a sudden stab of anger on behalf of Sebastian. It faded, for Penstemon had made the terms clear to all of them. He couldn't blame the man for standing by his game.

Had to take strong magic to bring five people back from the dead. Curiosity about that was what'd made James ask the question.

"I can't really explain it in a way that would make sense to you, I'm afraid," Penstemon added. "It's a bit technical."

"What would happen to us—us four—if you died?"

A look of shock crossed Penstemon's face. "Is that a threat?"

"No, sir. Just a question."

Penstemon looked out to sea again, his jaw moving tightly. "You'd return to where you came from," he said after a moment.

James nodded. That made sense.

He glanced behind him. There were a couple of people walking dogs down the beach a ways and a kid flying a kite, but no one near enough to hear them.

"I think Mr. Rothstein has it in for you, sir."

A smile grew on Penstemon's face, though he didn't turn. "I know he does."

"Do be careful, won't you? I don't really relish an abrupt return to Deadwood."

"He can't do anything to me without risking the same fate himself," Penstemon answered.

"Well, I wouldn't trust him too far, that's all. Canny as a snake, that one."

Penstemon's smile widened, and now he did turn. "Thanks

for your concern, Mr. Hickok. I do appreciate it."

"Call me James, if you'd like."

A glint of pleasure lit Penstemon's eye. "James. Thank you." He offered a hand and James shook it. "Call me Simon, then."

James nodded gravely. So the exchange of first names did still mean something, even though they were mostly used so casually now. He was glad of that.

Glad he'd come out here with Penstemon, too. Felt like there was a connection between them now, more than before. With a jolt of surprise strong enough to tingle down his arms, he realized that was what he'd been missing. Feeling connected with someone, with a friend.

He watched Penstemon, who'd closed his eyes again and stood breathing in the air like he was trying to inhale the ocean itself. Maybe the sorcerer got some sort of rejuvenation from the water. James smiled and shook his head a little, amused to find himself watching Penstemon's back at such a moment, and also glad to do it.

~ William ~

William sat in the back of the limousine, one arm around Alma and the other supporting a champagne glass, wearily content. They'd spent a lovely day touring historic buildings and museums and gardens and a lighthouse, and were now returning to the Black Queen for dinner and the continuation of the tournament.

William glanced at Joanie beside him, who was chatting comfortably with Mr. Rothstein. The gangster fellow had surprised William by agreeing to accompany them today, and had taken great pains to put Joanie at ease. He was behaving as a perfect gentleman, which was good, because if he gave the least sign of an inclination to mistreat Joanie, William would have to annihilate him.

How one annihilated a fellow ghost in temporary flesh, he had no idea, but that did not diminish his willingness. He supposed magical flesh was as vulnerable as normal flesh to the usual range of assaults.

Alma cuddled closer to him and clinked her glass against his. "Lovely day," she said, smiling.

William gave her a squeeze. "It certainly was, and would have been nowhere near as lovely without your company, my dear."

She chuckled. "Go on."

"Truth. I swear before God."

"Is there a God, Willy? I mean, did you talk to him, when you —?"

"Oh, no, heavens no. But I never got close to heaven, if you'll recall. Caught in one of those loops Penstemon mentioned."

"Very strange."

"Indeed."

William sipped his champagne and listened to Joanie and Rothstein talking. Rothstein was saying she should ask to go up to Penstemon's suite and visit his cats.

"Oh, no, I could never do that!" Joanie said. "I wouldn't want to bother him, he must be such a busy man."

"He wouldn't have to be there," said Rothstein. "He's got a housekeeper, doesn't he? I bet she'd let you in to visit the kitties."

"Well, I don't know—"

"No harm in trying, right? I say we do it."

Joanie let out a nervous laugh. Rothstein laughed, too, then reached for the champagne bottle to refill her glass. Didn't drink himself, which made William suspicious of his motives. Had to be something shifty about a fellow who wouldn't raise a glass with friends.

Rothstein's relentless persuasion had them all four in an elevator as soon as they arrived at the hotel, riding up to the top floor. William had to close his eyes briefly to quell the effect of the motion combined with perhaps a bit too much champagne.

The machine disgorged them into a wide, quiet hallway lit, as Runyon had described, all by candlelight. Joanie was captivated, and for that reason alone William went along. Poor girl; she'd had very bad luck, but seemed to be reviving under Rothstein's flattering attention.

They reached Penstemon's door and Rothstein stepped forward to knock on it. A moment later it opened, and a sharp-featured woman looked out.

"Mr. Penstemon isn't in," she said, and made to close the door.

Rothstein stuck his foot into it. "We aren't here to see Penstemon. Miss McCordle here just wanted to pay a visit to his cats."

Joanie colored a bit. "But not if it's any trouble—"

"We won't be any trouble," Rothstein said, bestowing a charming smile on the housekeeper. "Only take a minute, and it would mean a great deal."

The housekeeper gazed narrowly at him, then at William,

who added his mite by smiling back. With a great show of reluctance, she opened the door wide enough for them to come in.

"You can visit them in the kitchen."

"Thanks," said Rothstein, stepping past her.

William and Alma followed him and Joanie down a short hallway and into a vast living room. The housekeeper came right behind them.

"Oooh," breathed Alma at the view. To the right and left the walls were entirely glass, showing ocean on one side and glittering city lights, just now coming on in the sunset, on the other.

On the wall hung a portrait of a woman dressed all in white, her black, waving hair tumbling down past her hips. She stood in a rose garden, with a full moon overhead. Her beauty was beyond breathtaking; William gazed at her in open admiration.

"This way," said the housekeeper. "They'll come for a treat."

Joanie followed her through a doorway on the front wall of the room. Alma strolled after her, but William paused to watch Rothstein.

The gangster was walking about the living room, eyes taking in everything. He glanced up and gave William a smile that was somehow repellant, then followed the girls into the kitchen.

Three cats were already there, mewing and curving about the housekeeper's legs. She took a ginger jar down from a cupboard.

"Here, puss puss!" she called.

"Oh, they're lovely," said Joanie, bending down to pet a petite cat with white beneath its chin and on its paws. The others were all black. "What are their names?"

"That one's Corazon, because of the heart on her chest," said the housekeeper, taking a handful of treats from the jar. "Here, give her a treat."

"Hello, Corazon," cooed Joanie as she fed the cat a morsel.

"That one is Shadow, and that's Kitty. And here's Mishka and Festus," the woman added as two other cats hurried into the kitchen.

"Mishka?" said Rothstein sharply.

"Festus?" cried Joanie, looking up.

The two latecomers yowled for treats, which the housekeeper dispensed. Joanie had frozen, staring at the gray cat who limped past her to get to the food.

"My God," murmured William.

"Which one's Mishka?" Rothstein demanded.

The housekeeper raised an eyebrow, then picked up a black cat, showing a flash of white on its underbelly. "This one."

Rothstein took it from her and petted it. "Hello there, Mishka," he said in a low voice, smiling in a way William didn't like.

Alma nudged William and whispered, "Festus, wasn't that the name—"

"Yes, yes," said William hastily. "Indeed it was."

"Festus?" Joanie said again hollowly.

"It's short for Hephaestus," the housekeeper said. "On account of the limp."

Joanie stood up and took a step toward the gray cat. It glanced warily at her and ran away, back right leg thumping awkwardly.

"Oh, God!" Joanie moaned.

William saw it was time to take charge. "Well, lovely visit," he said to the housekeeper. "Very good of you to take the time, but you must be wishing us at Jericho so we'll get out of your way now."

He caught Joanie by the waist and propelled her and Alma back toward the living room. Cats scattered before their hasty feet.

"Come along, Rothstein," William said over his shoulder.

The gangster shot him a look of pure antagonism, then put down the cat he was holding. The smile returned to his face as he turned to the housekeeper.

"Thanks for indulging us. Nice place Mr. Penstemon's got here."

"Thank you," she said coolly, following him out.

She escorted them back to the entrance and held the door as they left. No polite chit-chat. No invitation to come back. She just said a brisk goodbye and shut the door behind them.

"Well, well," said Rothstein softly as the four of them headed down the hall toward the elevator. "So he sent his cats to fetch us. I wonder why."

William glanced at Joanie, who looked rather pale. Her mouth was pinched shut in a thin line.

"Don't suppose it matters," he said, trying to brush it off.

"Sure it does," said Rothstein. "Had to take a lot of effort. Why didn't he just send an employee?"

"No idea," said William. "So, ladies, shall we have dinner at the Diamond Grill again, or would you like to try another place? I think there's a Chinese restaurant—"

"Maybe he didn't think he could trust anyone else," Rothstein mused as they got in the elevator. "He wanted to send someone whose loyalty to him was unquestionable. After all, a famous dead gambler is a pretty unusual property. Might be worth someone's while to sidetrack us, know what I mean?"

"Not really, no," said William. He punched the button for the ground floor.

"What about that health-food place?" said Alma cheerily. "The Wikka Garden? That looked good."

"Sprouts," said Joanie in a dismal tone.

"Or the little bistro, Machiavelli's. Do you like Italian, Joanie?" William asked.

Joanie shrugged and continued to stare at the floor, seeming sunk in despair. William glanced at Rothstein, but the fellow was oblivious, lost in his shady speculations, no doubt.

Hellfire. He'd hoped Joanie had gotten over her infatuation. Knowing Festus was a cat should have furthered that process, he'd have thought, but the effect seemed to be the opposite. She was going to be a bundle of gloom for the rest of the evening.

"Dirty trick Penstemon played on you, wasn't it?" murmured Rothstein. "Sending a cat in human form."

He was looking at Joanie, not at William. She raised her gaze to meet his. William frowned, then the bell rang and the door opened and the noise of the casino swept over them.

"Look!" cried someone nearby. "It's Rothstein and Weare!"

"Sounds like a bloody law firm," muttered Alma. "Here we go."

A crowd surged around them as they stepped out of the elevator. Men and women in witch hats and long drapey robes, mostly black, crowded elbow to elbow with wolf-faced teenagers and green-skinned short people and a lot of other folk, strange and not, all clamoring for autographs.

William smiled and nodded and shook hands and scribbled his name over and over on scraps of paper and parchment and in one case, with a marker pen on a large, scantily-clad woman's astonishing bosom. Alma stayed close, flashing a brilliant smile that said, "Hands off" and keeping an arm firmly around Joanie's waist.

Somehow in all the hubbub Rothstein slipped away, William didn't notice when. At last the crowd thinned enough for them to escape. Pleading shortage of time, William bade farewell to the fans and hurried Alma and Joanie off to Machiavelli's, where an understanding hostess led them to a quiet, curtained booth at the back of the restaurant.

"Whew!" William said as he settled into the cushioned leather. "That was rather a crush."

"You're a bleeding rock star, Willy," said Alma, grinning. "I'm going to have to keep my eye on you."

"I'm yours alone, Alma, my dear." Realizing belatedly that this billing and cooing might make Joanie feel worse, William turned to her with a kindly smile. "Will you pick us out a bottle of wine to have with dinner, Joanie? You have such good taste."

Joanie sat blinking at the menu lying before her. "I want to go home."

"Joanie, love!" Alma put an arm around her shoulders. "Don't you want to stay and watch Willy win the tournament?"

Joanie shook her head. William tried to think of something to say, but comforting heartbroken women wasn't exactly his forte.

Alma picked up Joanie's menu and placed it in her hands. "Have some pasta, it'll make you feel better. Pick out something sinful."

A waiter arrived, a young man looking devilish in a black mustache and pointed goatee. The horns added to the impression. Had to be a trend, because William had noticed several individuals affecting this devil look, though this one had the best facial hair he'd seen.

The waiter set an antipasto platter in the center of the table. "Are you ready to order?"

"We need a minute," said William. "Bring us a bottle of your best Montepulciano in the meantime."

"Right away, sir."

The waiter gave a brisk smile and hustled away. Alma pushed the antipasto toward Joanie.

"Look, olives. Your favorite."

"I'm not a child," said Joanie resentfully.

"I know, love, but I just want you to feel better. It isn't the end of the world, you know. There's lots of fish in the sea."

Not the most adroit comparison, William thought, but he let it pass. Alma knew Joanie better than he.

He perused the menu and settled on veal scaloppini. By the time the waiter returned with the wine, Alma had coaxed Joanie into trying the antipasto and the two of them were giggling and making faces over the pickled hot peppers.

William gave his order for the veal, Alma ordered something spicy and unpronounceable, and Joanie chose lobster Alfredo, the costliest item on the menu. The fierce little voice in which she said it told William she hadn't forgotten her disappointment.

"After all," she said with a brittle smile as the waiter left, "Mr. Bloody Penstemon can afford it, can't he?"

She picked up her wineglass and took a large swallow. William sipped his, trading a glance with Alma. It was going to be a rough night.

"I still want to go home," Joanie announced, setting her glass down with a solid thump.

"I'll speak to Mr. Penstemon after the evening's tournament session, if you're of the same mind then," William said gently.

"Thank you," she said with dignity, then picked up her glass and swigged again.

He wondered what would become of Joanie, and of Alma for that matter, if he lost tonight. Presumably Penstemon would pay their way home to England or send them in his magical car-coach-jet thing. He worried, though. Alma would be all right, but he feared he'd done Joanie a disservice by bringing her along.

It had just been a lark. Sad how a bit of fun could turn so ugly. He'd never wished Joanie harm. Poor little thing, he'd bollocksed things up for her royally, hadn't he?

CUE INTERVIEW 3:

"You're the only player who has previous experience of poker tournaments, isn't that right, Mr. Runyon?"

"Well, I didn't play in them, I ran them, but yeah. I'm the only one that really knows Texas Hold'em."

"Do you think that gives you an advantage?"

"Sure it does. You know the game, you got an advantage. Those other guys are good, but—heh, heh. Good only goes so far, y'know?"

"What was your reaction when you were invited to be in the tournament?"

"Well, it took me a while to figure out what the hell was going on. I mean, for a while I didn't—well, anyway I was kind of disoriented at first. But I'll always play poker. Hell, I wasn't going to turn it down. And it's fun to be on the player side."

"What will you do if you win the tournament?"

"Finish up a few things. Go back to Vegas, probably."

"You're in a unique position, being the only player whose friends and family are still alive. Do you think you'll have any trouble going back?"

"Nah, I don't think so. I mean, they got DNA tests and stuff these days, right? So I'll be able to prove I'm me. Probably take some work to get my identity back, but that's what lawyers are for, right?"

"Assuming you're successful, what then?"

"Um. Well, you know, I'll probably retire, live a life of leisure, you know, ha, ha. Play some poker."

"Will you do anything differently than you did before your death?"

"Fuck, yeah. I'll stay away from bloodsucking bitch whores, that's what. Oh, do you have to bleep that? Sorry."

"What do you most look forward to doing after the tournament?"

"A couple of things…but you know, I mostly want to see my daughter, Connie. I just want to give her a great big hug."

"Well, here's hoping you get to do that. Good luck, Mr. Runyon. And now, back to the tournament."

~ Round Two ~

Arnold sat in the lounge, waiting impatiently for the unsavory individual—even now, he shrank from the word "witch"—to show up. He used the time to think over his plans.

He'd considered killing Runyon and the other two, but that would be messy and difficult and far less direct than simply getting control of Penstemon. That was his ultimate goal anyway, to control the sorcerer. The other poker players were incidental.

Control Penstemon, make him do his mumbo jumbo to make Arnold's body permanent, then proceed to take over his operation. Penstemon was too soft to take full advantage of the setup he had. Arnold saw lots of potential here for higher profit. He smiled as he thought about it, and took another sip of his tonic.

He'd thought about using the cats. Easy enough to get into Penstemon's suite and grab Mishka. Little minx. Serve her right for trying to put one over on him.

He wasn't sure Penstemon would give up everything to save a cat, though. Not worth the risk that he'd just write the cat off.

No, this way was better. Magic was Penstemon's biggest advantage. Arnold didn't have time to learn magic to compete with him, but fortunately his assumption had proved to be correct. Magic could be bought.

He glanced at his watch, frowning. Quarter to seven, almost time for the tournament.

The witch came in and made her way toward him with her stork-like stride. "Hiya, Mr. Big," she said, revealing the wonders of modern dentistry in a toothy grin.

"You're late," Arnold told her.

She folded her stilt-like legs and sat in the chair across from him, setting her purse in front of her on the table between them. "Good things take time. You wanted top quality, right?"

"Right. So what have you got for me?"

She glanced toward the bar where the bartender was hooking up a new keg to one of the beer taps. There was no one else in the place except for three old ladies playing a loud and rowdy game with some weird kind of trading cards at a table by the window.

Apparently satisfied that they weren't being observed, the crone opened her purse and produced two items: a small bundle of what looked like twigs and weeds that had a faintly foul smell, and a short, forked stick.

Arnold frowned. "That's it?"

"Yep. Drop the bundle in the person's pocket, then hold onto the stick while you issue commands."

"And it's good for how long?"

"Depends if the person's got any defenses. Your average witch, maybe take a day to overcome it."

"What about an extreme example? Somebody really powerful."

"Like Penstemon?" Her eyes glinted and she smiled unpleasantly. "No more than an hour. Maybe less."

"But it would control him?"

She nodded. "For a short time, yeah. Remind me not to be around when he breaks it."

An hour would be long enough, Arnold thought. Make Penstemon sign him on as a partner, make him do the magic on his body.

"I want a demonstration before I pay you."

She shrugged, glanced around the bar, then stood up and slung her purse over her shoulder. Arnold followed her out into the casino, where she strolled along between rows of slot machines. She pointed out a solitary woman wearing a baggy sweater with big, open pockets.

Arnold passed that one by and instead slipped the weed bundle into the pocket of a wizened little pointy-eared man in the next row. He held the forked stick up in front of the guy's face.

"Stand up," he said.

The guy stood up. The crone pushed Arnold's hand down to his side.

"You don't have to wave it like a baton. Just hold onto it."

Arnold stuck his hand in his own pocket, gripping the stick firmly. "Take off your coat," he said.

The old man took off his coat, and when Arnold told him to turn it inside out and put it back on he complied, then stood waiting for more orders. Arnold reached in the man's pocket, now harder to get to, and took out the weed bundle.

He strolled away with the crone, pausing in a soda fountain alcove at the end of the row. Glancing back, he saw the old man blink in confusion, then sit back down at the machine, jacket still inside-out.

"OK, sold," Arnold said softly. He took out his bankroll and peeled off ten thousand dollars, almost everything he'd made at the poker tables.

"And another fifty tomorrow," said the crone, stuffing the cash in her purse.

Arnold nodded. Tomorrow he'd have control of the Black Queen, and he'd send someone to dispatch this witch. Couldn't let her stay around, threatening to blackmail him whenever she liked.

She grinned, again flashing her large, long teeth. "Pleasure doing business with you, Mr. Big. Good luck in the card game."

"Thanks."

Arnold watched her lope away, then strolled back down the aisle of slot machines. He paused by the old guy.

"How much did she pay you?"

The guy blinked up at him. "What? Who?"

Arnold looked in his eyes and saw sincere confusion. "Never mind," he said. "By the way, you're coat's inside out."

He made his way through the casino to the elevators, where a crowd was waiting to get up to the tournament. He almost headed for the staircase instead, but since he was late he crammed into an elevator with a bunch of the rabble, smiling at them and answering their questions for the short duration of the ride, then escaping with a long stride that brought him to the ballroom door just as Penstemon was coming toward it.

"There you are! I was getting worried, Mr. Rothstein. I'd hate to see you forfeit the game."

Penstemon flashed a smile and motioned Arnold ahead of him with a broad sweep of his arm. No chance to slip the weed bundle in his pocket. Arnold suppressed his annoyance and went to the table. He could bide his time. There'd be other opportunities.

The others were there ahead of him. Four chairs now, with Runyon and Hickok on the short ends of the table while Arnold shared the long side opposite the dealer with Weare. Arnold took his seat as the red lights on the cameras lit up.

"Welcome back to the Black Queen Poker Tournament," Penstemon said to the cameras. The overhead screens showed his face a yard wide. He was standing between Arnold and Weare. Arnold leaned back a little in his chair. Penstemon took a step back.

"Four players remain to vie for the championship prize," he said loudly. "Dealer, put 'em in the air!"

It was the purple girl again. She dealt out the cards while Penstemon walked away. Arnold looked at his hand, which was crap, two-seven off. He folded it and kept an eye on Penstemon, who now was off in a corner chatting with the hostess, Gaeline.

Tonight her dress was all shimmering gold. Penstemon's suit was dark blue, with a burnished gold tie. Arnold wondered if they were a couple.

Maybe he could get to Penstemon through the girl? No, direct approach was the best way, but he had to get close to slip Penstemon the bundle, and Penstemon was keeping his distance.

Arnold gave it up for the present and turned his attention to the game. Chips went back and forth among the players, but there were no big bets at first. Everyone was warming up, settling in.

Arnold watched their faces. Runyon was still a bundle of tells, but Hickok had settled in to a steady, flat calm that was harder to read. Weare hadn't been very readable from the start, wily lawyer bastard. Arnold hated lawyers, except the ones he could buy. Those he didn't hate, exactly, though he didn't have much respect for them either.

He had an idea how he could rattle Weare. Glancing at the audience in the bleachers, he saw Weare's two girlfriends sitting in the front like last night. Arnold caught Joanie's eye, smiled and blew her a kiss. She ducked her head, looking self-conscious, then smiled shyly back.

Let Weare worry about that for a while. Arnold suppressed a grin as he glanced sidelong at Weare to see if he'd noticed.

He had. Weare called a big bet from Hickok, who took the pot with three sevens over Weare's two pair. Two of the sevens had been on the board, and Weare should have known better than to call.

Pleased with himself, Arnold raised the blinds on the next hand with an ace-king. Weare folded, Hickok called, and Runyon raised the bet twenty grand. Arnold gazed at him, decided his fidgeting meant he wasn't sure of the hand, and called the bet. Hickok called, too, and the flop was jack-ten-six, all diamonds.

Hickok checked. Runyon pushed the rest of his chips forward, about forty thousand.

"All in," Runyon said, looking up with a brutish frown.

Arnold had the king of diamonds. Runyon might hold the ace, but he didn't think so, not from the nervous way Runyon was clamping his jaws again and again, chewing on nothing. Looking at his own stack, Arnold decided it was worth the risk. If he lost, he'd still have over a hundred grand.

"Call," he said.

He looked to Hickok, expecting him to fold. To his surprise, the cowboy waved his hands forward.

"I'm all in, too."

Hickok's stack was only slightly larger than Runyon's, so

Arnold called the difference. Might as well, with the amount he had in the pot already. He could draw two more aces, or make the flush. Stranger things had happened.

"Turn 'em up," said the dealer.

Runyon showed a pair of kings and stood up, pacing nervously. That beat Arnold's ace-king, unless he paired the ace or got another diamond for the flush. Runyon let out a greedy laugh as Arnold showed his cards.

Hickok turned over ace-nine of diamonds. Nut hand. He'd win unless Runyon made a full house, which wasn't very likely.

"Shit!" Runyon said, stomping back and forth like a caged tiger. "Shit, shit!"

"Very nice," Arnold said quietly to Hickok.

The gunslinger glanced upward beneath the brim of his huge hat. "Thanks."

The dealer turned up a jack of spades, making a pair on the board. Another jack or the fourth king would give Runyon the win. The idiot was practically dancing, eyes desperate, hands in and out of his pockets as he waited for the purple girl to deal the river card.

Ace of hearts.

The crowd gave a roar of excitement. Runyon stepped back from the table, staring at Hickok.

"You fucking bastard! You fucking—!"

And then he began to dissolve. Arnold took out his pocket handkerchief and held it over his mouth and nose. He'd meant to close his eyes, too, but a slight movement to the side caught his attention.

It was Penstemon, crumbling something between his hands, blowing the dust away. A chill went down Arnold's spine.

Runyon's voice turned to a wordless howl that spiraled upward. His ghost drifted up, too, spinning, arms flailing as if he couldn't get his balance. Everyone in the place was watching him, and Arnold glanced again at Penstemon to see if he was distracted enough for Arnold to slip him the whammy.

No go—the sorcerer finished crumbling whatever it was,

dusted his hands, and signaled to Gaeline. She stepped in front of the camera and began giving the go-to-break spiel.

The dealer was counting up Hickok's stack. She looked up at Arnold.

"Seventy-nine thousand."

Arnold nodded and counted out the same from his own stack. She pushed it to Hickok along with Runyon's chips. That hand had made Hickok the chip leader by a good hundred grand.

Arnold riffled a few of his remaining chips, pondering whether he should have folded. No, it had been a good call. What had happened was he'd let Runyon distract him, and Hickok had slipped in the winning hand without his noticing.

He sighed and stood up. No point in worrying about it. He had other fish to fry.

Penstemon was talking to a couple of people from the audience, looked like bigwigs, dark suits, no weird hair or extra appendages. Arnold gazed at him for a minute, then followed Weare over to chat with the girls.

"Tough luck, Arnold," said Alma.

Arnold shrugged. "Win some, you lose some. Hiya, Joanie, how you doing? Care to come for a stroll with me? Protect me from the ravaging hordes?"

Joanie giggled, then stepped down and took his arm. Arnold strolled away, nodding over his shoulder to Weare and Alma. Weare looked suspicious.

Good, thought Arnold, bending down to whisper a comment in Joanie's ear about the Rainbow Girls, a set of seven giggly teens in the audience, each wearing a different spectral color with their hair dyed to match. Joanie had mentioned them earlier in the day. Arnold hadn't noticed them last night, and accused Joanie of making them up.

"I owe you a nickel," he said now. "You were right."

She smiled smugly. "Told you so."

"You sure did. Hey, Joanie, how'd you like to help me play a trick on Penstemon?"

"Trick?"

"Yeah, just a joke, you know. Get him back a little for the cats."

Joanie's eyes narrowed. "What did you have in mind?"

"I got this smelly herb bundle here," he said.

He made sure Penstemon wasn't watching, then withdrew the charm from his pocket and placed it in her hand. He slid his hand back in his pocket and around the command stick.

"Just slip it in his pocket, OK? Give him a stink."

"OK," she said, nodding. Her eyes looked a little glazed.

"Don't let him see you do it. Just sidle up close to him and drop it in when no one's looking."

"Yes." She nodded again.

"Good girl. Keep it out of sight for now. You're having a good time, right?"

She broke into a beaming smile. "Right."

He got her a drink and a soda for himself at the cash bar set up in one corner of the ballroom. The other people in line there were chattering about Runyon's wipeout. Arnold didn't comment, just smiled and nodded to the ones who congratulated him.

"Let's head back," he said to Joanie. He wanted to do this before the cameras came on again.

"OK," she said.

Too docile. He liked her better when she was shooting her yap off every other minute about some bit of historical trivia. Maybe he'd keep her around, dress her up, pamper her a little.

Trouble was, she was the honest type. She might think she had to rat on him, not that it would do any good. Once he got control, he knew how to keep it.

He guided her back to the stands, where Penstemon was still chatting with the bigwigs. He whispered in her ear, then leaned against the rail and watched her drift through the crowd, working her way toward Penstemon.

Arnold kept a tight grip on the stick in his pocket. He didn't want to get too close, but he wasn't sure about its range, so he took a few rambling steps that brought him closer to Joanie and Penstemon. He hoped to hell he hadn't negated the charm by handing it to Joanie—should've asked about that, damn it, but now it was too late.

He sipped his soda, watching Joanie intently. She sidled nearer to Penstemon, nearer. Within arm's reach now. Penstemon glanced up, saw her, smiled, and went back to his conversation. Arnold took another swig of his drink.

She had the thing in her hand, which she was holding at the small of her back while she chatted with a woman—he thought it was a woman from the shape—wrapped head to toe in bandages and wearing dark glasses. Penstemon couldn't see what was Joanie's hand, but others might. Arnold clamped his jaws shut on his impatience.

She edged nearer to Penstemon, not looking at him, just shuffling slightly sideways as she conversed. Almost close enough.

"Sweet little thing, isn't she?"

Arnold's heart skipped, but he managed to keep from jumping. Weare had come up beside him without his noticing. Bad—he'd have to pay more attention. That sort of thing could get you killed.

"Joanie? Sure," he said, angling his body toward Weare's while still watching her.

"You wouldn't disappoint her now, would you?" Weare said.

"Not sure what you mean."

Joanie was turning the herb bundle around in her hand. Hell, she better not drop it!

"I mean you wouldn't be thinking of taking advantage. You've got a hungry way of looking at her, Arnold."

Her hand slid down to her side. She was right next to Penstemon, facing slightly away.

Someone nearby laughed loudly, and for a second everyone paused to look. Joanie's hand came up and dropped the bundle into Penstemon's pocket. Arnold breathed a sigh of relief, then turned to face Weare.

"What do you take me for, some no-class two-bit loser? She's a good kid, I won't hurt her."

Weare smiled and gave a nod, looking very regal in his fancy old-style cravat. "Very glad to hear it, old boy. You know, I had to ask. She's my guest, in a way."

"Sure, I understand." Arnold flashed the shyster his best smile, then said, "Would you excuse me? Better freshen up before we get started again."

Without waiting for an answer he stepped away, striding in the direction of the hallway. He stopped before he got there, though, and stood behind one of the cameras, presently dormant and unattended. From there he could see Penstemon clearly. Joanie had drifted away from him again and was now chatting with the Rainbow Girls.

Arnold finished his soda, got rid of the cup, and slid his hand into his pocket. Closing it around the stick, he spoke in a whisper.

"Check your watch."

Penstemon stiffened for a moment, then looked at his watch. A flood of elation rushed through Arnold. He savored the triumph for just a few seconds, then spoke again.

"Say goodbye, then come over to the table."

He watched Penstemon's head bob, watched him shake hands with one guy, pat the other on a shoulder. The sorcerer turned around then and started for the poker table. His face wore a frown that seemed half confusion, half concentration.

He was trying to break the spell. Arnold's heart gave a frightened thump, and he gripped the stick harder. He'd have to make this quick.

Strolling idly toward the table as Penstemon approached, Arnold smiled and nodded as if they were meeting casually. No one else was near, but just in case he still whispered.

"Walk over to that rack of lights with me."

Penstemon moved stiffly beside him, eyes flashing anger. His lips were moving. Maybe he was trying to work a spell.

"Don't talk," Arnold told him hastily, and Penstemon

stopped.

When they got to the light rack, Arnold positioned them so they were mostly hidden from view by the equipment. Penstemon's frown had deepened.

"Show me the magic things you've got for us players, like the one you crumbled when Runyon lost."

Penstemon put a hand in his pocket and drew out three small, roughly round objects that were gray and lumpy like papier mâché. Arnold's blood went cold as he saw them. So fragile, so easily destroyed. They lay in the palm of the sorcerer's hand like little eggs.

"Which one's mine?" Arnold demanded.

Penstemon pointed to one and Arnold picked it up with his free hand. Step one, take away any power Penstemon had over him. He thought about telling Penstemon to crush the other two right then, but that would attract attention. He wanted to do this quietly.

"OK, do the magic to make my body permanent."

Penstemon blinked, then slowly shook his head. Arnold cussed under his breath.

"Why not? You can talk to tell me."

"I don't have the things I need," Penstemon said in a tight voice. "I have to do it in a power circle."

"Shit. Where's that, up in your suite?"

"Yes."

"Crap."

Arnold thought furiously, then glanced up at the big movie screens. They were playing his interview, and he was momentarily distracted by his own face large on the screen.

"OK, tell them to play another interview, then meet me out at the elevators. We're going up to your suite."

"I don't think so," drawled a low voice nearby.

Arnold jumped and turned. Hickok was standing there, holding his six-shooter aimed at Arnold's heart.

~ Endgame ~

James held Rothstein at gunpoint, wondering what the hell to do next. There was magic going on, he could tell by the cold prickling of his flesh, and he didn't know what to do about it. Somehow Rothstein was making Penstemon do things. From the look on the sorcerer's face he wasn't happy about it.

Penstemon started to walk away. James kept his gaze on Rothstein.

"Tell him to come back."

"Come back," Rothstein muttered, his dark eyes hard and angry.

"What are you doing to him?" James demanded.

Rothstein laughed then; a nasty laugh. "Go to hell!"

James had an urge to shoot him right then and there, but he resisted. "Take your hands out of your pockets. Show 'em to me!" he insisted when the gangster hesitated. "And if you try to give any orders to Penstemon, I'll blow you away."

He'd heard Rothstein talking about the little paper balls Penstemon had, how there was one for each of the players and how Penstemon had crumbled Runyon's. Just the thought of being that close to losing his body scared James silly. He pressed his left palm against his trousers to get the sweat off it.

Rothstein reluctantly took his hands out of his coat pockets. One was empty—he must have left his little paper ball in his pocket—but in the other he was holding a stick. James took a cautious step closer and held out his hand.

"Give it to me."

A frown creased Rothstein's brow. He didn't move.

"One word and I'll shoot, and if you don't give me that stick in two seconds I'll shoot anyway."

"Give it to him, Arnold," said a woman's voice nearby. "The

jig's up."

James was tempted to look, but he knew better than to take his eyes off Rothstein. The gangster looked, though, shifting his gaze to James's right, and his face went white with shock.

"Carolyn!" he said in a stunned voice. "What are you doing here?"

The woman stepped into view, and James risked a glance at her. She was all gray—one of the ghosts. Dressed in clothes of an unfamiliar style that clung to her, with a perky little hat and a fur stole around her shoulders.

"Nicky told me about the game," she said. "I've been watching with him and Meyer and a bunch of the others. All your old friends are here."

Rothstein frowned. Looked right confounded, he did. James hoped to hell he'd listen to the woman and give up the stick.

"Come on, Arnold," she said softly. "Play it out, huh? You know you can beat these guys."

Rothstein swallowed, frowning. He inhaled, then several things happened at once: his hand tightened on the stick, his gaze shifted to Penstemon, and he opened his mouth.

James pulled the trigger.

The shot brought all the chatter in the ballroom to a stop, except for the interview that played on. Rothstein's amplified voice rang out through the suddenly quiet room: "I prefer to be in control of my own fate."

Someone screamed, but it wasn't the ghost woman. She just shook her head, disappointed-like, and knelt beside Rothstein who was lying on the floor, back arched, bleeding as his mouth opened and closed, like a beached fish.

"Oh, Arnold," she said, caressing his hair. "Not again."

Shouting broke out and the crowd started to rush toward them. Penstemon dove for the little stick lying in Rothstein's slack palm. When he had it, he shot a glance up at James, then reached for Rothstein's coat, paying no mind to the blood that was everywhere.

"Excuse me, ma'am," the sorcerer said to the ghost woman as

he dug into Rothstein's pocket. He brought out the little paper ball.

Holding it in one hand, he looked at Rothstein and said, "I release you."

He crushed the ball, rolling it between his hands until it was dust. The crowd around gave a gasp as the magic started in. All the blood turned to little sparkling motes and drifted up toward the ceiling. The look of agony left Rothstein's face, and as his body turned to dust and floated off, the gray ghost that remained gazed calmly into the ghost woman's eyes.

"Carolyn," he said again. "I missed you."

She took his hand. "Well, I missed you, too, you know. I've been waiting for you."

Rothstein sat up and looked around. His gazed hardened as it fell on James.

"Sorry," James said, and he truly meant it. He'd never liked killing.

Rothstein stared hard at him for a long time, then broke into his dazzling smile. "Win some, you lose some," he said.

The smile hadn't got to his eyes. James knew he'd still have to watch out for this one. He was dead, but that didn't mean he was gone.

Rothstein stood, brushed off his suit, and offered his arm to the ghost woman. She took it and strolled away with him. They rose up over the heads of the crowd, who began to applaud. James saw that the cameras were recording everything. He hadn't noticed them come on.

As Rothstein disappeared into the ghost crowd, James took a last look around, then relaxed and holstered his gun. Penstemon was on his feet again, watching the gangster's departure. He looked at James.

"Thank you."

James pressed his lips together. "Sorry to disrupt everything."

Penstemon shook his head. "You saved your own life, and Weare's, and probably mine. I'm in your debt."

James shrugged. He didn't feel like killing a man was something he ought to be thanked for.

"S'pose I ought to withdraw from the game. Killing a player's against the rules, I figure."

Penstemon shook his head, a small smile coming onto his face. "It was self-defense. And anyway, it's my game, so I make the rules. Please finish it out, Mr. Hickok."

"Yeah, finish the game, Bill!" hooted a voice nearby. James didn't have to look up to know it was Calamity Jane.

The rest of the audience joined in, hooting and hollering and finally settling down to clapping in rhythm all together. Someone, probably Jane again, started yelling, "Wild Bill, Wild Bill," over and over again.

James gazed at them all and wondered what the hell he'd ever done to warrant all this fuss. Let that writer fellow publish stories about him, he guessed was how it had started. It all grew from there, and from the damn fool way he'd got himself killed in Deadwood.

Penstemon was still standing beside him. James leaned toward him so as not to have to shout over the crowd.

"Who was that lady Rothstein went off with?"

"His wife, Carolyn," answered the sorcerer.

James nodded. That made sense, then. "Seemed like a right good woman."

He glanced up at the chanting crowd, let his gaze run along the ghostly ranks above, who were also chanting and clapping and hollering and making a general fuss. The lights up there by the ceiling glared back at him, making him squint, making him think of the circus. The room was like a circus tent, in a way. He could almost imagine a high wire up there, among all the lights and cables...

"I say, old chap. Shall we get on with it?"

Dressed in his fancy suit with the ruffles at the sleeves and the old-fashioned neckcloth, Weare looked the complete gentleman. James guessed he himself looked like more of a rapscallion. Weare stopped a couple of paces away and made an elaborate, sweeping bow. The crowd roared approval, then went back to chanting.

James stepped toward Weare and held out his hand. They shook, and James caught the glint in Weare's eye along with the testing squeeze of his grip. The Englishman had by no means given up the show.

They walked together toward the table to the wild cheering of the crowd. Amber was there, waiting to deal, and they all three sat down to business as Penstemon stepped up in front of a camera.

"Arnold Rothstein has defaulted. Therefore, his chips will be removed from the table." He waved a hand casually and Rothstein's stack vanished. "We are down to heads-up play between William Weare and Wild Bill Hickok. Dealer, put 'em in the air!"

The crowd clapped and hooted, then settled down to watch. For a couple of hands James and Weare folded the blinds, both looking for winners. James watched the Englishman's eyes, which had a set and determined look to them at odds with his casual smile. Weare was playing for keeps.

Well, so was he. This was it—the final showdown. One of them would live on, and the other would go back.

Back to how it had been before? James chewed his lip as he watched Amber's pretty purple hands mess the cards around and then gather them up for another deal.

He didn't figure it would be like before. He'd been half asleep, then, and he doubted he'd forget everything he'd learned in the meantime, even if he did lose. He glanced at Penstemon, then at the hungry crowd in the stands.

His second card spun to a stop on top of the first and he lifted up the corners like they'd all learned to do from Runyon. Poor Runyon, gone back into the loop, he thought fleetingly, then his mind focused in on the cards.

Ace eight of spades.

He looked up at Weare, who had the small blind and the action. Weare shoved a stack of chips forward.

"One hundred thousand."

James matched the bet. "Call."

Amber dealt the flop: ace of clubs, queen of hearts, eight of clubs. A tingle went through James, not the cold prickle that meant magic but the ghostly touch of memory.

Aces and eights, queen kicker. He'd held these cards before.

He smiled inside but didn't let it reach his face. 'Bout time he found out whether this hand was a winner.

"Two hundred thousand," said Weare, pushing chips to the pot.

That was most of Weare's stack. James watched him, looking for signs of the gloat or the bluff. He could have a pair of queens or even aces, or two more clubs for a flush draw.

The Englishman's green eyes told nothing. Beyond him in the stands, Miss Alma and Miss Joanie were clinging together, and James felt a stab of envy.

Weare had everything to live for. He'd found a new love in this strange new world.

Whereas James had a bunch of what they called screaming fans, but not really any friends to speak of, except maybe Penstemon. He glanced toward the shadows where the sorcerer stood, quietly waiting. They were all waiting.

"Call," James said, pushing a pile of chips forward.

He only had a few thousand more. This hand would make or break one of them.

Probably he should have gone all in, that would have been the showy thing to do. He'd never been that much of a showman, though. He closed his eyes, suddenly feeling tired.

An excited noise from the crowd made him open them again. The turn card was on the board. Nine of diamonds.

James wanted to laugh, remembering the damn nine on the wall at the new No. 10 Saloon, and how he'd argued with the boss about it. He looked up for Weare's reaction and saw a tiny crease on his brow.

Not the card Weare had wanted, then. It made a straight possible. More than one way to win this one.

"Check," Weare said, leaning back and watching James.

James felt the elation of a sure win. Weare didn't have the straight, and James doubted he had a pocket pair to match a card on the board. James's two pair, the damn dead man's hand, were the boss cards, he felt sure of it.

He saw himself collecting the win, watching Weare fade to dust while the crowd roared and screamed. All except for Weare's two lady friends, of course.

Then what the hell would he do? Get a million dollars from Penstemon. Nice bankroll for a new start on life, but what the hell kind of life would it be?

He looked up toward the ceiling, past Jane and the other rowdies, up toward the back. The lights hanging up there made it hard to see, but still the back of his neck prickled as he glimpsed a silhouette that looked familiar. He stood up.

The crowd roared, thinking he was going all in. He hadn't done that, though. The cards were in his hands, his last few chips still behind the line.

"Fold," he said softly, and dropped the cards across the line.

He walked toward the audience, who were all staring at him, shocked to silence. He stopped when he reached the stands and turned his head to look back at Penstemon.

"I seen her. Took me a while. You're still looking, aren't you?"

The sorcerer gazed at him for a long moment, then slowly nodded.

"Hope yours finds her way here. She must be a hell of a woman."

Penstemon closed his eyes briefly, a crease of pain on his brow. James would love to know the whole story, but he had a more pressing matter to attend to.

"I'm ready."

Penstemon inhaled long and slow and reached into his pocket. James looked back toward the ceiling, squinting at the glare of the lights that shifted and softened as he felt the first tickling wave of his body going back to dust. He tried a step into the air and found he could do it, and broke into a grin as he strode up over the heads of the marveling crowd.

She came forward to meet him. She'd been waiting all this time, so patient, just like she had been in life. A solid, sensible woman, not a beauty, but she was beautiful to him.

"Agnes," he said, taking her hands.

She smiled back at him. "You done fooling around, James?"

He nodded. "I'm so sorry I failed you."

"Never mind," she said, and she took his face in her hands and kissed him, right there in front of everybody.

The crowd gave a wild roar. It faded into the crashing of the ocean, just like the hotel and all the lights and the crowd faded away around them as James and Agnes stepped into the sky.

About the Author

Pati Nagle was born and raised in the mountains of northern New Mexico. She has written over twenty novels in a variety of genres. Her short stories have appeared in *Asimov's Science Fiction*, the *Magazine of Fantasy & Science Fiction*, and in various other magazines and anthologies.

Her fantasy novels include the linked *Blood of the Kindred* series and *Immortal* series, as well as stand-alone titles. She writes historical fiction including the critically-acclaimed *Far Western Civil War* series as P.G. Nagle. She also writes the popular *Wisteria Tearoom Mysteries* as Patrice Greenwood.

Pati Nagle lives in the New Mexico mountains with her husband, two furry feline muses, and lots of wildlife. An avid student of music, history, and humans in general, she loves the outdoors but hides from the sun. She enjoys walking in the woods and looking up at the stars.

About Book View Café

Book View Café Publishing Cooperative (BVC) is a an author-owned cooperative of over fifty professional writers, publishing in a variety of genres including fantasy, romance, mystery, and science fiction.

In 2008, BVC launched a website, bookviewcafe.com, initially offering free fiction and gradually moving to selling ebooks of members' backlist titles, then original titles. BVC's ebooks are DRM-free and are distributed around the world. BVC returns 95% of the profit on each book directly to the author. The cooperative has gained a reputation for producing high-quality ebooks, and is now moving into print editions.

BVC authors include *New York Times* and *USA Today* bestsellers; Nebula, Hugo, Lambda, and Philip K. Dick Award winners; World Fantasy and Rita Award nominees; and winners and nominees of many other publishing awards.